Francis Henry Underwood

Man Proposes

A Novel

Francis Henry Underwood

Man Proposes
A Novel

ISBN/EAN: 9783337001001

Printed in Europe, USA, Canada, Australia, Japan

Cover: Foto ©Andreas Hilbeck / pixelio.de

More available books at **www.hansebooks.com**

MAN PROPOSES.

A NOVEL.

———————

BOSTON:
LEE AND SHEPARD, PUBLISHERS.
NEW YORK:
CHARLES T. DILLINGHAM.
1880.

MAN PROPOSES.

CHAPTER I.

THE warehouse of Prescott & Co. occupied the upper stories and lofts of a large granite building in Devonshire Street. The vast floors were supported by iron columns, and were covered with cases of goods laid out in orderly streets and lanes. A portion of the first story near the broad front-windows was sequestered by a mahogany railing, and was filled with desks, at which a dozen or more clerks were at work upon ledgers, bills, and invoices. There were tall men with eye-glasses and gray martial whiskers, precise in manner, and oppressed with responsibility; there were roly-poly boys that would be frisky if they dared; there were slender youths with yellow mustaches and lofty aspirations; and there were old fellows, stout and rubicund, who had long ago given up the hope of rising, and settled down to drudgery. Pens scratched away lightly and incessantly; great folios were turned over; letters were indorsed and filed. Without, a huge windlass raised and lowered cases; and the trucks in the street below were coming and going all day.

Prescott & Co. were selling-agents for a number of manufacturing companies, and carried on an immense business. The senior, Hugh Prescott, had a private room in one corner of the first floor; and the junior, Adolphus Gibbs, had a similar room opposite. In earlier days they had worked together: it was not so now. Mr. Gibbs had of late taken charge of the correspondence, and employed as private secretary Robert Prescott, a nephew of the head of the house.

As Robert is a person of mark, he should stand for his portrait. Behold him. He is tall, sinewy, and robust. His chestnut hair, abundant and wavy, falls in loose masses around a face of a strong and manly character. The lines indicate courage, probity, reserve, and, above all, a fine intellect. These impressions are heightened by his singularly expressive eyes, which are steel-blue in color in repose, but are lighted up to blazing points in moments of excitement, or softened at times by a not unmanly tenderness. It is the portrait of a person who should be considerably above the position of private secretary in a warehouse. At the bar, in the pulpit, or in a professor's chair, such a face and figure would have been in keeping with the place.

Mr. Gibbs was short, and inclined to corpulence; and, as he moved about, it was with an attempt to hold his solid and not very shapely head erect, or inclined slightly backward, as if he had been considering the scriptural question as to whether he could, by taking thought, "add a cubit to his stature," and had decided that he could. He might not have been ill looking twenty years before; but club dinners, and "business" as he understood it, had been distorting his features, and had given his eyes an unlovely gleam. His stubbly beard, which he persisted in wearing closely clipped, as if to show the fulness of his checks, added to the prevailing repulsive impression.

He came by the desk where his secretary sat, threw him a careless nod, and ejaculated a grunt intended as a substitute for a good-morning. Robert calmly and silently bowed, and meanwhile his long nervous hands were stoutly wrestling, one with the other, on his desk. Mr. Gibbs had apparently forgotten something; for in a moment he came out, and shut the door of his private room behind him. He walked between the desks, casting here and there a look that was like the ray from a burning-glass, or dropping a word that bit like a mineral acid. As soon as he was gone from the warehouse, there was a sigh of relief, so general, and exhaled in such perfect time, that one would think it had been rehearsed. Robert smiled, but mostly at the comic face of the nearest clerk, Gates Percival Amory, familiarly called Percy, or sometimes — apropos of Gates — nicknamed Bars. This young fellow had

full blue eyes that always seemed to be swimming
when they were not winking; a segment of the
arch of his round forehead was bordered by a
ridge of backward-growing hair, such as rustics
call a "cowlick;" his lips were pulpy and red,
like over-ripe strawberries, and his cheeks heavily
rotund. But there Nature had hesitated, and became a niggard in bounty; for his neck and chest
were slender, and his figure dwindled from the
shoulders downward, like a grotesque reflection
from a convex mirror. He was not an Antinous,
to be sure (somewhat grotesque, in fact), but had
a look of intelligence and spirit.

"Aren't you on speaking terms with your chum
Gibbs?" inquired Amory of Robert.

"As much as ever."

"That is, not at all, is it?"

"Something like that. If I expected to stay
here, I should say no more. But I think you are
discreet, and I will"—

"Unfold the secrets of your prison-house. Go
on."

Robert, not heeding the interruption, continued
gravely: "Kings fed their pride by having captive kings as menials; Roman consuls decorated
their triumphs by leading conquered princes in
chains: Gibbs, who is more moderate, is satisfied
with the practised pen and the enforced silence of
a college graduate."

"That sounds like a part in a play. You have
been rehearsing this. It shows that you are
galled."

Robert smiled in spite of himself; for he *had* been making mental comparisons, and the formal sentences, though newly formed, were not spontaneous. A rigid thinker, his utterances were apt to be bookish. He went on: —

"I am not only his secretary, I am his pen and penwiper, his chair, his footstool, his door-mat. I am to do only as I am bid."

> "'Yours not to make reply,
> Yours not to reason why,
> Yours but to do and die,'"

broke in the irrepressible Amory.

"When he comes, I am not to speak to him, not even to say, 'Good-morning.' I am forbidden ever to address him on any subject, unless in direct reply to his question. When I have answered, I am dumb. I must ask no question in return, nor any explanation."

"This is monstrous! Why, the Sultan is more decent than that! You are a slave. We will have you included in Lincoln's proclamation, and emancipated. Emerson shall write a hymn for you. Why, —— his chuckle-head! — Gibbs's I mean. I beg your pardon, — I know you have studied divinity ; but really one *must* swear."

"But this is not all," continued Robert. "He hedges himself with observances. There is a rule for every action. I haven't the liberty to move, to look at a newspaper, to touch a letter-file. In his presence I am not to sit, unless requested. I stand at the window and wait while the great man, leaning back in his chair, meditates, or gives his orders. I come when he calls; I stand silent until he speaks. Having heard what he has to say, I go. At my own desk, even, I am not to remain seated when he speaks to me. I rise to hear him."

"Any thing more?"

"Yes. I have my orders, that, if any one inquires for Mr. Gibbs, I am to make one of these three answers: 'Mr. Gibbs, is within,' 'Mr. Gibbs is out,' or 'Mr. Gibbs is engaged.' No matter what other questions are asked me, I surrender my rank as a free moral agent, and repeat, like a parrot, the same sentence as before, as the case may be, — 'Mr. Gibbs is within,' 'Mr. Gibbs is out,' or 'Mr. Gibbs is engaged.'"

"That's true. I heard you answer a man so the other day, and I remember thinking you were either uncivil or stupid. Well, upon my word!"

"You will think this a severe ordeal for a proud man; but I have not been so much humiliated, even by these petty tyrannies as by my share in the moral transactions."

"Moral transactions? What have morals to do with selling goods?"

"True enough. That is an axiom. I should explain. Mr. Gibbs, I hardly need say, is far too shrewd to allow any lies to be written, — out-and-out lies. But he would tear a secretary to pieces if he wrote the exact truth, — unless the exact truth were so improbable at the time as not to be believed. So the letters are skilfully studied. There is an evasion here, a slight false suggestion there, a reticence on some vital point beyond. There is a lie in the letter always, but *so* skilfully put!"

"Ah! I see. In tuning a piano the difficulty is to dispose of the 'wolf,' the sum total of discord between the upper and lower octaves. So the tuner distributes it from the top to bottom of the scale, making every chord slightly imperfect, but in the end getting rid of the 'wolf.' And you have to temper all *your* octaves, do you?"

"Something quite like it."

"If lying and meanness were catching, like small-pox — gracious, what a pickle you would be in!"

"Catching or not, I am determined to leave. I shall go to Eaglemont, and help father get in his hay, and in the fall go back to Andover for my degree, or go abroad. You know I expect to become a missionary."

"Yes," said Amory with a sigh, lamenting in his heart the sacrifice, as it appeared to him. Then, after a pause, "You speak of helping your father; but did it ever occur to you that you might do a good turn by helping your uncle?"

Robert looked fixedly at the clear blue eyes of his friend, as they alternately swam and winked; and, without a word being spoken, a ray of intelligence was sent and returned.

Robert reflected. Then Amory, too, suspected the designs of Gibbs! He thought of his good and generous uncle, — a man so esteemed, that to be "as honest as Hugh Prescott" was a proverb on 'change. He wondered if Gibbs did mean to ruin his old partner — if he had the power. Then he remembered the troubled looks of his uncle. He had seen that Gibbs more and more took the direction of affairs, and quietly ignored the senior. He remembered the costly style of living in his uncle's house, the superb receptions, the profuse hospitality. He thought of the pride of Mrs. Prescott, — of her carriage, dress, church, and concerts; and he thought with indignation (as he had often done before) of the habits of her son Roderick, who was pleased with the distinction of being the most extravagant member of the Arlington Club.

Yes, these expenses for his wife and step-son had perhaps exceeded his uncle's income, large as it had been.

But what could he, Robert Prescott, a poor theological student, do for this uncle in his emergency? He had been willing to work for a year to recruit his finances; but to continue — under Gibbs — in abject slavery, bound to a business that he had no taste for, to give up his manhood, his intellect, his moral nature, his mission as a preacher? It was not to be thought of.

Besides, his uncle had not taken him into his confidence, and evidently did not think him enough of a man of business to be consulted. Yes, it was best that he should return to his profession. What should detain him? He felt at liberty to resign his position, and to leave on short notice.

But, after all, he did not exert his will; or, if he did, the universe was a solid wall around Boston, and he could not get out. The divinity student was in love. He did not know it; only at the thought of going away there was something tugging at his heart, — some glistening lines, as fine as spider's threads, floating in air, yet potent as the invisible forces of nature; and it required no long observation to perceive that the figure towards which the traction tended was a young lady just out of her teens, whose rich color of tea-rose, and soft dark hair and eyes, were like a dream of an Italian painter. The longer he meditated, the more tangible grew the lines that stretched out to him, and led back to the image. "Edwards on the Will" failed to elucidate the mystery.

But the situation was a delicate one. He did not know the girl's parentage, nor any name for her but Phœbe; for so she was called in his uncle's house, where she lived on terms of intimacy, if not of equality, and where she had lived from early childhood. It was Phœbe simply whom he loved. She might be Phœbe Maloney, or Courtney, or de Guiscard, or Della Torre. His uncle, Hugh Prescott, had not legally adopted her; yet he and his wife treated her as a daughter, and gave their hearts to her as few parents do. She was barely twenty, wholly unspoiled by the world, sweet and equable in temper, simple in manner and speech. So he had found her during the year he had been teaching her Latin. These traits occurred to him now in flashes of memory; and above all he remembered an unwonted maturity of character, in which the charming dignity of the woman was blended with the joyous nature of the child.

She was inaccessible as a star. Could he go to the uncle, without any settled purpose in life, and ask him for the darling of his heart? Could he ask Mrs. Prescott, who was a devotee of propriety, — Boston's chief god, — for a young girl with braids of hair down her back, still studying music and languages, and he without an establishment, or the means to set up one? Dare he make his suit to Phœbe even? Would this fresh and lovely girl be content to share his lot as a poor preacher, or perhaps as a missionary to the heathen?

The desire alone was on one side, and a dozen solid objections on the other.

And then Roderick, the gay impertinent — what if his mother had plans for him? What if she had reared this charming young woman for her future daughter-in-law?

Between all these difficulties and dangers the young man was sufficiently perplexed.

The whole circle of doubts had, however, been traversed in an incredibly short time; for, as he came down from the upper sphere, he saw Amory standing on the same foot, leaning on his tall desk, and contemplating a certain writing which was arranged in sections of four parallel lines, quite unlike any mercantile formula.

Amory's large blue eyes turned towards Robert with a puzzled look.

"It doesn't come. Three lines are passable; the fourth is bad, incorrigible."

Whereupon he whipped the sheet of paper into a drawer. Robert was only partially recovered, and he wearily observed, "Mr. Gibbs is late in coming."

Amory, however, was sailing on his own tack, blown by a wind which Robert had not felt, and said bluntly, "If you go up to Eaglemont haying, I have a mind to go with you."

"You go haying! You'd wilt sooner than the grass, and be glad to crawl under a windrow to get out of the sun."

"Doesn't your father have help in haying?"

"Oh, yes! sometimes. I have always helped him so far; and sometimes Mary rakes after the cart."

"Does she, indeed? Ah, what a pretty idyl! And haymaking is something so fragrant, — grass all dewy, and mixed with sweet red and white clover. And then Mary rakes after the cart? In a sun-bonnet, of course; and the sun-bonnets are so jolly,—like sugar-scoops. Mary must look charming in a sun-bonnet. The scoop would look as if it had been successful."

Robert meantime was far away. The long and shining lines were drawing at his heart again, and he was thinking of the peachy bloom that glowed and wavered upon cheeks of tea-rose.

"I suppose I should have to go to church if I went to Eaglemont. It isn't respectable in the country not to go to church. Uncle Solomon and aunt Zeruiah always go, don't they?"

"My father and mother never stay away from public worship," said Robert, recalled from his vision. "In haying-time, though we are tired, and would like absolute rest, we go for the sake of example. Father sometimes nods on a hot day before the preacher gets to 'thirteenthly.'"

"I like your father, Mr. Prescott," said Amory respectfully, "and I must beg pardon for calling him uncle Solomon."

"Everybody calls him so, though he isn't old."

"And your mother, too, seems wonderfully good and just; though I wish she"—

"I know what you would say: she has an Old Testament way with her. But the poetry and old-world stateliness of the Hebrew Scriptures seem to have taken possession of her."

"And Mary—well, the young ladies in these hill-towns have sweet and charming manners—in a sun-bonnet, raking after a cart"—

The conversation came to a sudden close. As

a covey of partridges is hushed when the hawk sails overhead on widespread wings, so the small-talk ceased when the short, heavy step of Mr. Gibbs was heard. All were as diligent as if to enter figures in blank books had been the special end of their creation.

The junior paused at Robert's desk, and asked if Mr. Prescott had come. Being answered in the negative, he said in an irritating voice, —

"Late. Better attend to business. Need for him."

Robert and Amory exchanged glances, and went on with their work.

CHAPTER II.

It was true, as Mr. Gibbs tersely remarked, that Mr. Prescott was late in getting to business. His breakfast was over; and he sat in a small room adjoining the open conservatory windows, smoking a cheroot while he looked over "The Advertiser." The house stood on Mount Vernon Street, fair to the sun; and the windows would have been flooded with genial light, had not the rich but sombre Egyptian draperies interposed to make a fashionable gloom.

It was June, and nearly everybody had gone to Nahant, or Newport, or Mount Desert, — everybody whom Mrs. Prescott cared to know, — but up to this time Mr. Prescott had been unwilling to leave. Madam was seated near by, busy with a pile of soft Berlin wool, that looked as if it were the end of a rainbow that had been tangled in spooling. The air came in from the conservatory, cool, dewy, and fragrant; and the light on the lady's face was flecked with soft green shades.

Mrs. Prescott was what people call a fine woman, with clear complexion, large humid eyes, and a well-rounded figure, so becoming to a dame of forty-five. Something in her manners and habitual expression testified to her English origin; and in truth few women of American birth at her age retain such fresh features and elasticity of movement. Her luxuriant, ruddy-brown hair was lightly streaked with gray; and, while a part of its abundance drooped on both sides of her face, the remaining strands were gathered and coiled above her head, and, with laces and a soft pink ribbon, formed a striking and becoming coiffure. Her husband was a man of near sixty years, of medium height, plainly dressed, but exquisitely neat, and remarkable only for the singular depth and brilliancy of his eyes. His features were subdued in expression, — a habit formed by steady thought and by the exercise of caution in business; but his eyes, and the lines about his mouth, showed at once the quickness of his intellect and the impulsive generosity of his nature.

"Really, Mr. Prescott, it is time for us to leave town. The summer is coming in earnest, and we can't stay longer."

"June, my dear, is the finest month in the year in Boston. Just think what a glorious resort the Common would be at this season if it were only in Newport." Here the cheroot was raised to an angle of forty-five degrees, bearing east by south towards the lady.

"But it isn't in Newport; and it might as well be built over, for all the good it does us. *We* can't walk there."

"And why not, my dear?"

"Why, you know the malls are always filled with country cousins, and strollers that have nothing to do, and people that go holding each other's hands; and the seats are occupied with queer, staring couples." There was a shrug or shiver of disgust.

"Part of the entertainment, my dear. These strange folks make the walks a study. And they can't spoil all the fresh air, nor use all the green shade, nor monopolize the blue sky."

"No; but refined people like privacy. These low cads and shop-girls would make the finest park vulgar. No lady in society is ever seen on the Common, except in crossing to St. Paul's on Sunday morning."

"So much the worse for them."

"But truly, Mr. Prescott, can't we go to Newport, — or perhaps to Narragansett?"

"*You* can go, my dear."

"Of course I shall not go without you. Is it business, or what is it, that makes you want to stay after everybody has gone?"

"I haven't a doubt that a census would show as many people in Boston now as in winter, perhaps more."

"You know I don't mean that. Our set makes the world for us, — our church, our club."

"If the population were less by one, and I could name that one, I might go."

"Is it a riddle? 'Less by one!' What one?"

"Gibbs."

There was a volume of meaning in his look as he uttered the word. Mrs. Prescott looked at him with a puzzled expression,—an expression that soon deepened into pain as she saw in the depths of his clear eyes the strength of his feeling.

They were silent for a moment; but swift currents of sympathy coursed to and fro. After a while he went on, as if talking to himself,—

"Gibbs is a devil-fish skulking at the bottom of the sea. His eye takes in the opportunities, and he has tentacles ready for unwary fish."

"You frighten me. How can a junior partner harm the head of the house?"

"It remains to be seen which of us is the head. If he gets the upper hand, I don't look for any sentiment on his part, nor any forbearance. The interest of Gibbs is all that interests him."

"So we must lose the summer for the sake of Mr. Gibbs?"

"*I* must. I don't intend to be absent a day."

Mrs. Prescott sat fuming in her feminine way, much like a large spoiled child; and her husband went on smoking.

In an alcove connected with the drawing-room, on the opposite side,—an alcove of some size, lighted from above, and specially constructed for the grand piano,—Phœbe was running over a new song, humming the air at times, and then disentangling knotty places in the accompaniment. Tints of rose in the draperies of the alcove cast a warm reflection upon her face; and her luxuriant hair showed fine points of light, relieved by deep masses of shade. Her fine soft eyes were fixed on the music, her lips curved apart in her eagerness; and the exercise of her faculties, and her delight in the composition, were seen in a heightened but still refined glow, and in a rapt expression which painters strive to imitate, but which is never seen in life except as the sign and seal of genius. So she sang and played, by turns, with all her soul.

Mr. Prescott, as he sat, could see the illuminated profile of his darling, although most of the alcove was in a rosy shadow. The music was interrupted now and then, and Phœbe's face would wear a look of impatience. By and by it appeared that the leaves of the song were turned by another. Was it a fancy, or did she once or twice raise her shoulder, with an urgent feminine shrug, as if to be rid of some annoyance? The leaves were turned again, as if by some meddlesome hand interfering with her practice. Then once or twice she turned her head as if to hear something, and meanwhile her face showed successive waves of color. More interruptions followed; and soon all the variations in the scale of expression were seen, as if curiosity, vexation, dignity, shrinking, and then terror and anger, animated her in turn.

Mrs. Prescott had put down her work, and was looking at the plants in the conservatory windows. Mr. Prescott still affected to smoke; but the che-

root soon lost fire, and he chewed the end of it
with silent fury, until it became a shapeless wad
of tobacco.

The piano had ceased, and the voice of song
also; but Mr. Prescott saw, rather than heard,
Phœbe talking in a low voice, but with an electric
energy of manner; and meanwhile her eyes lost
their sweet look, and her cheeks grew velvety red.
She was no longer a girlish St. Cecilia, but was on
the eve of some angry outburst.

Mr. Prescott, whose senses were sharp, and
whose deductions were quick, was at first inclined
to blaze out with an oath. But he thought of his
wife, and he hated a scene, and therefore restrained
himself. He only rose, and yawned audibly, and
made some intentional bustle by overturning an
ottoman, jarring his chair against the table, and
then walking with some energy across the drawing-room, as if going to the alcove.

He did not enter the alcove: it was not necessary. Phœbe came out with a swift step, and,
half hiding her reddened and tearful face, slipped
into the hall, and ran up the front-stairs. The
step-son Roderick also came out from the recess,
calm and self-possessed, whistling the air of the
new song, and, sauntering towards the conservatory, took a cheroot, and lighted it. Then with a
pleasant nod to his step-father, and a by-by to his
mother, the young man crossed over to the hall,
selected a fanciful stick, and went out. The most
careful observer would have failed to detect any

sign of compunction, or any consciousness of impropriety. He looked as composed, and void of offence, as a cat just from a cream-pot.

Mr. Prescott regarded him silently, but not with his usual calmness. On the contrary, his jaws were firmly set; the full veins showed in his temples; and his eyes were almost phosphorescent. But he sat down again, smoked rather furiously, and seemed struggling with painful emotions.

"I wonder how long this is to go on," he said at length, thinking aloud.

"What is it, my dear?" asked Mrs. Prescott.

"Roderick is twenty-five, isn't he?"

"Yes: twenty-five last October. You know his birthday is the anniversary of Trafalgar, when his great-grandfather, the admiral"—

"Yes, I remember. But he isn't an admiral, nor on the way to become one. And what he will arrive at is the question."

Mrs. Prescott looked inquiringly at this abrupt turn.

"As we have brought him up to do nothing," he went on, "I suppose the best thing we can do now is to get him married off. That is the phrase, I believe,—married off,—like the periodical sales of surplus live-stock."

"I hope he will marry some time; but he is young yet, and he should have his pleasure."

"Oh, never fear! he'll have that, married or single. Do you think he has any notion of settling down?"

Mrs. Prescott was somewhat embarrassed. For her part, she had decided that her son should marry Phœbe, if she could bring it about; but she did not like to put her thought in words.

"Since I have adopted him, and he is no longer a Courteney, but Roderick Prescott, I am responsible for him; and I confess that I don't like to see the frivolous period spun out too long. He is a boy no longer."

"His great-grandfather the admiral was a gay youth too."

"So I have heard; but a sea-fight sobered him."

"And made him glorious."

"Yes, I know. You see, my dear, if I am to have a bout with Gibbs " —

"Must I always hear of that man? Isn't it enough that I give up Newport on his account?"

"Not at all. I must consider those I have to lug with me. Roderick doesn't count for help. He is among those that have to be carried."

Mrs. Prescott did not feel at ease. Her husband's remarks were barbed arrows in her soul. She did not exactly cry; but her breathing was short, and her color came in pulsing tides. "While you talk of what you have 'to carry,' you are grudging a share for Phœbe too, I suppose?"

"I grudge nothing to any, — neither to Phœbe nor Roderick. Every one, however, has to be considered. And, speaking of Phœbe, what is she doing now?"

"She reads Virgil twice a week with your nephew Robert, and she has lessons in music and Italian from Signor Belvedere: that is all."

"Hm! Robert is a fine fellow. Belvedere, too, seems a gentleman."

"Phœbe is wonderfully prudent and self-respecting."

"So I believe," — thinking with renewed wrath of the recent scene.

"I think she is fond of Roderick," — this with some caution, in a tentative way.

"Of Robert, did you say?"

"No, my dear: I said she was fond of Roderick."

"Yes, I've no doubt. She ought to be very fond of him."

"They have been brought up like children together."

"Yes; like a terrier and kitten, — paw and claw."

"And I have been thinking" —

"And I too."

"Ah! you think Robert should look for a rich wife?"

"If I live, and struggle through with Gibbs, Phœbe will want nothing. I shall see to that."

"She is a dear girl."

"I have said a thousand times she is like my own flesh and blood."

"And Roderick is not" (apprehensively).

"No; but I shall look out for him."

The steady look meanwhile was like the sight of a rifleman. Mrs. Prescott could not penetrate her husband's thoughts. All that he had uttered was open and free; but still she felt there was something in his mind that she could not divine. She shifted the topic of conversation.

"Don't you think we should make another effort to find out her parentage?"

"No, my dear. We should only come upon some good-for-nothing adventurer, who would want to sell her, and, if he could not drive a good bargain, tear her from us. But we have a right to adopt her, and in about a year she will be her own mistress. So she reads Virgil with Robert? Well, she might do worse."

"I suppose Robert will soon be leaving the office."

"Probably. His year is about up."

"I am sorry he doesn't join the church, and be ordained by a bishop, instead of throwing himself away. I can't bear to think of him as a — as a — sectary. How noble he would look in the robes! He has a better figure than father Carlton. And such a charming spiritual expression!"

"Better not let his mother hear you! Aunt Zeruiah, as the country people call her, would tear the robes off his back. 'Mark of the Beast' would be her mildest phrase."

"I heard of some very unkind words she said because we had the altar candles lighted in our oratory at the solemn music on Good Friday."

"Well, it was a little sentimental, wasn't it, to have a string quartet playing dolefully by candle-light, and the family and friends sniffing as if at a funeral?"

Mrs. Prescott looked a mild reproach.

"By the by, when Roderick comes in from his walk, ask him to step down and see me before dinner."

When alone, Mrs. Prescott had plenty to think of. She was anxious for her son, whose hold upon her husband's regard and affection she saw was loosening. She lived chiefly for the graceless youth, and had shielded him often from his step-father's anger. She loved the girl Phœbe too: but it was interest that prompted her to desire her marriage with Roderick; for she felt sure that Phœbe would some day have a good share of Mr. Prescott's property, and it would be so comfortable not to let it go out of the family.

Various reasons had combined to keep the girl in seclusion. She had not been acknowledged as a daughter. She was not a Prescott, nor any thing but "Phœbe." She attended no parties or balls, had no friends among the young ladies who lived in the neighborhood, no confidant nor intimate. Having a quick mind, perhaps more reflective than observant, she lived in an interior world of romance, peopled with great and heroic men as well as beautiful and brilliant women. The only persons of all the living she knew (besides her old foster-mother, Mrs. Maloney) were those of Mr.

Prescott's family, his nephew (her Latin teacher), and her music-master, Signor Belvedere. These were but few; but they formed Phœbe's world. In such a life the character of each friend becomes momentous. In such a life an ingenuous girl may become frank and outspoken like Miranda, without a thought of overstepping the line of delicacy.

Mrs. Prescott knew little of Phœbe's interior world; but she was conscious of having neglected a mother's duty towards her, and hoped to make late amends.

But the chief subject of her thoughts, and the object of her fear and dislike, was her husband's partner Gibbs. This feeling did not arise from any real knowledge of the man: it was only because she saw the success of his schemes would lower the position of her family. And without her establishment, her church, her son, and the Plato Club, the world would be empty, and life not worth living. Gibbs, in this view, was the sum of all evil. She was in terror; and what made it agonizing was the sense of utter helplessness.

CHAPTER III.

Signor Belvedere's apartments were on the
third floor of a fine but old-fashioned house,
whose windows opened upon a pleasant vista of
grassy slopes and full boughed trees. Two rooms
and a closet sufficed for his modest wants. In
one was an upright piano in ebony case with gilt
ornaments; in the other a capacious sofa, that
might be a bed in disguise. In both rooms there
were book-shelves in every nook, and along the
base-boards; brackets supported antique casts;
pictures, sketches, and prints covered all available
spaces upon the walls; and, instead of curtains,
exquisite flowering plants in pots of majolica
filled the windows, not wholly obstructing the
prospect, but tempering the light by soft green
glooms, and filling the air with delicate scents.

To a stranger the rooms were full of pleasant
surprises. Though seemingly devoted to elegant
ease, if not to luxury, they contained sufficient for
the ministry of common needs. The porcelain
stove (a German contrivance) had bright sauce-
pans and kettles stored away in its pagoda-like
top. In the wall there were panels that swung
open when touched, and showed glass and china,

silver-ware, and table cutlery. An ottoman in a corner, if examined closely, proved to be both a wash-hand stand, and an ice-chest. Behind rows of books were receptacles for eggs, macaroni, canned mushrooms, truffles, and sweetmeats. A bamboo reclining chair was also a library table, with drawers for stationery and letters. The litter and annoyance which usually attend housekeeping, and which make life odious to sensitive people, were wholly wanting. In short, the rooms, though packed with ingenious contrivances, like a London dressing-case, seemed to the casual visitor to be steeped in the air of delicious idleness.

Signor Belvedere was above fifty years of age, tall and spare, but active and graceful. He wore a full white beard, and his iron-gray hair was closely cut around swelling temples; while above rose his bald head like a dome, — a fitting crown for a noble figure. He would have been a vision of antique beauty, but for the large bulbous glasses that shaded his deep-set gray eyes. But not even the glasses could conceal the fire and softness of the orbs, nor the full, dark lashes that fringed them. It may be added that he had the exuberant feeling and taste of an artist, and the serene manners of a prince. Something of finesse and caution belongs to all the race that produced Macchiavelli, and Signor Belvedere was naturally velvet-footed in movement; but a more ardent soul than his was never pent in clay. He seemed to have stepped out of a picture of the middle ages, at a time when art, poetry, and knightly courtesy were born.

He had completed his morning toilet, though not without some trouble. The laundress had ironed off a shirt-button, and he was fain to secure the plaits of the bosom, white as snow, and unstarched, with a quaint mosaic brooch. The bit of color showed fairly under the soft waves of his snowy beard. "It is unusual," he said to himself as he looked in a mirror; "but it is not-a unbecoming."

One black silk stocking had a hole in it. "'A solution of the continuity,' as-a my friend the philosopher would say." He could mend it, if there were time, as he could turn his hand to any thing; but breakfast was to be accomplished. He took another stocking: that had a hole also; but luckily, as he observed, after thrusting his thin, nervous hand into it, "the apertures" were "not co-extensive nor co-terminous." So he drew the one long, slender, glossy stocking over the other, triumphant. "In-a my slippers," said he "the hole will not-a show." The slippers of leopard-skin were perhaps incongruous; for every other part of his costume was black and unobtrusive.

Opening one of the cupboards, of which the room seemed as full as a stage-scene made ready for a Christmas pantomime, he set a few dishes upon the table. His alcohol lamp was already burning, and there was a supply of boiling water ready to be dashed upon his fragrant coffee, freshly roasted and pounded, and to fill the coddler for his eggs. He raised a small slide, fitted in grooves at the end of a wooden tube that inclined forward, and let an egg roll out. He looked at the date pencilled upon the shell, and saw that it was recent; then he let another roll into his hand. By this means every egg in the inclined tube that served for a repository had been turned over, — a wise precaution, as every observing housekeeper knows.

An orange, the two coddled eggs, a roll, and a cup of coffee, — a large Sevres cup, — furnished him an ample breakfast. It was half-past nine, and time for his pupils. He did not indulge in smoking until after dinner. From the closet he brought a something that looked like a small churn operated by a crank. He put in it the few dishes, poured in hot water, and in a moment the cleansing was accomplished. His fingers were as delicate as a queen's, and his ingenuity had been devoted to saving them from contact either with dirt or hot water. Viands and dishes were put up; the secret recesses were closed; the room put off its workaday air, and, but for the faint lingering fumes of coffee, was as odorless as a gallery of sculpture.

There was a slight tap at the door. Signor Belvedere rose and opened it, holding it open with stately politeness for his visitor. A tall and beautiful girl entered with a light step, and with only a faint smile of greeting.

"Good-morning, Miss Phaybe. You are quite-a punctual."

"Yes, professor. I started early; and, for a longer walk, I came by the path under the lindens. I have been enjoying the fresh air, and I thought I might be late."

"How oft-en must I request you, my dear youngg lady, not to call-a me 'professor'? Ever-y player of guitar, or snapper of castanets, or boxer, or hitter of shoulders, ever-y quack and boot-a-black in this great country, is 'professor.'"

His speech was rapid and energetic; but his eyes were corruscating in merry twinkles, and his white teeth glistened under the curves of his mustaches. On her part, there was an evident effort in her politeness and in her assumed cheerfulness.

"Pardon me!" she said. "I spoke without thought: I know better. Yet you are generally called so."

She was standing by the front-window, as if to turn her countenance away from the light. The brilliant greenery in the window, studded with blossoms, and flecked with sunlight, formed an appropriate background for an enchanting picture. This the quick eye of the artist saw; but there was something in her manner that excited his surprise.

"Take a seat, Miss Phaybe. You are perhaps agitated. It is far from the street, and there are many stairs. Your breath comes with-a difficulty. Please to take a seat."

She hesitated; and her looks, though dark and sad, were inscrutable. The color seemed to heighten even while her teacher was regarding her.

She was in girlish dress, — a light fawn-color with scarlet edges; but she had never seemed so tall before. She appeared to rise visibly to a stately height as she stood there, so that the rather short skirt began to look out of place. Her full and naturally brilliant eyes were now charged with emotion, but inflamed and tearless. The plain chip hat, and the full shining braids of black hair, did not seem to belong to her: it was as if some queen of tragedy had put on the head-dress of a schoolgirl. This was not the bright and cheerful creature whose coming had always been like a sunbeam. She was persuaded to sit; but she did not remove her hat, and she kept her roll of music in her hand.

"Some-a thing troubles you, Miss Phaybe," he said. But here he checked himself, with the thought that it was not delicate to invite a young girl's confidence; and, changing the intended sentence, he added, "but we will try the les-son. It is a lovely melody; and, in the high and pure atmosphere of Mozart, we will-a forget whatever is annoying."

"I cannot sing," she said. It was as if all the sorrows of all her sex had found expression in those three words. Her look was not so melancholy as it was abstracted, or perhaps indicative of a slowly receding storm of anger.

Signor Belvedere was puzzled. He opened the piano, ran his fingers lightly over the keys, struck handsful of pathetic minor chords, and then, as if after struggling with them, wrested the secret sorrow, and turned them perforce into new and joyous combinations. Leading up to the melody of the lesson, the piano sang it like a prima donna. It was a call, he thought, that the heart of a singer could not resist. He looked at his pupil with an eloquent interrogation as he was ending the strain; but she shook her head, and dropped her eyes.

"I don't know that I shall take lessons — at least now. I am going away — I must leave my, — that is, Mrs. Prescott. I — I may have to care for myself, and there will be no money for lessons." There were no sobs, only the same steady, unreadable looks.

He left the instrument, and sat down near her, looking at her fixedly but tenderly. "And pray what has happen-ed? Mistress Prescott loves you like a mother, does she not?"

"Yes; Mrs. Prescott is good to me. I ought to like her for mere gratitude, and I do like her. She is kind."

"She is religious?"

"Yes, she is devoted to her church. I suppose you know she has a room with stained-glass windows, and religious pictures, and kneeling hassocks for morning and evening prayers, — an oratory."

"Engleesh!" said the teacher with a comic shrug.

"I suppose so. You know she was born in England, and has relatives living in Lancashire. If you are much with her, you will hear of her family, especially of her grandfather, the Admiral who fought at Trafalgar."

This coldly critical tone was quite unusual. Phœbe was naturally affectionate, and inclined to playfulness; and it seemed now as if she were piqued, and seeking reasons to justify her ill temper.

"Mr. Prescott — is he not good also?"

"The dearest good man that ever lived. He is all goodness. I am sorry for him."

"You are-a — sorry for him, eh?"

"Yes. His partner is Mr. Gibbs. Do you know him? I think Mr. Prescott is afraid of him. Mr. Prescott is domestic, and cares little for fashion. And the stepson" —

As she paused, the teacher's eyes wore a keen look. "And-a — the stepson?"

"The stepson Roderick, who now has the stepfather's name, is a person of whom" —

She set her lips firmly, and was silent.

"And-a the stepson is the person with whom Miss Phaybe is angry?"

What she thought was unutterable: what he *was* the course of the story may show. As he then appeared to her, he was a person for whom she felt something like contempt. His slight and elegant figure was before her, as when, dressed in faultless costume, he was sauntering towards the club. She had marked his smiles for people of condition, and his polished indifference or insolence to others. She had seen his levity, and his respectful disrespect to his parents; and she had felt an aversion to any personal contact with him which could be expressed only by inarticulate sounds and by certain urgent feminine adjectives. She believed him a smooth hypocrite, a selfish seeker of pleasure, without conscience or honor. Not that she had cultivated the power of analysis, or could have put in due phrases her view of his character. That was the way he had affected her.

Her silence was significant, and the teacher made a tack.

"You have been my pupil, Miss Phaybe, four-a years; is it not so? And before that — before you lived with Mistress Prescott — where was your home?"

"Mrs. Maloney, a washer-woman, brought me up. I do not remember my parents. I have only a faint recollection of the looks of my mother."

"I shall-a respect Mistress Maloney from this time. There are many noble people of the Irish race, but it is evident that you are not-a one of them. Your figure, your eyes, the contour of your face, your complexion, are more trustworthy as evidence than a register of baptism. The English have a blunt but expressive saying, 'Blood will tell.' You have, as I read you, the hair and eyes of an Italian mother, and the height, the erectness, the profile, and the brilliant complexion of an English father. But it-a does not matter. You are a good girl, and my dear, splendid pupil; and I am proud of you."

Phœbe's eyes began to grow misty. The conjectures as to her parentage did not interest her greatly; as all previous inquiries in her behalf had been baffled, and she had settled into contented ignorance. But her teacher's sudden tenderness touched her.

"And I shall give you lessons so longg as you will come. If the worst comes, — and who but the All-Wise knows what *is* the worst? — you can singg. You will have success. You will captivate." Phœbe still meditated. "I suppose," he continued, "that it has lately come to the knowledge of some young gentlemen, that you are no longer a tall and large schoolgirl, that you are a young lady, and handsome, — a per-son to be lov-ed."

His tone was airy and pleasant; but the words brought a deeper flush to her cheeks. She hastily sought to parry. "I might give lessons — to beginners," she said, "or sing in a choir."

"Ah, that is easy, if you do not-a — get married. While you singg, you must give your life to your art. Per-haps you will prefer to marry? There is a beautiful vista in the future for every young lady, — her own especial private vista; but at the end of ever-y one is a church with a bridal party coming out of it, — and she knows who is wearing the orange-blossoms."

She almost smiled at his raillery, but soon became grave again. "I hope to get something to do, for I *must*. I cannot stay with Mrs. Prescott."

"Don't be rash, my dear young lady! We must not-a give the world more to talk about than we can-a help. The stepson Roderigo may be a gay impertinent; but his mother"—

"It is his mother who schemes for him. If any one were likely to share Mr. Prescott's fortune, as, perhaps, I might, she would try to unite that share with her son's. She has even told me so." It was in a swift, angry way that she spoke, and to her great mortification the moment after.

"What frankness! It is-a like the sweet simplicity of the golden age! And so you do not-a love him?"

"I detest him more every day. When he did not appear to notice me, I liked him better."

"And so you have blossom-ed into his-a lordship's notice, eh? I am not-a your father confessor; but is this all?"

She thought it was much, and more than enough; but she did not answer his question. She remembered vividly that her protector's nephew, Robert Prescott, had manifested a most eager interest, not only in her studies but in her welfare, and had seemed bent upon giving himself the sole charge of her future, whether she would or no. Signor Belvedere was not her father confessor, and she only blushed in silence.

Signor Belvedere observed her slight confusion, and forbore. But he returned with his fatherly advice.

"My dear youngg-a lady, it is a very important step. I beg of you take-a time to think. Do not count on getting new friends like the old ones. A new social status is not always practicable, if desirable. There are per-sons now, — old fellows, to be sure, — who will-a consider your welfare as their own. Remain, I ask you, — as a father, I ask you, — remain with Mistress Prescott for a few days, a week. I cannot-a say what I will do; but I will do something. Who knows but the young man Roderigo will go to the war? All the young fellows are going; capitanos, colonels, in plenty. Perhaps he, too, will march away, vhistling, 'The girl I left behind me.'"

She did not answer. Her mind was so fixed in the idea of seeking a new home, that her teacher's arguments had no force. No matter at what cost, she must get away. She felt that she could not meet Mrs. Prescott nor her son. But her resolve, like the secret of her disquiet, was kept in her own breast.

"And what of the other young man, — the other Prescott? I have seen him but once; but I shall not-a soon forget his picturesque face, his athletic form, his flowing brown hair, and eyes of steel-blue."

It was still in a light and pleasant tone that he spoke; but the effect was evident. Phœbe's confusion was increased; but in a moment the expression of her eyes visibly softened.

"He has been a divinity student," she said with some effort, "and he intends to be a missionary."

"A missionary! *in partibus infidelium.* And so you don't want to go to Asia, no, nor to Africa, nor yet to convert the heathens of Roma, or of Paris. And perhaps you do not aspire to be the sposa of a priest at all?"

Phœbe struggled with some rising thought, but answered in a mild voice, "Perhaps I shall have a career of my own. I hope to follow my art."

"Brava! But I am afraid, after all, you will follow your heart."

Phœbe laughed: her rigid ill humor had begun to soften. The master rose and went to the piano. Once more he played the chords of *Voi che sapete,* and looked wistfully at her. She came to his side, and began the song. The unusual excitement had given a new energy to her nerves. Her lovely face was radiant with the heightened feeling. Her breast heaved with deep and sustained respirations. Her voice poured out in grand volume, but obedient in every swelling wave to the control of the mind. The phrases were exquisitely marked, and blended into an artistic unity. It was the magnificent utterance of a cultured singer, who, though long trained, had never before put forth her strength, and had never apparently been conscious of it. In one step she had reached the pinnacle.

When she ceased, there was a silence that tingled. The master had inadvertently moved sidewise to the sunny window, and was looking at a rare Japanese plant decked with sweet-smelling white blossoms. As he returned with a sprig of glistening leaves and blossoms in his hand, Phœbe noticed that he had furtively put away his handkerchief, and that his usually serene features showed the liveliest emotion. A mocking-bird, that up to this time had been good-humoredly piping some simple notes over his seeds, now struck up a brilliant strain, shooting through scales and variations with dazzling rapidity, trilling as if his little heart were throbbing with ecstasy, and then lapsing into tones of delicious languor. It was a gay counterpart of the song, — the bird's version of the sentiment against the young prima donna's.

Signor Belvedere, pointing to the cage with an assumed gallantry (for in his heart he was so enraptured that his joy was like a pain), exclaimed, " My bird, Miss Phaybe, saves me the necessity of compliment. What I could not utter, his songg has exemplified. It is not to every one that this intelligent feather-ed critic gives his praise. Believe-a me, I never heard bird or damsel singg so before. Wear this little flower, if you will. It will fade; but I shall not-a forget." He turned his back and whipped out his handkerchief, and then added, " I have something of cold in-a my eyes."

She was so much affected by his sudden change

of manner and by the intensity of feeling in his tones, that she could not utter a word of reply. She silently grasped his hand, then flung a kiss to the bird, who was still trilling and caracoling gayly, and lightly stepped down the stairs as if descending from the heavens.

"She is a good girl," he soliloquized, "and she is an inspir-ed singer, one born to reveal the glory of music to the world." He looked at his watch. It was eleven o'clock. "Two more pupils this morning. Oh the thick ugly voices! I cannot-a bear them. After that song — those notes of an angel? No. The air is clear. The east wind has blown away the dull odors, and has left a sweet breath in heaven. I will promenade. No more lessons to-day."

He selected a Malacca stick from the sheaf of fencing-foils suspended over the mantel, put on his invariable black coat, and walked out.

CHAPTER IV.

ROBERT PRESCOTT in his heart was chiefly a poet. He was devoted to his intended calling, and sincerely religious; but he looked at religion, as he did at nature, through the medium of imagination; and with him truth and beauty were harmonized. He had never wrought out a stanza; but duty in any guise to him looked noble, and the world was always a pictured poem. The bright flower of poetry in youth is love; but before this the severe student had not recognized it. His pupil in Virgil was but lately developed from a tall and rather awkward girl into a magnificent woman; and the amateur grammar-master fancied himself the first to observe the phenomenon.

There is a spring every year; but when the warm days come, and the poplars have a sheen of silver, and the horse-chestnuts are seen in an emerald haze, — when the pear-trees are studded with white clusters, and the apple-trees spread their tops like huge pink bouquets, it seems always as miraculous as if it were a special display of the Lord of gardens. Year by year, too, these ungainly schoolgirls, with short dresses and long braids, with unshapely arms, and apparently large fect, are developed into the roundness, the sweet dignity and grace of young womanhood; and every one witnesses the change with a new surprise.

Robert Prescott thought from the first that he had never seen a girl that promised to become so fine a woman. She appeared sensible, modest, delicate to a fault, and capable of enthusiasm. Through the year this conviction had grown stronger; and now, at the time of this morning walk, he was conscious of trying to suppress a glowing and all-absorbing passion.

It is apparently the belief of some that every man when in love loses his intellectual character and power of expression, and that he must necessarily stammer out his passion in short pointless sentences, such as the shallow and thoughtless use. It was not so with Robert Prescott. Accustomed to silent meditation, animated by one great and absorbing purpose, accustomed to blend all thoughts and delights with the service of God, accustomed, too, to thinking in set phrases, as if framing homilies or prayers, his exuberance of poetry and piety appeared to have been thought out beforehand; when, in fact, his strong and steady flow of speech was but the fusion of all feelings and ideas in a solemn yet uplifting love of the Divine Being.

It was not for such a man, when once aroused, to content himself with timid monosyllables in the presence of his beloved. He had broken away

from the office of Prescott & Co. by some resist-
less impulse, and strode out for a walk. As he
neared the Common, the elms seemed to wave him
a welcome, and the long brown malls opened invit-
ingly. Cool airs played with his hair as he raised
his hat under the shade; and the peace of the blue
heaven came through the open-work of leaves.
He was mentally putting things in order for a
return to his higher duties. The image of his
pupil, spelling her way through the Latin lesson,
or singing in her grand and natural way, he would
not allow himself to contemplate. He compelled
himself to think of his preparations and his departure, — perhaps to a foreign land.

But there was a figure not far distant, moving
with a graceful step, and it began to grow familiar. Should he turn, and walk the other way?

Phœbe, after leaving the master, walked briskly
along, her steps keeping time to the inspiring
strains that still rang in her ears. She did not
wish to meet the family in such a state of excitement, for she knew her cheeks were like blood
peaches; and, in truth, the more she thought of
it, the idea of returning home at all was insupportable. She had no definite purpose beyond
that of enjoying a walk and of considering what
she was to do; and she entered the Common, and
turned into a narrow path that led to a broader
mall under old trees veiled in tender green. The
birds overhead sang incessantly: it seemed to her
that they knew their auditor, and rejoiced in her.

Sparrows hopped along on either side, looking up at her saucily, and now and then stopping to flutter over a dusty spot as if taking a sand-bath. Nursery-maids with stout arms, and with faces unwrinkled by care, were pushing jolly young aristocrats about in perambulators. Pigeons cooed and loitered, or strutted and sidled, and came up fearlessly to get the crumbs which the children threw. But Phœbe met no one whom she knew; and she enjoyed the luxury of the grateful shade, and the cooling wind upon her still glowing cheeks. If one wishes to be unobserved by the world of fashion, a shady mall among the loveliest sights and most soothing sounds is the safest retreat.

She had not brought her meditations to any point, but was still drifting in a sea of revery, when she was aware of a firm, springy step behind her, every moment coming nearer. Instinctively turning, she saw Robert Prescott.

Phœbe's look, as she paused for a moment, was unmistakably one of frank surprise and pleasure; but Robert was disconcerted and unready. The sense of coming difficulties oppressed him. The very sincerity of his respect for womanhood, and the fervor of his hidden affection, made him hesitate awkwardly. He had always envied in men of the world their easy and triumphant approach to women, and was vexed with himself that he, who had a right to be unabashed, and frank in manner, in the presence of the best, should never be able to do as he would.

Hs took off his hat, bowed, and smiled; but a tutor in "deportment" would have seen much in him to criticise.

"You come from your lesson, I suppose? How delightful that I meet you, and on this day, too, when I am about going away from — from Boston!" It was out, though he had just resolved to leave that piece of news till the last.

She answered with a sweet gravity, —

"Are you going away? Isn't it sudden?"

"Yes, my going is rather sudden; though I have long intended it."

"Just think! I shall miss the last of the eclogues!"

"How happy I should be in parting with you to miss nothing more than the eclogues!"

"Oh, surely I didn't mean that I shouldn't miss you too! You have always been very kind. I thank you very much."

"I don't deserve the least thanks, if you are thinking of the lessons. It was pure pleasure, and I was wholly selfish. I wish the lessons had been twice as many, and" — As he paused to look at her, she cleverly avoided the expected turn of the sentence.

"Does Mr. Prescott, your uncle, know of your going?"

"Perhaps not yet. I have just written my resignation, and left it on Mr. Gibbs's desk.'

"They will miss you at the office."

"In business, Phœbe, no one is missed. Another

man will sit at my desk. Every thing will go on as before. Among friends the case is different. It is pleasant, — and sad too."

They walked on in silence for a moment. The self-denial he had imposed upon himself began to give way before the rising current of feeling. Hardly knowing what he said, or whither his passion was leading him, while a luminous paleness overspread his face, he faltered out in a helpless way, —

"If I might hope, Phœbe — yes, I am sure you must know my secret: I must have told it a thousand times as we read together. My eyes have betrayed me, I know, and my voice. O Phœbe! while I taught you Latin, I was studying a far deeper lesson, — a lesson so absorbing, so momentous! A life-time wouldn't be enough. You must have seen it. I have struggled against my feelings in vain. I thought I could be brave; but now, with my solemn duty before me, and upon the point of separation, I am the most wretched of mankind."

He looked at her beseechingly as if he would read her soul, and find there some encouragement. She did not speak. With a still more earnest tone, he went on, —

"If I were thinking of myself alone, I would risk every thing, but the favor of my Divine Master, for your sake. But I have to consider others. You are the idol of my uncle, and I would not win the heart of his darling without his full consent. May I ask him, Phœbe? With all my soul in my words, may I go to him, and ask his forgiveness for robbing him of you?"

The situation was delicate. She could not tell him of the occurrence of the morning, and what was now in her mind; but she said earnestly, —

"Don't, I beg of you, don't go to Mr. Prescott!"

"But he would not object, — not long, — if — if he knew your happiness were at stake."

"I cannot say that — cannot say that my happiness depends upon any one. I am not happy."

There was a sense of loneliness in the tone.

"My dear Phœbe, you don't know yourself. If ever woman was " — He checked himself. "I mean to say that love and marriage are divinely appointed, and belong of right to the purest souls. Your noble nature will know, must know some time, what it is to love."

"I don't know how it may be. I haven't thought. of it."   This in a low and innocent tone.

"May I not hope that at least I do not repel you, that you would think me deserving — in a measure — of your affection?"

With perfect sincerity she answered slowly, —

"I have not thought of you, — not in the way you speak. You do not repel me; for I respect you, and trust you. I have not thought of any other feeling towards you."

What she did *not* say was, that she felt herself at a distance from him; that with her respect and trust was blended the reverence due a superior being; that his powerful mind and high principles, to say nothing of his grave ways, made him unapproachable; and, above all, that his chosen profession was associated in her mind with painful solemnities, — with the repression of music and natural gayety, and with the shadows of unending gloom. If she thought of him with admiration, it was blended with awe. Now was the moment when the want of sympathy was a barrier almost like that between the seen and the unseen world.

"And so you look up to me?"

"Yes, I must."

"I might say the same. I have perhaps some gifts that impress you; but I am very flesh and blood, brother to the humblest; and, when I see a pure and gentle soul like yours, I look up to it with the longing of a child for a star."

"You don't do justice to yourself. Your whole life is above mine."

"This is the inexperience of youth, Phœbe. You are cultivated in your own way. Your feelings are the same."

"I don't think so. I have often listened to you. You read as no one else does; and you find what others do not see, — even in a sunset. You seem to have a world of your own."

"This is cruel, to place me on an eminence where I do not belong, and to leave me there alone. If you please, I'd rather come down from the pedestal."

Nothing was so stimulating to Robert as the idea of a comparison or of some form of reasoning; and for the moment his feverish pulse subsided while he endeavored to argue with her about the harmony of different "spheres."

"Even if I were such a being — I won't say such an idol — as you set up, should I find my other self in a woman of masculine force and fibre? Not so, my dear Phœbe. It is a beautiful paradox the Creator sets before us, that the touch of a gentle girl's finger is as potent as the grip of an athlete. Did you ever read Jonathan Edwards's letter to the young lady whom he afterwards married? — and you know what a Titan in mind he was. There is nothing more tender, more beautiful, even in Shakspeare. It breathes the fragrance of love, and you seem to see blossoms of poesy springing up among the simple words."

While Robert was philosophizing, Phœbe's agitation had time to subside. She delighted in his talk, except when it took a strong personal turn. She had nothing against clergymen — in the pulpit. The rustle of a black gown, when too near, made her shiver.

"Perhaps you think me gloomy. I may appear so; but my thoughts are bright to me; my soul's horizon is all glorious. I say it with all my heart, only the religious man has the full sense of the loveliness and the poetry of nature; and it is he who has the highest and least selfish love for woman. Gloomy as you may think me, I am full of rapture, even to be near you. For you are so beautiful as I look at you, — your noble head, your sensitive eyes — every fibre in me is trembling with delight."

She felt strangely moved by his impassioned manner; but still with every sentence there was a rustle of the black gown. He, too, felt that he had been sailing on the wrong tack; but his strong soul would not mind the helm. He was not urging his suit wholly *as a man:* though conscious of the disadvantage, he seemed trying desperately to carry his theological opinions, his chosen profession, and himself, all together, and win her acceptance of the whole.

As Phœbe appeared absorbed in contemplating the smooth gravel of the mall, he went on : —

" I often think of the Providence that led me here, and to meet with you, the one I would have chosen from among all living. My leaving off study for a year was a cross; but now I see it was a blessing. My parents — you will go some time to Eaglemont, and see them — have toiled and saved and prayed for me, not that I might be rich or great, only for the glory of God. For my success nothing was considered too great a sacrifice. They were content to live meanly, so that I could be fitted for the ministry. I don't feel worthy of such love."

It was in a tender, almost pathetic tone he spoke; and sentence had succeeded sentence as if he were impelled by some unseen power. But

Phœbe still felt no sense of *nearness*, and manifested no wish to reply. He began to think again that such a high and holy strain might not be the means to win the heart of a bright young woman just out of her teens.

"I don't know that I should repeat these things; but I can't help it. I seem to be untwisting the inmost strands of my being; and I find my love for the dear ones, and for *you*,— for you, my darling" (somewhat falteringly spoken), are twined with the greater Love which is given us from on high. There they are, all the strands together. I cannot simply say I love you. I *do* love you; but I seem to be held *with you* in the Almighty arms.

"Tell me," at length he said, almost despairingly,— "tell me how I can touch your heart! I know you are not cold. I am the one at fault. I am the drifting iceberg, bringing a chill into your sunny atmosphere. You have different associations. God has been for you an awful name perhaps, and you shudder at hearing it, while I am warm in his pervasive light."

"I don't think I look at things as you do," she said; "but the Creator does not seem to me an awful being."

"Even the highest natures differ in their conceptions of the Infinite: to some his power is revealed; to others, his love. Two souls may not have an identical view, but they may yet love each other fervently. But why can't we drop theology? and let me say once more, 'I love you.'"

She had been quite willing that theology should be dropped, but not desirous to hear his confession over again.

"I can't help thinking of one thing," she said with some hesitation. "I think of the future,— yours and mine. I can't think the Creator is less pleased to hear me sing than to hear the birds."

"Surely not. Music in itself is pure, refining, ennobling. But I want you first to feel an interest in me; and, if you think my purpose holy, you would have an interest in that too. But I don't even press that now. I want first your love. I will leave the future to take care of itself under the guidance of Divine Wisdom. Believe me, Phœbe, I could die for you. 'Greater love hath no man than this, to lay down his life for his friend.' You see, I can't help quoting Scripture."

"But I don't want any one to die for me," she answered with a faint smile. "If I ever have a lover, I want him to live for me."

"My dearest, I cannot give you up. I wish I could show you my heart of heart: it has but one image, except my blessed Lord's. Every thing about you suggests beauty and perfume and goodness. I have seen you visibly blooming like a rosebud. I love you. I have never felt the thrill before, and it can never come again."

"I wish I could thank you. I hope I am grateful; but love, they say, comes unbidden. If I *don't* love you, how can I?" She felt a little twinge here, as if this were an unmaidenly expression; but he had pressed her sorely, and she was driven to frankness. She did not wait for him to reply, but continued, —

"I beg of you, don't urge me! While I listen, I am a bundle of feelings; but that must pass. I must be myself. I should be miserable as a clergyman's wife. You almost take away my breath; you are so earnest; but I fear that *you* are yourself the reason I don't love you."

"But in time you would sympathize with me, and have the same joy that I do."

"I don't know. But, Mr. Prescott, this is hardly fair, is it? I mean, it is not kind to continue this. It is hard to bear."

Hitherto she had walked slowly, generally with her eyes fixed on the ground, and had spoken in low and tremulous tones. Now that she had begun to make a more active resistance, or self-assertion, she raised her head, and, for the first time in her life, confronted the tall lover with something of a courage like his own.

"Did you ever think," she continued, "that I may have my own necessity, and perhaps my aspiration? that I might have the feelings of an artist, and that I may become a public singer? While you were attending a prayer-meeting, I might be on the stage of the concert-hall or opera."

His countenance fell. She saw her advantage.

"My teacher has praised me this morning,—praised me to vanity, perhaps,—and I feel sure I shall sing. I may have to earn my own living."

" Why, you couldn't think of it ! You surely will never leave my uncle?"

" I am sorry to say it; but I think I shall try to find another home. Even if I stay, I might be unwilling to give up my ideal. You would feel pained, would you not, if any one were to ask such a thing of you? It would be as if your father and mother, and your sweet sister, had lived for you in vain."

This was a new view. In the conception of two beings becoming gradually alike in thought and life, it is generally the woman that is expected to assimilate. The young man tried to think how it would look for him to give up the ministry to become the husband of an opera-singer. It was dreadful. In all his previous meditations, if there had been any moulding to be done, woman represented the clay, and man the potter.

It was with a great gasp that Prescott said, " I see the gulf between us. I have already said too much. I had hoped your feelings would change ; but I see that cannot be. I shall go into the Master's field ; but I shall go alone. Birth and death, and a love like mine, happen but once. Farewell !"

" Don't ! " she said eagerly, — " don't say those despairing words. You will be happy, as you deserve to be."

His face resumed its solemn expression, but seemed to be illumined by an inward light. His voice faltered. "Do not leave my uncle," he said: "you have a home with those who love you. As a singer, and among strangers, I dread to think what may happen, — what indignity you may suffer."

"One may suffer indignity anywhere."

The words brought an explosion like a thunderbolt. "What! — Roderick? Has he dared " —

She felt her head droop, partly in regret that she had allowed such a hint to escape. "I beg you, be silent," she said.

"Infamous, silken reprobate!" he continued, grinding his teeth. "But perhaps he will get a commission, and go to the war: I have heard it intimated. But I pray you, don't leave my uncle. He doats on you, depends on your love. I don't know what the future is to bring forth; but I have misgivings. I suspect and fear Gibbs. I am afraid the time is near when uncle will need the aid and sympathy of all who love him. Sing, my dear Phœbe, if you must, but don't leave him." Here he halted for a moment.

"You just now said 'Farewell.' You are not going to leave at once?"

"Yes, at once. We have rambled wide; but here is the end of our path. Here I must leave you — forever. Pardon me if I don't come to the house to say good-by. I shall drop out of the city quietly, and be forgotten." With a sudden rush of emotion he said, "May the great Father of us all have you in his holy keeping! May your heart be always like a lily in his sight! God in heaven bless you!"

It was like the invocation of a saint. His eyes were tearless, but unspeakably tender, and the glowing light came again to his face as he turned away.

A sensation almost of awe fell upon her as she heard his parting blessing, and saw his rapt soul in his eyes; and she exclaimed, half aloud, "Oh! why could I not love that noble man?"

CHAPTER V.

IF Phœbe had lingered, she would have seen on the mall two persons in earnest conversation, whose meeting at such an hour, and away from the business quarter, would have given her cause for thought. Hugh Prescott, her kind protector, and his stepson Roderick, were slowly pacing the walk. The elder walked slowly, as if carrying some unusual burden. Of the young man some hint has already been given. He was a pattern of the reigning mode in dress and manner. Elegance and an air of studied indifference were plainly visible in his features and carriage. The conversation was a long one, and it need not be wholly reproduced. It covered the usual topics of discussion between rich parents and prodigal sons; such as horses, billiards, clothes, jewelry, wines, cigars, clubs, and accommodation notes. The elder was vehement: the younger was provokingly cool. The elder wished the youth to know that "the last straw" was not a fabulous growth, but an actual entity: the younger, who had passed through many similar crises, believed that his mother would bring the enraged step-father round, as she had often done before. He made vague promises of amendment: but the father put no faith in him; he felt that the youth could be pinned to nothing; it was time that he should know the worst.

"Roderick," said the elder with a deep and earnest tone, "I blame myself greatly for what you are. You are an aimless boy, without fixed principle, or sense of responsibility, without useful education, and contributing nothing to the world, not even a good example."

"*Fruges consumere natus,*" interposed the youth, with a satisfied smile.

"I am glad you remember three words of Latin," said the father sharply. "I wish I had put you in the counting-room, given you a moderate salary, and made you live on it. The time has come when you might have been of use. You have naturally good parts, and I need help. I am pressed to the wall. But *you,*—you are a butterfly; and I need a man with energy, soul, stability."

There was something in the tone of this speech that awakened the young man's curiosity, and repressed the gibe that he was about to utter.

"Yes," continued Mr. Prescott, "if you had been trained to business, and had given to it half the zeal you have wasted on extravagances, you might perhaps even now do something."

The young man remained silent; and the elder went on:—

"I took Mr. Gibbs as a partner, because he had

shown ability as a business man, and because I thought that gratitude, if nothing more, would attach him to my interest. I took him, without capital, fifteen years ago. To-day he has three hundred thousand dollars; and I — I hate to say what I have. You have spent a mint of money. And your mother — well, I won't reproach her: she thought my purse had no bottom. She spent for flowers alone, for that last reception, nearly a thousand dollars; and next day I had to go, hat in hand, to a bank director to have a note extended. What the clergy manage to get out of her for charity, I groan to think of. Our house is the resort of professors, foreign celebrities, unsettled preachers, and the talkers of the Plato Club. But all things have an end. We have spent our income, and more too. It has come to me through my nephew, — and, by the by, I am sorry such a level-headed young man is going to be a preacher, — it has come to me that Gibbs, who has long been secretly plotting to get me under his thumb, has been intriguing with the corporations owning the mills, whose accounts we have, and expects to force me out, and be himself the sole agent. This he will do, when he is ready, by demanding that the partnership cease, and calling on me to buy or sell. He thinks I can't buy; and, as matters now look, I surely can't. The result will be that I shall have to retire, — an old man without business, without capital, the husband of a once fashionable lady, and the father of a prodigal son."

Roderick hoped the matter was not quite so serious. Mr. Prescott went on: —

"It is just so serious. The information my nephew gives me, though only vague as to details, tallies exactly with the observations of Amory the clerk, an honest though scatter-brained fellow, and explains some cautious suggestions I have had from friends in the business. In short, Roderick, my ruin, your ruin, the ruin of the family, is near at hand. For myself I have a little place in the town where I was born, not far from my brother's farm on the old hill in Eaglemont. I can live there. But your mother? — and you? Now, while I have the money, I offer you a draft of five hundred pounds to go to Europe with, or," he continued hesitatingly, "if you should *want* to go to the war, — mind, I don't advise it: God knows I would not put you in the way of a rebel bullet, — not half so soon as I would risk it for myself. But many of your set have gone; and, if you *do* want to go, I will get you a commission, — that is, if I can, — and give you a handsome outfit. I don't want to have you here walking about, or tapping your boots with a Malacca cane, when I have to suspend payment. I wish you to make your choice. You can go up to Eaglemont (the house shall be your mother's, and I will furnish it comfortably); you can take your five hundred pounds, and go abroad; or, if you feel inclined, freely and without any urging of mine, to volunteer, that course is open to you. But something is to be done at once."

"I will volunteer," said Roderick suddenly.

"God bless you!" said the father, with a dash of emotion. "You have the pluck of the old admiral, your mother's grandfather. I will see the governor at once, and get you a commission."

But here Mr. Prescott's face assumed a serious look: his eyes began to glow, and his breath came fast.

"There is one matter which I must speak of; but it wrings my heart. I am deeply pained to confront you: I would rather lose all I am worth. While it was doubtful what your decision would be, I would not bring it up. I would not use this — this wickedness that I suspect you of — I would not use it as a weapon against you, — to force you away, to expose you to danger. But when you manfully accepted, when you showed that you had some good stuff in you, I thought I *must* say it — must give you a warning, I will call it, in place of an accusation. For it is something that touches the very core of my heart. I mean Phœbe, my darling, my pride. This morning I saw you — saw something that staggered me. Your manner was gay and off-hand; but it did not deceive me. The girl has beauty and modesty; but she is a woman, and has a heart. You were trifling with her. What you said, God only knows. I don't inquire: I don't wish to know. I know what you *did*, and that you made the quick color come in her cheeks, made her eyes drop in shamefacedness, continued your advances or innuendoes, or whatever they were, until she rose in wrath, until she cast upon you the swift glances of anger, of mortified, insulted, indignant virtue, and rushed away. I saw it all, sir. I cannot be mistaken. I fear to lose her. I fear you have outraged her feelings so that she will leave us. And this, sir, was the one strong, irresistible motive I had to separate you from the sweet girl whose tender feelings you have injured. All I have said about my affairs is true to the letter; but if I had millions I should require you for the present to live elsewhere. A man of my age and standing, sir, does not permit a dependent woman, either of high or low degree, to be trifled with, if he knows it."

All this invective came like the torrent that rolls down the valley when a dam gives way. The stepson could do no less than quail before the angry looks and vehement reproaches. He tried to excuse himself, insisted that his conduct was misunderstood, and that he meant no dishonor.

"I take you at your word," said Mr. Prescott stoutly. "You meant no dishonor. Then tell her so, in the words and with the deference of a gentleman. You are going away: let the girl and your mother and myself have cause to think kindly of you. You are to be a soldier: be without reproach, as without fear. God knows I wouldn't be rough to my wife's only son. Let us be united in feeling at home. The outside world has trials enough for us without these."

"I will apologize to Phœbe, and with all due deference," said Roderick earnestly.

"Do it, my dear boy, and make me happy. I must leave you: I have an appointment with Gibbs."

If Roderick was not the darling his mother thought him, he surely was not quite the villain that Phœbe supposed. As his step-father had intimated, his useless life and indefensible conduct were in a great measure owing to his neglected education and to the absence of good influences. He had associated solely with young men who had no duties to perform, and no responsibilities to bear. In their company he had learned the flippant speech and supercilious manners that mark fops and profligates. The dignity of labor, the worth of character, the virtue of man and of woman, the duty owing to society, these were topics never mentioned in his set, except with gibes and laughter.

So Roderick had grown up, ignorant of every thing useful, familiar only with elegance, learned in club amusements and etiquette, wearing the cool manners of old reprobates and young dandies, regarding his mother as a person to be flattered and cozened, and his step-father as one to be treated with just enough respect to secure the regular allowance. As for Phœbe, he had never bestowed upon her a thought, any more than upon a pretty servant-maid, not, at least, until her dawning beauty had given some emphasis to his mother's prudent suggestions. Then he began to notice her, to admire her in his lawless fashion, and to delight in bringing blushes to her cheeks.

He was a tolerably worthless person as he stood; but he was not without some good impulses, and it would have been possible even then to make him an honest and reputable member of society. But his mother was occupied with her visiting-list, her church, her oratory, and the Plato Club; and she did not know that she was rearing a polished heathen in her own house. Roderick behaved well at table, was never drunk, — in her sight, — went to church with her on Sunday mornings, and performed well his butterfly parts in the refined circles which made her heaven upon earth. That was all she knew.

She was ignorant as yet of his conduct towards the orphan under her charge. She had come to admire the girl, and, as we have seen, had set her heart upon her marriage with Roderick. She supposed that the young Sultan had only to throw his handkerchief; for, of course, no girl in any station would think of refusing an offer from a young man with such personal and social advantages.

Now Roderick must let his mother know that he had not only got a deserved repulse, but had forfeited the girl's respect, and, moreover, that he was going to join a regiment for active service. It was a sad message he had to carry. The situation sobered him, and set him to thinking of various practical matters in new lights.

CHAPTER VI.

ROBERT walked swiftly at first, but soon short-
ened his steps, and, with bowed head and bent
shoulders, slowly traversed the malls, making a
long circuit, and returning without premeditation
to the place where he had parted with Phœbe.
The uprooted tree floating in the current of a
river, when it reaches the broad and deep eddy
where the black water lazily circles, yields to the
force, and all day describes its planetary orbit,
rushing down on one curve to be swept slowly
back on the opposite one. Robert's mind was
such a whirlpool, deep and uncontrollable; and
upon it floated the flower of his love plucked up
by the roots. Still swept the black eddy; and,
though the contemplation was maddening, he
could not for one moment free himself. It was
as if a requiem were chanted in the recesses of his
brain, — mournful chords that never would modu-
late, melodies like the wail of a mother over
her first-born, and all blended in a never-ending,
always-beginning movement.

While in this mood, he was unconscious of the
lapse of time, of his own surroundings, of bodily
wants, and of the presence of mankind; but he

was made aware of companionship in his walk. Roderick, fresh from the meeting with his step-father, and at once sobered and softened in feeling and manner, came up with Robert, and touched him lightly on his arm. Robert's eyes while in repose had something of the vague and wonderful depth which elderly people remember in the look of Webster. They were contemplative, humorous, or tender, by turns; but in moments of excitement they blazed with an intolerably fierce lustre. For one instant the habitual deep and melancholy expression was turned upon the new-comer; then, as the parting came to mind, and the terrible hints given by Phœbe were re-called, and it became evident that this was the sleek beast of prey that she was fleeing from, the fierceness shone like an electric flash.

"Is it YOU?" he said. They were simple words; but Roderick probably never forgot them, nor the look and the tone that accompanied them.

The glance was like flashing a sudden light upon a burglar, and the tone was contempt, wrath, and defiance. It was certainly more like the spirit of the pugnacious Peter than of the gentle John. There was still a good deal of the "old Adam" in this young Christian.

Practised man of the world as he was, Roderick was surprised, stunned; but policy and inclination combined to make him patient. "Why, Robert,—Mr. Prescott, I should say,—you go off like a torpedo! We have been friends. Can't we remain so?"

"A torpedo isn't *intended* to hoist its friends," said Robert coldly and deliberately.

"Then let us see why we are *not* friends."

"I cannot be a friend to one who would sully maiden innocence."

Roderick felt the thrust, and began wondering how his rough and luckless wooing had been noised abroad. Not by his step-father, certainly not; his mother did not know it: then by the girl herself! The process of reasoning was short; or rather conscience, like lightning, ran over the lines to the inevitable conclusion.

Roderick had the power of thinking on his legs; or rather his natural sprightliness played in the inner chamber of thought a kind of running accompaniment to his speech. Even as he began his excuses and deprecatory exclamations, his mind was darting back, and making wonderfully acute deductions as to the meaning and implication of the confidence between a rather sedate young preacher, and a tender, shy, and thoroughly modest girl, such as he knew Phœbe to be; a confidence, too, that admitted the possible mention or the hint of an indelicacy. The intimacy was certain; and the fact was not calculated to inspire courage, or fluency of speech.

When Robert launched his arrow, he had paused, and was leaning against a tree, throwing out meanwhile the light of his steel-blue eyes. Roderick was determined not to be angry, but to stand on guard, to parry, and at last to palliate and belittle

the offence. So, without wincing, he exclaimed,
" As a general principle nothing could be more
correct.   Your friend *could not* sully maiden innocence."

"But haven't you attempted it?"

There was a dangerous directness about this
man.

" By no means. I, a destroyer of innocence!
On my soul, no! Pardon me, you are a clergyman, or soon to be; and I am not, and must
speak in the way of the world that is not over
nice. I don't pretend to have been a Joseph."

"I believe you have not been."

"But don't wear that awful frown. You look
like a prosecuting attorney harpooning a lying
witness. I am not the criminal you think."

" Have you not driven a friendless girl from
your father's house and your mother's protection
by your shameful treatment?"

"Not that I know of. Of course you mean
Phœbe,—a young lady that I am very fond of,
one that my mother loves as her own daughter.
And, with the feelings I entertain, I shouldn't be
very likely to attack rudely the lady I hope to
marry."

During the last sentence, which was uttered
more slowly, the "harpooning" was done by the
other party. Roderick watched the effect of his
stroke, and was pleased to see that it touched a
vital point in his adversary. All the poetry,
purity, affection, and pride in Robert's strong

nature, rallied for the defence of Phœbe against this monstrous claim. Though lost to him forever, the thought of her in the arms of this rival was worse than the doom of Jephthah's daughter.

" *You*," exclaimed he in a sudden fury, — " *you* to win the heart of an angel like her! She is a lily; and your hands are foul. She has a soul; and your heart is a void. If all the world conspired with you, God himself would interfere to prevent the unnatural union."

" You preachers have a comfortable way of keeping God as a kind of reserve-corps. But you will have to fight your own battles without divine aid. You know *you* can't win the girl, and I assure you *I will*. We can at least understand each other. Let me add that a pint of wine at a late breakfast sometimes makes the blood a little unruly: that is all. I *was* a little hasty. I don't mind saying it, since you know so much. But a woman easily forgives an impulse which her beauty provokes. Don't be uneasy about me. I will make it all smooth. I should like to be friendly with you. I have not known you as a rival. I did not know that you felt called upon to defend the lady's honor."

Give Roderick time enough, and he would talk down even Satan. He had flanked the adversary, but now feared he had pushed his triumph too far, and he hastened to conciliate.

Robert was drawing deep breaths, and was contemplating the easy escape of his wily foe. His strong convictions were unchanged. He did not regard what Roderick said, and he did not care much for what he did; but his whole soul abhorred what he believed Roderick *was.*

"You make a very plausible statement. You are not deficient in tact and cunning. I have my opinion, nevertheless. As you say, I may not win the girl; but I pray devoutly she may be delivered from you."

"Don't trouble yourself about me. I don't need your prayers, nor does Phœbe. I shall shake off the habits of a man about town; and when I come back all new, with a star or two on my shoulders, we shall see. Girls are not implacable. Let us see, is it to India you are going?"

Robert would have been puzzled to explain his sensations. Physical violence was not to be thought of. Christian meekness was quite out of place. He simply drew himself up, and replied, "My intentions, I believe, do not concern you. I shall go where duty leads me."

"Quite sorry to leave you under such a cloud; but it would be cowardly not to let you know my aspirations. I could sneak in, you know, and capture the girl without fair warning, especially as you had shown your hand. I bear no malice. You'll think better of me when you know me. And so you won't shake hands? Well, I for one won't be uncivil. You have my best wishes — in every matter except one."

Roderick walked off with almost all his old

gayety, leaving his rival fixed to the spot where he stood, and full of the most maddening reflections. Robert had yet to learn that the fine-spun theories of poets and ethical philosophers with regard to the triumph of truth and sincerity are delusive. The habitually false, who have the art of making the worse appear the better, get along quite as well in the world. As the high souls are uncommon, and as people in general know nothing of the absolute purity of such characters, their simple and direct speech is regarded as an affectation. Men do not credit the existence in others of a higher standard of truth than their own. Therefore the plausible insincerities of Roderick were as likely to gain credence as the unswerving nobility of Robert. The rigid virtue that could not accommodate itself to the sinuosities of Mr. Gibbs, and give a fair outside to lies in trade, was only mocked at. Even Mr. Prescott the senior probably considered his nephew squeamish. But no one, probably, not even the sorely-tried Phœbe, could understand the grand self-truth which would not allow of any wavering from duty to gain the prize more coveted than any object this side of heaven.

From the hated world of business as represented by Gibbs, from the false social world of which Roderick was a type, and from the unappreciative soul of the girl he had chosen, Robert turned away to commune with himself and his Creator.

Roderick went to his usual haunts, — to the Minerva Library to see what new novel had come out, to the hotel where out-of-town friends called, and, lastly, to his luxurious club, the Arlington. There, among kindred spirits, the affairs of the day were talked over, and the military news was discussed. It is but just to say that he seemed to have a more earnest tone, a sounder fibre in him, and a sobriety of judgment that was vastly to his credit. He met returned officers, some wounded, some invalids, and the incidents of the service were discussed. It was soon known that he was going to have a commission in a regiment, — a regiment of blacks; and the ordinary banter was hushed. He was becoming a hero. He saw it in the eyes of his friends, and the consciousness re-acted upon himself. He was steadied by thought of the weight he was to carry. But still his thoughts often returned to the fair girl; and he wondered, if, after all, he would carry out his plans.

" Who knows a woman's wild caprice? "

CHAPTER VII.

IF Mr. Gibbs was not in a good humor when he went out, he was still more grim on his return; for, on going to his desk in his private room, he picked up a letter, and read the resignation of Robert Prescott. "Humph!" said he, running over the lines, "resume my theological — hm — business wearisome; will settle with my uncle; expect to go abroad — hm — canting fool!" He tore the letter to shreds, and put them in the waste-basket.

It was not the gracious air he wore when he entered his "swell" church, or when, arm in arm with a man who had a grandfather, he walked through the fashionable streets. He mused: "So young Prescott has gone. Well, he had brains, and wrote for us in a style that did credit to the house; but too honest, too squeamish. Letters needn't *be* honest: they should only seem so. Prescott wouldn't swerve a hair. Troublesome. Wanted always to tell the whole. Bad to show your whole hand. One card at a time; let your adversary play to *that*. Time enough then to play another. But I wonder who will take his place? Shall I try Scraggs? No: he owes me on a mortgage; mustn't let him get too near; couldn't squeeze him if there was any intimacy. Dobson? No: he is too sharp. If he got any points in the business, he'd use 'em for himself. Boric? No: he goes out for a cocktail at twelve. Cocktails are for after-hours, and at the club. Amory? Yes, Amory: why not? He is vain; but he writes well. Honest? yes; and not so sharp as to make his honesty a thorn."

Mr. Gibbs went out towards Amory's desk, and motioned to him. Amory shivered. The truth was, he was ambitious to shine as an author; and, though he had never neglected his duties as clerk, his desk contained no end of sonnets, epigrams, and couplets in various stages of evolution, besides (if the truth must be told) a variety of studies for advertisements, — a species of composition which the prudent youth found more profitable than writing verses gratis for the newspapers. He feared that his secret delights had been observed, and that he was now about to get a raking. Moreover, he had been absent two afternoons a week, for some time, on his own business, without formal leave, although he believed that Mr. Prescott had either sanctioned his absence, or condoned the offence. Amory felt much like a schoolboy summoned to the master's private room; but Mr. Gibbs had been considering his policy, and was almost cheerful in his greeting. He even motioned to his clerk to sit, — an unprecedented condescension. Full of wonder, Amory seated himself, and waited.

"Well," said the great man, "strange things are happenin'. Robert Prescott's gone."

The clerk nodded.

"Goin' to preach; goin' to the heathen—hm. Boston's good 'nough place for me."

No reply appeared to be called for to such a self-evident statement.

"I sh'd like to travel, though. Went to Yerrop once, about twenty years ago. Was hauled about to see ol buildin's,—all out of repair,—rickety from top-ston to under-pinnin'. If I go again, I sh'd try to enjoy myself,—go to the operer, hear music, and see the people. The Bible says the proper study of mankind is men and women. They ain't heathen, though,—them broonets in the Hague and Brussels! Silky hair, like corn-silk, skins that show the blood clear through, an' pale blue eyes,—them's my colors. The women in Italy with rhubarb complexions, and eyes like great blackberries, make you think of the pictures by Michel Anglosaxon. Too much development. Didn't like 'em,—pictures nor women."

As Mr. Gibbs was never to be corrected, not even when he made $2 + 2 = 5$, Amory did not venture to comment upon the eccentric views of nature and art. The merchant appeared to have some idea of establishing a basis of sympathy between himself and a man of known taste for literature and the arts.

"You don't paint, I s'pose?" Amory shook his head smilingly.

"If I had time, *I* sh'd like to patronize music. Some people run wild about paintin'. Talk about a thousan' dollars a square yard! Wy, there never was any such vallue in any square yard of paintin'. You can sometimes git good picters on the sidewalk in State Street for ten dollars, all framed, with clouds and woodses an' water an' boats, — jest as good, jest as good. I take more to music. I s'bscribed for the big orgen" (here he felt of his pocket sympathetically). "Makin' tunes is like makin' somethin' out o' nothin'. Try to whistle, and you get into somebody's tune: if you get outside on't, you're nowhere, — lost. You can *say* somethin' new; but, when you whistle, it's somethin' old. It's a smart feller that picks up the notes layin' round, and puts 'em together so as't they stick."

Mr. Gibbs had been watching his clerk; but the face before him was as if it had been made of china. He had not struck the young man's fancy yet.

"I've a mind to bring up one of my boys to be a Be-thúven. Why not? Don't you think that's an idea? I might have him write histry, like Motley; or pōtry, like Longfeller: but it's more of a thing to be a Be-thúven, — more grand like, more kinder distangay. Do you ever compose any music?"

"Not at all."

"Thought I'd seen things in rows like gridirons, on your desk, — long gridirons with peeps on 'em?

Oh, ah! somethin' else? Pŏtry, I've no doubt.
I know you have somethin' *here* (tapping his cor-
rugated brow with a pudgy finger).

Amory blushed, and replied rather nervously
that he *had* written a few verses now and then,—
out of office-hours.

" You study too? "

" Yes, a little natural science."

" Well, I'm glad it's nateral science. There's a
lot that's unnateral. Histry, too? "

Amory nodded, curious to know how this excursion through the arts and sciences was to end.

" I've been asked to take hold of a new bank
(I'm drector in three now); and they said — some
of em — they was goin' to call it the Sam Adams
Bank. Now, I want know who in —— was Sam
Adams? Any relation to young Sam on Battry-
march Street, or to them stuck-up Adamses down
to Quincy?

Amory modestly gave the desired information,
and added that it was proposed to set up a statue
of the orator.

" Oho! A statoo! Why, that'll give the bank a
good send-off. Histry doos come in now an' then.
And you can write somethin' sensible about com-
merce an' the like?

" I hope so," said Amory.

" Hm. And so you can rattle off on paper in
good style? Put in long words that sound well,
and don't mean any thin'? Let a feller down easy
that we wouldn't wanter trust? Keep people

from gettin' too familiar and over-drawin'? Oh, I know. Style's every thin'. Manners and cere-munny keeps vulgar folks at a distance: so doos style in writin', — somethin' in that. Yes, writin' has its place. Couldn't do without it. Though genrally, when a feller writes too well, he can't do nothin' else *ez* well. It hurt Choate, this bein' litry, and it hurts Hillard. The quiet ones that don't spread themselves on paper 's too much for the litry fellers. No offence to you. *We* shall run the machine " (tapping once more the ugly brow), "and I think yourn's the hand for the pen. What d'ye say ? "

The end of this oration was signalized by a keen look from the twinkling eyes, and a forward movement of the bulky body; while two stout hands came down as props upon the short chunks of knees. The sloping line of the back, the pose of the head, and the expression of face, reminded Amory of a toad. But the question was none the less embarrassing for its comic aspect. The first impulse was to refuse bluntly. Mr. Gibbs repre-sented nearly every thing that he detested. Even at a distance the decent hypocrisy due to an employer was difficult: to keep up the show of respect at close quarters would be a hard task. Mr. Gibbs did not merely inspire silent aversion, but active dislike to the very border of hate. Amory felt almost like fighting when the head of the enemy was thrust towards him.

Mr. Gibbs, who had expected an instant and

joyful acceptance of the offer, was surprised to find Amory hesitating. To make the declination less offensive, the young man expressed doubt of his ability, especially as the successor of so able a correspondent as Mr. Prescott's nephew, the divinity student. Mr. Gibbs blurted out "Pshaw!" and "Nonsense!" But, the longer he talked, the stronger the aversion grew in the soul of the honest little man; and at last, being pushed to the wall to answer yes or no, he said *no* civilly but decidedly.

Mr. Gibbs was naturally angry, and started up. He was not in the habit of being opposed. He drew himself up to his full height of five feet six, pursed out his cheeks, and, while the color deepened in his coppery nose, he exclaimed, "Very well, sir. You leave this house. The cashier will settle with you. Go!"

He opened the door, and pointed outward with a short stout finger.

Amory was quiet and firm. "I believe," said he, "I am entitled to a notice, and am not to be put out of doors in this way. I was hired by Mr. Prescott, and I don't believe he would see me dismissed without cause."

"I will let you know that *I* am master. *That* for Mr. Prescott. Get out, you beggar!"

The next instant Mr. Gibbs was lying on the floor with a contusion on the back of his head, caused by the edge of the desk which he struck in falling. Amory did not follow up his advantage, but stood on the defensive, with his fists clinched, glaring in every way at the clerks who had rushed towards the scene. There was pain or surprise on the faces of some, but suppressed merriment was evident in more. The elder men got Mr. Gibbs up, looked at his head to see the extent of the injury, and placed him in a chair. His rage and astonishment, to say nothing of the fall, had literally made him speechless.

Meanwhile Amory held his ground, disdaining a word of explanation, until presently Mr. Prescott appeared. The sharp look of inquiry which the senior cast upon the group was answered at once by Amory.

"He had just discharged me for no cause, and without notice. I thought that was enough; but he then called me a beggar, and I knocked him over."

"Very wrong," said Mr. Prescott, but without any great emphasis.

Mr. Gibbs had recovered enough to gurgle out, "Call a policeman!"

"No need of that," said Amory. "I'll appear at court, and pay my fine — with pleasure."

"Arrest him!" said Mr. Gibbs fiercely.

"What is all this about?" asked Mr. Prescott.

"I dismissed him," said Mr. Gibbs.

"And for what cause?" inquired Mr. Prescott, nettled at the assumption.

"Because I chose," replied the junior, straightening up, and settling his chin in his collar.

"Mr. Gibbs," said the senior in a deprecatory tone, "any thing in reason, you know. And, after what has happened, of course he must go. But you will hardly desire — if you think of it — to give such an answer to me. Amory was entitled to a fair notice — until his act of violence; and I am entitled, as the head of this house, to a respectful answer."

The face of the junior, which had been paler than usual on account of the shock, seemed to blaze, all at once, with recollections of limitless burgundy and brandy. The rigid wrinkles about his eyes encroached upon the limited surface above his stubbly beard. Perpendicular furrows shot up between his eyebrows. His temper was uncontrollable; and, with a husky voice, he shouted, "The head of the house be d——d! This firm is dissolved. Time will show who is master."

"This is extraordinary language," said Mr. Prescott; "but I am not altogether unprepared for it. — Remain, Mr. Amory, a moment. An interview that begins with a storm like this should have a witness. — So, Mr. Gibbs, the mask is thrown off. You announce the dissolution of the partnership. It is a little sudden, but, perhaps, just as well. Notice to the public, of course. Usually the notice gives the new arrangements also."

"The new arrangement will be 'Gibbs & Co.,'" said the junior, with protruding lips.

"Possibly," said Mr. Prescott. "But there are

a few preliminaries, such as an inventory, a transcript from the books of the assets and liabilities of the firm."

" All prepared, Mr. Prescott.   The whole thing is ready in my desk, — inventory to date, schedule of bills payable and receivable, private account of Mr. Prescott, ditto of Mr. Gibbs."

" A little time may be necessary to verify statements covering so many items."

" As much time as you want.   But the dissolution is a fact.   Your rights are what they are. Figures will show. — Confound that desk!   How my head aches ! "

" What do you propose ? "

" I might say that to you.   Buy, or sell."

" When would you expect the payment to be made, if I conclude to buy ? "

" I won't be unreasonable.   It's a large sum. It would take some time, — say a week."

" Monstrous ! " said Mr. Prescott.   " You know the richest man on the street would find it a task to produce so much money, — money, I say.   People talk of such sums, but they don't often see them.   There hasn't been such a sum paid over in settling a firm's accounts, in money, — mind, I say in money, — for years."

" Well, make it a month."

" Call it three."

" It's all the same.   Let it be three."

" If the old Corinthian had not given out," said Amory aside, speaking now for the first time.

Mr. Gibbs heard the remark, and, sore as he was, howled with derision, "The Corinthian! a humbug copper-mine! Why, I've got certificates enough to line a trunk. By George, I'll sell 'em to my barber for shaving-paper!"

Mr. Prescott winced. It was he who had persuaded Gibbs to invest with him in that disastrous venture. The shares that Mr. Prescott had "placed" with his friends had left marks everywhere like blisters. Some actually thought he had "unloaded," had knowingly sold the stock after its worthlessness had been proved, — just as the promoters of the Pewter File Company did, swindling credulous friends out of their hard earnings. This was a very sore subject with Mr. Prescott; for he was a man of honor, and not a man to "unload." He had fully believed in the Corinthian, and had not only put his money in it, but had persuaded his friends to do so. But it had given out, as Amory said. There was not an ounce of copper in the hill that would not cost the price of two ounces to get it to market. It was a hopeless wreck. The certificates were pretty specimens of engraving; and people kept them, as they kept Kossuth's Hungarian bonds, mementoes of a pleasing delusion. No wonder Gibbs sneered.

"Gather 'em," said he. "You are out of business, Amory. Gather the bonds. Get 'em all together; and perhaps the paper will help pay your fine, you puppy!"

Mr. Prescott was going to speak; but Amory respectfully waved him back, saying, " I am not quite without resources. I can pay the fine, and I can earn a living. I should be better pleased to serve Mr. Prescott without a salary than his partner *with*. I am glad to take my leave. Goodby, Mr. Prescott. May we meet under happier auspices!"

Mr. Prescott was so much absorbed in this sudden turn of affairs, that he scarcely listened to Amory, and scarcely returned his farewell.

"The mill accounts," said he to Gibbs, "are they at your beck and call? May not the directors of the Pequot, or the Miantonomo and other mills, possibly have something to say?"

"Let him carry the accounts that can get 'em," said Mr. Gibbs doggedly, rising, and sopping his wet handkerchief upon his head.

"Amen!" replied Mr. Prescott. "You are playing for a large stake. You may win, because I may be unable to raise such a sum of money. But I don't believe you will get the mill accounts; and, if you don't, you will have lost the game. You will have shown your bad temper, your ingratitude, your baseness, in vain."

The attitude of Mr. Prescott as he uttered these words was neither aggressive nor petulant. The words came from his lips in tones that were free from the exaggeration of wrath. Mr. Gibbs was full of rage, almost ready for violence; but as he cautiously looked about, standing within sight of the clerks, he saw that something of the conversation had been overheard, and that he was closely watched; and he knew that an assault upon the "head of the house" might lead to very unpleasant consequences.

So the two men separated, — the one to rejoice over the success of his first move, the other to meditate on the chances left him. The younger man affected no sense of delicacy, no sentiment of honor, no feeling of gratitude. He had neither. He was a rich man, and he had become rich in the usual way; namely, by always taking the biggest slice in the dish. A fine-souled man with regard for his fellows, one who waits that others may have their share from the bountiful platter that Nature sets out, will be apt to see the dish swept clean before his turn comes.

And the elder was too proud, too well acquainted with the way of the world, to make a single reference to the past. It was of no consequence that he had given Gibbs the opportunity to rise, or that Gibbs owed every thing to him: the only question was, what Gibbs's interest was *now*. In dealing with such a "business man" in the present year of our Lord, if one has the advantage over him, it isn't advisable to throw it away.

CHAPTER VIII.

IT was nearly time for dinner, and Mrs. Prescott
was weary of looking at the clock. After Phœbe
went to take her singing-lesson, a foreign bishop,
one of the celebrities of the time, called, but
only long enough to exhibit some relics which he
designed to carry to the next meeting of the Plato
Club. He had a bit of stone from the holy sepul-
chre, the dagger and a lock of hair of Lord Byron,
and a roll of parchment from a monastery on
Mount Athos, containing a fragment of a pseudo-
gospel in Greek, in which were related the spor-
tive miracles wrought by the infant Jesus while at
play with his fellows. The stone was a fraud, the
relics doubtful, and the manuscript a forgery;
but Mrs. Prescott had a surfeit of piety and sentiment in looking them over. The day had waned.
Roderick had not come home, though that was not
unusual. Mr. Prescott was also late. But Phœbe
had never failed to return to lunch before. It was
surprising, and was becoming a matter for alarm.

Phœbe, as we know already, had few acquaint-
ances, and scarcely any friends, outside the family.
If she had a relative living, she did not know it.
When Mrs. Maloney formally surrendered the

charge of her, it was understood that visits were to be as infrequent as Christmas and Easter. The barefoot and ragged regiment in Mrs. Maloney's neighborhood had, of course, lost sight of their old companion; and the young ladies of her own age in society knew little more of her than if she had been an upper servant or seamstress. The position of a dependent had its trials; but they had not only been borne without complaint, but had been ignored. Beside her protector's family and her teachers, she was absolutely alone in the world.

Some dim consciousness of this had begun to form itself in Mrs. Prescott's mind. As she had virtually assumed the place of a mother, she felt that she could not much longer delay public acknowledgment and a formal presentation of Phœbe to her circle of friends.

But where could she be now? She had sent a servant to Signor Belvedere, and had learned that he was not at home. She was beginning to be nervously anxious.

Mr. Prescott and Roderick happened to enter the house together. Not having rehearsed their parts, each threw a meaning glance at the other as they passed into the sitting-room.

"How late you are!" said Mrs. Prescott, rising, and greeting her husband with the usual kiss.

"Quite sorry, my dear," he replied; "but it couldn't be helped. Business has been troublesome to-day."

Roderick, fearing that a scene would ensue if

his step-father were to be precipitate, gave him another warning look. Mr. Prescott, who was still greatly agitated, observed the caution and returned it.

"There is something between you two," said Mrs. Prescott. "You look at each other strangely."

"Have patience," said her husband: "there is no cause for alarm."

Her expression indicated extreme distress. Ashy pallors and shadows trembled over her face ; painful wrinkles gathered and stiffened upon her forehead and around her eyes; and her lips seemed ready to utter a moan. She turned to her son, and, with a pathetic voice, explained, "Roderick, tell me what is this? Suspense will kill me."

Mr. Prescott drew her to the sofa, and tried to soothe her; but the nervous agitation increased.

"Won't you wait, dear mother," said Roderick, "and let us talk of affairs in the morning?"

Her reply was scarcely articulate; and it was evident that something must be told her, — either she must hear the truth, or be put off by some evasion.

"My dear mother, if your ancestor the admiral were living, and if he were, as I am, an American, if he were twenty-five years old, and without wife or child, and his country needed his sword, what do you think he would do?"

The mother looked at him wildly, but continued sobbing.

"I have no doubt what you will say, my dear wife," said the elder, "when you have time to reflect. Roderick has stated the case well, and we shall see if you have not some of the old Anglo-Saxon spirit."

At length she found words to say, a gasp at a time, "It may be a proud thing — afterwards, but terrible while the danger — is near — and I can't give up my boy — no, not for the fame of Nelson — and my ancestor too. Stay with me, Roderick!"

" I didn't intend," said Mr. Prescott, "to let this matter out this evening. I meant to take a proper time and a smoother way. But we men are not very artful; and, while we thought we were as secret as quails under a bush, you read us both at a glance. But it is out. Be cheerful, my dear. All our young men are volunteering. Roderick will go with the best youth of the city. He will come back with the stars of a general. How proud we shall be of him! He couldn't stay at home. Pray what excuse would he have? He will have a captain's commission in a new regiment. When it is organized, he will probably be major or lieutenant-colonel. You will get over your natural trepidation, and will rejoice that he inherits the spirit of your grandfather."

The mother felt a secret thrill at these words: but the sensation was transitory; the natural instinct was too strong, and she could not repress her thick-coming sobs. It is not well to attempt to repeat the disjointed phrases, or portray the unreasoning grief of a mother's heart.

Roderick moved his seat next to her, and held her hand, while her head fell on his shoulder, and the tears rained down.

Mr. Prescott walked the room, and wondered whether he had been too stern, whether he should have favored the young man's volunteering, whether any lack of affection had mingled with the sense of duty in his talk that morning. His own lip quivered, and his breath came short, as he saw his wife's distress. It was useless to say, "Cheer up;" for the current of sacred grief, like the summer rain, must have its course. He waited, uttering now and then a soothing word, until Mrs. Prescott raised her head, calmer, though still tearful, and asked him if he had seen Phœbe. The question stabbed him to the heart; but he was more on his guard, and he resolved not to show his secret thought to her again. By a great effort he replied that he had not seen her since breakfast. He did not look at his wife as he spoke, still less did he look at his stepson. Not if he could help it, should she drain this other cup of grief in which there would be such a mingling of shame.

The situation of the young man was pitiable. His mother was already prostrated with her sorrow, and it needed all his and his step-father's care to soothe her. The morning's conversation with the elder left no doubt in his mind as to the cause of the girl's absence; but he could only remain silent, since the worst conjecture could hardly be more painful to the mother than the truth. Mr. Prescott maintained a steadfast silence also; while his wife recalled every incident of the last few days, set up one baseless theory after another, and, finding none satisfactory, finally lapsed into a gloom from which nothing could rouse her. One grief she might have overcome, but the two weighed her down. Mr. Prescott wondered what would have happened to her if the third tremendous fact, their impending ruin, were also to be made known. "This must come to her gradually," he thought. "I will be wise. I will fit up the old house in Eaglemont; and, after Roderick is off, I will persuade her to go up and spend the summer there. We will be cheerful. We will have some young people;" and then his fancy came to a halt, for he thought of Phœbe, and was again in the slough of despond.

At length Mrs. Prescott rose mournfully, and walked slowly into the hall, and up the stairs to her chamber. Both the husband and son by a common instinct respected her grief, and let her pass without a word; only the young man, stealing into the hall, caught her hand tenderly as it rested upon the baluster-rail, and kissed it.

It was a gloomy dinner. Flowers fresh and dewy were in the large silver dish in the centre of the table, and miniature bouquets stood by each plate. The man-servant stood in respectful silence,

as the two men, with heavy hearts, took their
places. The two women whose beauty and spirit
had always enlivened the table, and made the dinner-hour the brightest of the twenty-four, were
absent. The one was stricken with an incurable
wound; and the other — where was she?

Mr. Prescott after a time motioned away the
servant, and said, " This is a bad business, this of
Phœbe's going away. We must find her. I *will*
find her, and I will bring her back if I bring her
in my arms." He spoke low, but his eyes glowed
with strong emotion. " But don't think I will
betray you. You have behaved handsomely. Only
let me find her. I will make all things smooth.
We must have her back, for your mother's sake
and mine."

In the space of an hour Roderick had done more
serious thinking than in all his life before. Still
he could not talk. The family was encompassed
with troubles that were largely due to his own
faults and errors. He could say nothing in face
of the present and the coming calamities; and the
ordinary topics of conversation seemed foolish and
impertinent. But he had made up his mind to do
his devoir as a son and a soldier. He was determined, as far as he could, to atone for his follies,
to implore the forgiveness of Phœbe if he could
only find her, and to leave behind him the memory of duty and honor.

Still he could not talk. A deep sense of regret
for his extravagance and his aimless life, a sense

of burning shame for his lawless conduct towards a pure and high-minded girl, filled all his soul. The step-father saw the struggle in the young man's face, and brooded over the gloomy situation, feeling that the one gleam of hope for the future was to arise from the chivalric deeds of the repentant prodigal. "Roderick," he said at length, "I think you are wise to go in the infantry. You are scarcely strong enough for cavalry service. Your command will be black, but perhaps more tractable. You will have much to do in the next few days. You are to get your equipment, and begin the study of tactics. You will have no time for any thing else. I will set on foot every possible inquiry for the poor girl." His voice choked as he spoke. He went on in a calmer tone, "I thought of your wants after we parted. I drew a check for you, and then, when I came to reflect, it seemed small; and as I am getting old, and am beyond the little vanity of jewelry, I thought the diamond studs your mother bought for me were of no use to an old fellow, and especially to one who is soon to be a hermit in Eaglemont, and I sold them. So here are the two checks, enough, I hope, to pay your bills, and fit you out as an officer, and my son, should go."

Roderick looked at his father's shirt-front. True enough, there was a set of plain ivory studs in the place of the brilliant gems he had been used to wear. He sobbed aloud, "This is too much. I don't deserve it."

"Pooh, pooh!" ejaculated the elder, striving to carry it off as a matter of no consequence: "I don't need the things; better they should serve some useful purpose." In fact, the sacrifice was little to him, as he had worn the bawbles to please his wife. To the young man it seemed quite different, for he tried in vain to imagine such self-denial on his own part.

"I never saw how grand and good you were before," faltered the youth. "If I live, I will deserve your regard, your affection, my dear, dear father!"

"Oh, don't cry!" said the father, brushing off two or three glistening drops from his own cheek. "It isn't worth a tear, nor a thought. Don't cry!" And his own features were struggling to keep up an outward semblance of stoicism.

They sat long at the table. Their hearts had been opened each to the other. They discussed the momentous events of the day. Roderick saw himself, his step-father, and the world with new eyes. Tears sometimes clarify the vision.

Mr. Prescott looked at the changed face, and again and again reproached himself that he had not, years ago, by daily intercourse and by the power of sympathy, seized hold upon the boy, and retained his influence up to manhood. He judged rightly that it was in a measure his fault that he had let go his grasp, and allowed a difference to grow between them, until their lives were unalterably divided.

For this passionate repentance which we have seen, and these sudden good resolutions, were not feigned. The youth, though he may have broken every moral law, was not wholly base. His life was the result of a vicious education. His habits had been formed in the society of dandies, idlers, and spendthrifts. His notions of the honor of man and the purity of woman were such as too often prevail among our gilded youth. It is only in a virtuous home that young men see the true and the immutable relations of society, and learn to live for noble ends. Heaven pity the youth whose training has been solely in a fashionable club !

"Now, if we can only find Phœbe!" said Mr. Prescott. "I know, Roderick, this is a painful subject. I don't refer to it to harrow up your feelings, but I can't keep her out of my mind. Not that I think she will come to serious harm, she is too circumspect and too high-spirited ; but I fear she will do some quixotic thing, — try to teach or sing, or even go into some house as a servant. I ache to think what she must suffer. And by to-morrow your mother will be frantic."

Roderick was silent.

"We won't continue this conversation," said the father. "Leave me to break the matter to your mother. We may not meet in the morning. I must have an early breakfast, and prepare for what is coming. Gibbs will be fierce after his knock-down.—Plucky little fellow, Amory, though

I am afraid he precipitated matters for me when he sent Gibbs reeling. Good-night."

Roderick rose, and grasped the friendly hand, stammered some inaudible words, and then fell back into his chair to reflect.

CHAPTER IX.

MR. PRESCOTT went early to his office. The sweeper had scarcely finished dusting the office furniture. The morning letters lay on the chief clerk's desk, unopened. Amory was at his desk, of which the lid was propped up, and the drawers out, clearing the receptacles of his private papers. There was a look of half-comic resolution on his face. His ripe and pulpy lips seemed to have grown solid. Even the cowlick on his broad round forehead appeared to stand up more defiantly than usual.

"Ah!" said he. "Good-morning, Mr. Prescott. I was afraid it was Gibbs."

"And so you are really going? Have you any thing to depend upon?"

"It is very kind of you to think of that. Gibbs wouldn't care if I had to go to the Island."

"Do you want any thing for your fine and costs? After all, it was my battle you fought."

Amory laughed. "No, I thank you, I have plenty; and, if the judge is reasonable, I sha'n't complain. The knock was worth all it will cost. I am comfortably well off. My mother owns a little house. We have been very prudent, and I am glad to say I have saved something."

" On a thousand a year ? "

" Yes, on a thousand a year.   And I have spent a hundred the last year for lectures at the Polytechnic School too.   But then I have earned something," here his tone grew confidential, " by writing.   I was named for a poet, — a dangerous experiment on the part of parents.   Napoleon was made a butcher by getting a present of a. toy cannon when a child, and I got a fatal lurch towards poetry by being called Percival.   The toughest thing that can happen to a man is to have a longing and taste for something he has not the talent for.   My poems were published in ' The Evening Tea-Table ; ' but I never could *sell* one for a sixpence.   Thinks I, this will never do.   No talent is worth any thing that doesn't bring in something, that doesn't bear on the question of bread and butter.   The sky over me was full of butterfly thoughts; but they didn't light.   The actual lines I wrote were a great ways from the unspeakable things I imagined.   But I am boring you with my gabble ? "

" No : go on.   It's early.   I like to hear you.   It is a relief."

" Well, I'll be short ; though generally, when a man says that, you may look out for a long stretch. I want to show you how helpless a fellow is when he can't catch his butterflies.   Look at that scribbled sheet of paper, its usefulness gone — as paper.   Some fellows wouldn't show it, because it is a record of failures.   But I'm not ashamed to

show it, for there is an *idea* in it, — without form,
but not void; and that is more than you can say
for many finished verses. There are four lines
together. There are three. Then see the scrawls,
the erasures, the blots. That's me! Do you
want the history of that effort? Read that first
quatrain:

'Brave little birds on the telegraph wire,

'Motionless dots on an air-spun line,

'Breasting the wind as its surges rise higher,

'Would that your trust and your patience were mine.

"Not bad, are they? only the last line is rather
pious and humdrum; but I couldn't get the
rhyme in any other way. Well, now look at that
group of lines, and that: —

'Snow crowns the window caps, ice paves the street

'Elm branches groan o'er the desolate malls,

'Still on your airy line hold your firm seat,

'Waiting the signal —

'Now on the portico fluttering come

'Tiny feet hopping, sharp eyes askance

'Warily pecking

~~Harrowmild~~
' Trees writhe & moan like the maniac king

~~up goes the sash and~~
' Till out of my window the signal I fling
—A—

~~in their long sleep are 'aid.~~
' Insect and worm out of reach are asleep
—A—

" But they wouldn't come into shape. You see,
I was looking out one day at the sparrows that
rode on the wire opposite my window. No food for
them; insect and worm asleep; the earth in icy
mail. When I raised the sash and whistled, they
fluttered down to the roof of the portico, hopped
saucily up to the window-sill, gobbled the crumbs
with *such* a funny voracity, and then flew back to
swing in the wind again. Then I thought how
the messages of love and death, of crime, battles,
politics, and business from all over the world, were
coming under those tiny feet, and the little souls
were unconscious of the momentous thoughts that
were rushing like lightning over the wire they
clung to. And then I thought that men here
on this planet, which is only a great electrical
machine through which the thoughts of God are
pulsing, creating diamonds, it may be, or causing
earthquakes or tidal waves, were really unconscious as the birds. Well, a great many such fan-
cies flitted over head, — butterflies, I have called
them, — and I wanted to catch them. As I said,

they wouldn't *light*. See how I wrestled here, and here! No use: I was stuck, like a fly in honey. I kept the thing three months. I sat down to it every few days, and vowed I *would* accomplish it. But I didn't, and there is the sorry-looking sheet."

"They say that poets only express what other men feel," said Mr. Prescott.

"Yes; and after a while I concluded to leave the job to them. For myself I gave it up. As I'm going away, I don't mind saying, that, in the cause of bread and butter, I made a more effective use of my faculties. You see how the great tailors and the furniture-and-carpet men come out in rhymed advertisements: well, that pays, — pays as well as the poetry of the ' Pacific.'

Mr. Prescott laughed immoderately. "Why, you don't say that flowery flummery stuff is yours?"

"Perfectly willing you should laugh. I know what it is: I don't flatter myself a particle. I know it is bosh. But I am not above earning an honest penny. I have paid for the Polytechnic Lectures by that bosh, and saved a good bit besides. And the lectures are *not* bosh."

"Pray what have you been learning at the Polytechnic School?"

"To use my eyes and my faculties. I have been digging into natural science. But never mind now. I am a fool to be talking of my nonsense when you must have so much upon your mind. My papers are gathered, — a precious lot they are, — and I am going. I think I shall take a trip out West. Perhaps, in that region of vast distances, my faculties may have a late expansion, and my mother may not have named me Gates Percival in vain."

"If I should carry on the business alone, would you come back to me?"

"I don't know. I am afraid you won't vanquish the beast (beg pardon), won't get the better of Mr. Gibbs. I think of you more than you will ever know. There is nothing under heaven I wouldn't do for you. But I can do you no good here, perhaps not anywhere." Amory here assumed a reflective air, and talked in a tone that sounded like philosophy. "Besides, I am not satisfied with business. What is business? Self-ishness. Any Christianity in it? Any honor, such as even a Pagan like Cicero would approve? Not any. Three partners are together: two of them think they can get along without the third, and they crowd him out. He is crippled, and his life's prospects gone. Do the two care? Not *much.* I have never seen a transaction in this house, never seen a letter written (begging your pardon), that was not based solely upon self-interest. Natural, you say; but where does the Christianity come in? Mr. Gibbs is merely acting on this rule, 'Look out for yourself, and devil take the hindmost. Make what you can out of every man, and, when you can get no more out of him, drop him, kick him out.' Mr. Gibbs owed every thing

to you. What does that matter? Business is
business. He has capital enough of his own, and
doesn't need you. Brains he can hire; not mine,
however. He can't hire *me* for the tenth part of a
second. I think of Falstaff, and his catechism
about honor, and I say about ' business,' ' I'll none
of it.' If you succeed, it is because you are not
troubled by Christian principles, nor hedged in by
honor, nor softened by sentiment. Cussedness
wins, with the cutting edge kept dead ahead."

"And this is what you have learned in my
counting-room?" said Mr. Prescott seriously.

"Not here especially, and never from you; but
these notions, though men don't advocate them,
because they have an ugly sound nakedly stated,
— these notions, I say, are in the air. Your great
merchant, like Stewart, is only the one overgrown
pickerel in the pond, swallowing every smaller
fish he can seize. I say, in short, that the rule in
business is to look at every question solely as it
affects your own interest."

"You may say the burglar and pickpocket do
that."

"Oh! that is extremely silly — on the part of the
thieves. There are laws against what are called
crimes, and prisons for the fools that are caught.
Your good business man doesn't break the law, —
unless he can do it safely, not he; and he has his
lawyer to tell him how far he can go."

"Well, well!" said Mr. Prescott, " this is a singular commentary. It seems that I am rightfully

overthrown, that I am only the engineer 'hoist with his own petard.' "

"Don't for a minute think, Mr. Prescott, that in this way I justify Gibbs. Dash him! I should like to knock him over again, and then wring his neck, an ungrateful, treacherous, arrogant beast! But I see how men like him construe the law of business, which is only selfishness, and how they count their very baseness an honor. I don't know that I shall ever go into business again: if I do, I'll come to you. If there is a Christian man in the street, it is you; and I am afraid that is what's the matter."

"Thank you, Amory. I knew I was sure of your good wishes."

"There is another matter, Mr. Prescott," and the young man spoke in a lower tone. "You may remember — or, I should say, you have heard, perhaps — your niece in Eaglemont, Miss Mary, your brother Solomon's daughter. I saw her here last Christmas; and, before I go West, I might take a run up there. Picturesque old place, isn't it? I think I might fill out that mutilated poem if I were on the old hill, looking down."

"And with Mary sitting beside you for a muse!"

"Don't jest, please, when her name is mentioned."

"Well, and as to the young lady?"

"I have a letter from her. It seems they are looking for Robert. He left here yesterday; and I suppose is going to sail for India, or China, or some other heathenish place "—

" To introduce 'business' views among the innocent natives," suggested Mr. Prescott.

" Oh! he's in dead earnest. Your nephew is a man of a million. He is as lovely as John, as fervent as Paul, and brave as Peter. His head is above the clouds like a mountain-top; and the light of heaven shines on it."

" That sounds like a quotation from one of your poems."

Amory actually blushed. It was, in fact, a thought from a sonnet he had sent to the fair maid of Eaglemont.

Mr. Prescott thought a moment. " Amory, you can do me a favor. Tell my brother Solomon that we are going to pass the summer in the old house, the one half way down the hill. Ask him to get Bissell the carpenter to go over it, and put it in order, and then let Lane give it a coat of paint outside and in. I would have the garden spaded and raked, and the fences mended. See that the whole place is in decent order. You might give them the benefit of your advice, though I have no doubt the mechanics will be faithful: 'business' views, as you state them, have not yet reached Eaglemont."

Amory was only too happy to be of service to the man to whom he was bound by so many ties, and whom he regarded with a feeling that was little short of veneration. He now was ready to go. His hand-bag of letters and manuscripts was strapped, and yet he lingered.

"Mr. Prescott," said he, "you have three months in which to decide. Suppose you try to find a partner, and make a new combination? You may raise the money, and euchre Gibbs."

Mr. Prescott shook his head. "I am afraid not. I am getting old. As you have been saying, I fear I don't understand business. It was different when I began. I got the seven companies for whom we sell when my word was as good as my bond, and every mill-agent and treasurer knew it. Now affairs are changed. The mills need money, and the selling agents have to raise it for them. It is a case of the servant becoming greater than his nominal master. The corporations have got to give their affairs into the hands of those who can supply their wants, and their wants grow every year. Gibbs can raise five dollars to my one. He is lucky, believes in himself, and others trust to his star. I shall have, perhaps, some sympathy; but I shall have to quit the street, sell the house that my wife thinks so much of, and go into the country. Exit Prescott."

"Still I beg of you hold on to your three months. You can never tell what is going to happen. Gibbs may die."

"No chance of that. He is tough as a bull."

"So was Eben Fancher; but dinners at the club, and a carriage back and forth, did for him. Surfeit and laziness, physical inactivity, I mean, will do for any man. Gibbs will go the same road, and they'll find him some day a dead load in his coupé."

"I can't speculate on such chances."

"No; but you bide your time, and take the chances that come. Good-by, Mr. Prescott. You will hear from me. God bless you, sir, good-by!" The resolute little man walked off stoutly, but with a quiver on his lip that Mr. Gibbs, who was coming in, attributed to an emotion which the discharged clerk never once felt. The partners, recognizing each other with a nod, withdrew to their several rooms. Mr. Prescott marshalled his beggarly assets, and, after trying in vain to put his mind to business, went out to take a stroll.

Mr. Gibbs watched the senior through the crack of the door, and chuckled as he saw his heavy step, and noted the deepening lines about his eyes. Does the stock operator sorrow for the man caught in his toils? Does the hunter sorrow for the stag brought down by his rifle?

CHAPTER X.

Up to the moment that Robert Prescott left her
with that tender benediction, Phœbe had been
uncertain what she would do. When she left
home in the morning, she had determined not to
return, but to find some other place to live. The
advice of Signor Belvedere made a strong impression upon her, and she was almost persuaded to go
back to Mrs. Prescott. Then came her interview
with her lover, Robert, and it was very trying to
her. His personal magnetism was very strong.
His intellectual character gave his love-making a
tone which might seem unreal ; but to her it was
sincere and spontaneous. The spoken words had
a tender and winning quality, something that is
beyond types to represent. So strenuously had he
pressed the matter, that she was utterly weary and
overcome when left to herself. Furthermore, with
the recollection of this man, strong in mind and
heart as in body, with the sense of his purity,
straight-forwardness, and generosity, the contrast
between him and Roderick, the elegant sensualist,
was too painful to be considered for a moment.
With every remembered trait of the one, the idea
of the other grew more repulsive. She had parted

with the man whom she reverenced: could she return to a companionship that she loathed? The strong and poetic man was solemn, and perhaps repellent: the gay and graceful man was corrupt and insincere, and they were the only admirers she had ever known. She walked on, unobservant of streets, while these thoughts revolved in her mind. She thought of Mrs. Prescott's concern for her absence, of her alarm perhaps, and of a search being made for her. She thought of Mr. Prescott's surprise and distress. Once or twice she half resolved to turn, and find her way back. Then came the thought of the unspeakable; and her eyes flashed again, her mouth was firmly compressed, her bosom heaved, and she strode on among foul faces and evil eyes, through districts as unknown to her as Africa.

In a narrow street, now mostly filled with shops of mechanics, there was an old-fashioned brick dwelling, whose ample doorway and carved pilasters bore witness to the wealth and position of its original occupants. The house seemed to have withdrawn from the noise of the neighborhood, relying upon the grim brick wall at the street-line as a barrier. Through the open fret-work of the iron gate in front, the windows might be seen closely blinded. There was no bell-pull, only a grim lion's-head knocker. There was once a paved carriage-way at the side; but grass and weeds had covered the regular lines of cobble-stones with thick, dusty tufts, and the great gate that used to be opened for carriages had been nailed up for a generation. A brick building at the rear of the yard, on the right of the house, held the old family coach; but it had been fastened in an original way by a contrivance of nature's own. A horse-chestnut tree had grown up in front of the door to a goodly size, and closed it effectually. However, it was no matter; for the ancient yellow coach within was the home of rats, and was festooned with cobwebs. No one had seen it, apparently for years, except a few urchins, who at times had scaled the fence, and looked in at its faded splendor through the crack of the door.

Phœbe stood and looked in at the gate. This was better than to go back to the poor and comfortless home of Mrs. Maloney. This was a place of which she had often heard; because it was the residence of an eccentric lady, Miss Thorpe, who was a friend of Mrs. Prescott, and had sometimes attended the sessions of the Plato Club. A sudden impulse seized the girl. Of all the women she had ever known, Miss Thorpe seemed to her one of the most original and most attractive. Not that she felt the sympathy of likeness: she knew that Miss Thorpe was in every respect a contrast. But she knew that Miss Thorpe lived alone, with only one servant, and that she was regarded as the most actively, indefatigably charitable woman in town.

Phœbe opened the gate and walked up the path, and then with a sensation of dread raised the ponderous knocker, and let it clang against the solidly panelled door.

She was admitted by a good-natured looking Irish woman, with broad shoulders, ample chest, wavy chestnut hair, and mild blue eyes, — the very counterpart of her old friend, Mrs. Maloney. The servant evidently recognized Phœbe's face as being a familiar one, and showed her into the drawing-room.

A serene little woman came into the room. She was perhaps forty years old. Her features were smooth, and her complexion delicate almost to transparency: her gray hair was brushed back from her face, and its luxuriance gathered in a classic coil behind. Very slight in figure she seemed, but not weak or fragile. Her face wore a look of dignity and gentleness. Her dress was a neutral-tinted silk, plainly made. Her linen collar was fastened by an antique cameo brooch; but, excepting a plain seal-ring on her right hand, she wore no other jewelry. But these details, which occupy so much space in description, came to the eye at a glance; for never was there a picture more harmonious than the stately little lady presented. Figure, face, expression, carriage, and costume belonged together, and had been fore-ordained from the beginning.

How to address such a person! What could a homeless girl say?

Fortunately Miss Thorpe remembered her visitor, and with thoughtful kindness made her wel-

come. The few minutes of preliminary common-
places often serve an important purpose; and
Phœbe was very soon able to turn the conversation into the channel in which her tumultuous
thoughts were tossing about. So she told Miss
Thorpe what she remembered of her earlier years,
and of her residence with Mrs. Prescott. She
spoke with enthusiasm of Signor Belvedere and
of her progress in music. She spoke modestly of
her hopes and of her vague plans for her own
support, and added that, first of all, she wished
to get a home, and then to get pupils in singing.

"Does Mrs. Prescott know of this, — of your
coming to me?" Miss Thorpe had noticed the
expression of pain in her face, and now saw it
grow more intense.

"Oh, no! My coming here was a pure accident. I had heard of your house, and knew it
from description, and I came in because I had a
pleasant recollection of you. If I had not happened to pass here, and to think of you, I don't
know where I might have gone."

"Then I infer that you are leaving Mrs. Prescott?"

"Yes. And this is the most painful thing, that
I can't tell you why. I beg of you don't ask me.
But I must say, for fear you will think ill of me,
that I don't leave for any fault of mine, — not for
any quarrel or difference. I know Mrs. Prescott
is looking for me at this moment, and will be surprised and grieved that I don't return." The tears
began to start.

"But you will not go back?"

Phœbe shook her head in silence.

"This is very singular," said Miss Thorpe, as if in soliloquy, "and I don't know but I ought to see Mrs. Prescott."

"I pray you don't think of it. If you wish it, I will leave you. If you distrust me, I *must* leave you. I only want a short time to think, to plan, to get a good home, and get started as a teacher. I don't wish to be dependent upon any one. Pray don't speak of going to Mrs. Prescott. I cannot bear it. I am not a runaway child." Her sobs increased.

"Pray how old are you, miss?"

"Nineteen, nearly twenty."

"Old enough, certainly, to know your own mind. And I do trust you, and will help you, — not perhaps wholly in the way you expect."

Miss Thorpe had been rapidly making a superficial analysis, and it ran something like this: "A good face, as well as a handsome one. Eyes clear and truthful. Head fine, large, and well-balanced; temperament, though, is very sanguine. A dangerous glow of feeling. Tendencies towards sensuous art. Susceptible to pleasure, and liable to its retributions. Good reasoning faculties. May escape the weakening of moral tone caused by indulgence in music."

"The truth is, Miss Phœbe," she went on, "I am not sure about your career as a singer, — I mean I couldn't advise you to follow it. Music

should be only an occasional amusement.   It is re-
bellion against reason, because it is an indulgence
in an emotion.   An emotion may control an infant,
a savage, a Southern negro; but reason alone con-
trols an intellectual being.   Without the control
of reason, the soul is at sea.   There are musical
emotions, and emotions of the beautiful in art;
there are so-called religious emotions, and others
still stronger, not so often mentioned.   I am not
sure that all emotions are not correlated, and glide
into each other like the forces of nature.   But
this is a philosophy you have yet to learn.   To
teach piano — yes; and the art of singing — yes,
up to a certain point.   But the delirium of song,
especially of the passionate sort, is to be avoided."
She looked as steadfast as a piece of sculpture as
she uttered these sentences.

Phœbe felt that she was encountering a new
force.   Mr. Prescott was always sensible, and
sometimes energetic; Mrs. Prescott's nature was
receptive, easily pleased, fond of superlatives, too
indolent for consecutive thinking; but Miss Thorpe
was quite another person.   Here was a woman,
who, with the sweetest tones and the most delicate
feminine emphasis, was letting fly definitions and
distinctions, and creating a new metaphysical
world.   Phœbe was at once interested, piqued,
and nonplussed.   She tried to measure herself
against this active, tireless nature.   It was impossible.   In "thought's interior sphere" Phœbe had
almost every thing to learn.

"But you look fatigued," said Miss Thorpe, "and I dare say you are hungry. I envy you fresh and hearty young people your appetites." She led the way, and they walked into the next room, and sat down to lunch. Miss Thorpe took a cup of tea, a slice of toast, and a small piece of honey in the comb. Phœbe was indeed hungry, and could have devoured the delicate portion given her in a moment; but she instinctively paused when she noticed Miss Thorpe's slow and dainty manner, and she could not help wondering what those full rows of beautiful teeth could be doing so long with those little bits of bread. Miss Thorpe had brought herself to regard appetite as something not quite in harmony with a spiritual organization, and therefore to be repressed, brought to a minimum, like the other unavoidable accidents of this mortal life. But, now that she looked more closely at Phœbe, she said, "I don't believe you breakfasted, either. You need food and rest."

She rang a bell; and, when the servant appeared, she ordered a slice of steak broiled, and would hear of no objection on Phœbe's part.

"I cannot quite make up my mind to do without animal food, Phœbe, — we will drop the 'Miss,' if you please, — though I seldom eat it more than twice a week. But I must say I have some compunctions about eating flesh. I feel that I am an abettor of murder when I taste it. I have never seen any answer to the gentle creed of Goldsmith's hermit: —

> ‘ No flocks that range the hillside free
>   To slaughter I condemn :
> Taught by the Power that pities me,
>   I learn to pity them.’ ”

Here the slice of steak came in, not a very formidable one as it seemed to Phœbe.

Miss Thorpe went on. “ Eat, my dear girl. I like to see you enjoy it. Some Malthus of herds will give us the other side of the argument, — as to flesh-eating, I mean. But it is against our finer instincts, against mercy, and, I am afraid, against justice, to take life without necessity. But I forget that my philosophy may spoil your appetite.”

Phœbe wondered who Malthus was, and why he was opposed to eating beefsteak; but she thought she would not inquire then. There were books everywhere in the rooms; and she promised herself she would read some, enough, at any rate, to enable her to understand what Miss Thorpe was talking about.

After lunch Phœbe refreshed her tear-stained eyes with water; and, as the sorrowful look faded, her beauty shone out like Cowper’s rose “ just washed in a shower.”

It was settled, that, for the present, she was to remain with Miss Thorpe, and that a letter should at once be sent by Phœbe to Mrs. Prescott. The arrangements for the future were to be afterwards discussed. A boy was found to carry the letter; but as he was thoughtlessly paid beforehand, and quite liberally, he could not cross to the fashionable quarter where the Prescotts lived; until he had "treated" a number of the gamins of the neighborhood to peanuts and ginger-snaps, and had cut up a number of antics besides. When fairly ready, the little rascal could not find the letter, but was not honest enough to make known the loss. For this reason Mrs. Prescott (as we have already seen) did not hear from Phœbe.

Lest it might be thought that Miss Thorpe's mode of life was dictated by parsimony, the reader should know, that, though the lady had an ample income, she spent little of it upon herself; and, as she kept a minute account of every day, — diary and petty cash-book together, — the entries for the day just closing will best show her character.

"MEM. — To market: beef, thirty cents; bread, ten cents; one pound butter, fifty cents; two oranges, ten cents. Shoes for Bridget's sister, three dollars. Tickets to Hertz's Concert (blind) one dollar. 'Loaned' the Rev. —— —— (a good man and bad manager) ten dollars. Gave Phœbe for spending-money (till she earns some) five dollars."

All the pages of that diary show a like disparity, — a linnet's rations for herself, the bulk of her daily expenditure in bounty to others.

When evening came Phœbe was shown to her chamber. It was neatly furnished with a fine old-fashioned dressing-bureau, easy-chairs with chintz covers, and handsome curtains. A cool and pure air pervaded the room, renewed by a swinging window-pane and an open fireplace. There was a portrait in oil on one of the walls, somewhat resembling Miss Thorpe, though younger and rosier. On the white counterpane were a woman's garments, too large for the slender hostess, and apparently made for a fuller and statelier figure.

In spite of all she had gone through, Phœbe slept peacefully. The face in the portrait smiled on her as she woke; the eyes followed her as she made her toilet, and put away the delicate cambric robes she had worn; and the lips pouted out a kiss as she left the chamber.

CHAPTER XI.

THE civil war had been for some time in progress: the line of battle stretched half across the continent. It seems now like a hideous nightmare to recall the havoc that attended those eventful years. The alternations of hope and despair, the continued filling-up of shattered regiments to be again decimated, the capture of forts, the loss of men-of-war, the awful but indecisive struggles between armies such as no European captain ever led, — this has been an experience which even now is hardly realized, except by the actors in the terrible drama, and which all good men must hope will never come again to us, nor to our children. The two contending sections were equally matched in muscle and endurance; and, if there had not been a disparity in numbers and in resources, the struggle might have been protracted as long as a man was left on either side to fire a gun.

The first alarm called off the adventurous, the unemployed, the ambitious. As the war went on, the plough went deeper into the soil. Men of maturer years and established position enlisted. Lawyers and judges, merchants and gentlemen of

leisure, felt the solemn call. Studious and schol-
arly men listened to the boding drum-beat, and felt
their hearts throbbing in response. Silken gallants
left their clubs and their social pleasures, and
cantered off gayly to the rendezvous with death.

One may be certain that the excitement was
deep and pervading when a youth like Roderick
Prescott was ready to go into the field, and content himself with a soldier's fare. However, a
good number from his club had already gone.
Some were still in service as staff and line officers;
some were at home wounded; some were recruit-
ing; some were in captivity; and quite as many
were lying under Southern soil. Roderick was
naturally brave, and the thought of danger was
almost an attraction; but he had never before
exhibited so much activity or spirit. He knew
that his acceptance of a command in a negro regiment put him in double peril; because the enemy
had proclaimed that no quarter would be given to
the colored troops, whether officers or men. Roderick had not *chosen* this service; but at the time
no other new infantry regiment was forming; and,
as for the old regiments in service, the great and
wise governor rarely gave commissions except by
promotion.

Roderick, like the majority of young men in
society, had no politics, least of all any sentimental politics. His company consisted of so many
rows of machines to load and fire muskets: their
color was of no consequence. There were others

who were moved by AN IDEA, among them, conspicuously the hero for whom Fort Wagner will stand as a monument forever. Roderick went into training with eagerness. It is astonishing how much can be done in a short time by one who gives his whole soul to the task. In a very few days he mastered the elementary facts of military discipline; and then he followed up resolutely the practice of a sergeant, a lieutenant, and a captain. The great hall where much of the preliminary drill went on was his home: afterwards he lived in the suburban camp with his soldiers. Temperate, earnest, and indefatigable, he advanced in knowledge and in the development of a soldier's character, till he won the admiration of all. There was no talk of "blue blood," nor of "playing soldier." Every man who handled a musket respected this severe and resolute officer. The stoutest radical had to admit that this man of birth and breeding, with soft hands, and effeminate manners, had the sturdy Saxon pluck in him. The metamorphosis of the dandy into the officer was complete.

Mr. Hugh Prescott was the person most astonished by the change. He had frequently visited the armory, and afterwards the camp, in company with his stepson, and was gratified by his proficiency, and proud of the respect he saw accorded to him. Roderick was so much occupied, that he had little time for his mother's society; but his demeanor towards her was tender and respectful.

She gradually became accustomed to the idea of parting from him, and was able to converse with him calmly; and she devoted her time to the preparation of elegant and useless conveniences which she supposed would adorn his tent.

Roderick's opportunity to make his peace with Phœbe had not yet come. He was naturally reluctant to make his apology conspicuous by calling on her at Miss Thorpe's house; and his step-father, on further consideration, had thought best not to insist upon the girl's return until after the regiment had left for the seat of war.

Daily the town was stirred up by the beating of drums; and the fife's shrill music rose over the noise of the streets. Squads of serious, eager men, paraded, carrying the beautiful national flag, and followed by all eyes as they passed. The war was a tremendous fact, and was brought home in all its weight and terror to every human being. At length the colored regiment was filled up, the commissions were issued; and Roderick, who had been promised a captaincy, was appointed major.

The day came when the regiment was to leave for the seat of war. A stand of colors was to be presented by the State authorities, and there was to be a review and a glorious " send off." The regimental flag had been made by ladies, — the mothers, sisters, and wives of the officers. Quarter-masters and commissaries had completed their long and tedious preparations. The line was formed; and, amid the long roll of drums and the piercing notes of wind instruments, the grand salute was given; and while a thousand muskets and a thousand dark faces gleamed at " Present arms!" the governor and staff came forward. With them came a great orator to make the presentation speech, — a man somewhat past his prime, but still in the maturity of his brilliant powers. He took the silken flag, and addressed the officers and men. His voice and his enthusiasm rose with the occasion, until his thoughts took form in glowing words. He touched the chords that have swayed men in all times. His face was pale, inspired by great thought and strong emotion; and many of the officers shed unwonted tears as he finished. Every listener fancied himself a hero while under the spell of this eloquence.

The ceremony was over. The regiment was allowed half an hour's recreation. Arms were stacked; and soldiers went to the lines in the rear to say a good-by to wives, daughters, parents, and brothers. In those precious, terrible moments, what agonies of love and anguish were suffered! Of the thousand brave men that stood at the lines, looking forward cheerfully to the grim future, and soothing the grief of those left behind, how many now are wakened to any music! Most of them lie in far off-humble graves, many without a stone, their last resting-places known only to the infinite pitying One.

Meanwhile the officers, their friends, and the authorities, were to meet in a marquee for the final leave-taking.　The marquee was pitched on the brow of a gentle hill overlooking the parade-ground; and thousands of citizens — men and women, who had gathered to witness the thrilling scene — were in close ranks' on the grass near by. The officers had dismounted, and were approaching the line against which the multiude swayed. Conspicuous among them for his graceful form and soldierly carriage was Major Prescott.　His step-father was near the tent, and the two met in silence with a strong hand-grasp.

For a moment neither could speak.　At length the elder, pointing to the tent, said, —

"Your mother, at the last moment, changed her mind, and came."

"She is here, then?" said her son. He was rather sorry. He had parted with her in the morning, and he feared a scene.

"Let us not sit down to cry," said Mr. Prescott. "We don't want any refreshment, and it is better to pass the time in a way to divert your mother's attention.　Go to her, and propose a walk on the parade-ground."

The suggestion was a good one.　The young man hastily collected his faculties, and, in a light and jaunty manner, entered the tent, and approached his mother.　Taking her hand, he proposed to saunter about in the open air. She looked like one without will or self-control.　Her face told of unutterable things. She took her son's arm, and the three walked slowly out into the open plain. They passed for some distance along the line without speaking. It was a perfect day. The grass was a beautiful carpet, and the trees around were still in their freshest robes of green. Suddenly Roderick was aware of the presence of persons who recognized him. Within arm's length, but outside the line, stood Miss Thorpe and Phœbe. He was surprised, and deeply moved. The elder lady wore the usual pearl-gray suit of silk, and a bonnet that would have become a fair Quaker. Phœbe, whose fine classic features, cream-tinted complexion, and lustrous dark hair, made her so conspicuously beautiful, was attired in a gauzy robe that it would be prosaic to call yellow, but which borrowed the delicate hues of the jessamine, and, where the folds hung in masses, had the rich, deep color of the dandelion. Her ornaments were pale coral. She was a vision such as nature repeats once or twice in a generation, to show that beauty is not the creation of the painter, and to keep alive the tradition of the golden age. So might Egeria have appeared to the ravished Numa. So Clytie looked, bursting from the heart of the sunflower. So Diana was revealed to Endymion. The lover re-creates the past; and nymphs, naiads, and graces people his waking dreams.

It takes but a glance to sweep over these details. But Roderick probably did not see them at all, but only perceived the harmony and the instant total impression. His position was most painful. He was beset with difficulties. He felt that he really ought to love Phœbe, in spite of the wrong he had done her. He would have fallen on his knees abjectly to ask her forgiveness. This was his only opportunity. But there stood his mother, and there was the placid but vigilant Miss Thorpe. The mother had never known of the indignity, for the two men had kept their counsel.

Mr. Prescott exclaimed, " Why, Phœbe, you wicked, perverse creature! Come in here! — Roderick, let the guard pass the ladies in! — Why, you runaway, you naughty girl! you have broken my heart. — My respects to you, Miss Thorpe; but you can't love this ungrateful darling as I do. You are not a childless old man: you don't need her." He apparently was determined to admit no reply, but kept the reins in his own hands, and went on: " To think, Phœbe, that I see you again, and looking so charming! I was afraid you might have fared ill. God only knows what might have happened to a friendless girl in the streets. Now, after this ceremony is over, you will go back with us. No compulsion, only you must. I am Sir Anthony to-day, and put up with no nonsense."

Mrs. Prescott meanwhile had seized Phœbe's hand with fervor, while her features were struggling with hysterical emotion. Phœbe scarcely uttered a word; and, though she showed in her eyes a warm affection, the color mounted to her face, and crimsoned even her ivory neck. The memory of her fierce wrath was coming back. Mrs. Prescott saw this, and noticed, too, that Roderick was moody and silent. She did not correctly interpret the scene. In her opinion Roderick had proposed marriage to Phœbe, and had been rejected. The theory received confirmation in her mind from every look of the young people. This, then, was the cause of Phœbe's leaving the house, and this the reason why her darling son was going to the war. All for a girl's black eyes he was going away to be shot. She had not trusted herself to speak, but kept her mouth rigidly shut. Her breath came quicker. The tide of feeling swelled higher, and surged in her heart. More and more her expressive features told of the struggle within. It could end in but one way. She burst into an uncontrollable passion of weeping, and between her sobs exclaimed, "O Phœbe! is it for you, that I am going to lose my son?"

Her husband and Roderick in vain strove to soothe and quiet her. The current could not be checked; and Mr. Prescott, not to imbitter the little time remaining with unavailing cries and reproaches, led her a short distance away, hoping that she would recover her composure. Roderick seized the moment, unmindful of Miss Thorpe, although her presence colored his phrases, and put a check on the expression of his feeling. It was an effort such as he had never made before.

"Miss Phœbe," said he in a tender and respectful tone, "I am going away, and may never return. I hope for the best; but I know the risk, and mean to face it without fear. I wish to leave behind me in the memory of — friends — a — I wish them to think of me as one whose errors — as one who meant better than he sometimes did. There are things that a man don't forget, can't forget, can't excuse himself for."

Here Miss Thorpe said simply, " Phœbe, if you will excuse me, I think I will join Mrs. Prescott."

Roderick was properly grateful; but Phœbe was less so, in fact, she appeared rather annoyed.

" O Phœbe!" he went on, " you have come to a beautiful womanhood so suddenly. I thought of you only a short time ago as a schoolgirl: now you are so stately in your ways. I can't tell you how you affect me as I am with you. I could worship you. But when you are away, as often as I try to think of you, there comes a cloud over your face, — I see you turning away in anger. I confess to myself that your anger is just; but it kills me. There are things I should like to wash out with my tears; and, if they didn't do it, I would pour out my blood."

Phœbe had listened pityingly. She was thinking more, however, of the distressed mother, and feeling that her resentment had actually driven the young man to despair.

" Say to me that you forgive me," he said.

" I do forgive you," she replied solemnly; " but to forget is sometimes out of our power."

"I know," he said almost bitterly. "But when one says, 'I forgive, but can't forget,' it shows that the forgiveness is not very hearty."

"I do forgive you," she repeated, "and I shall try to think of you as you are to-day. You won't be offended, will you, if I say you haven't always been so? It isn't the fashion for young men to be serious. I used to think you studied to be disagreeable, it was such a thoughtless manner you affected. This is the time for truth, and you must bear it. But to-day, Roderick,—I can't say— You are like another man. It was not this Roderick that grieved and wounded me."

There was a tremor in her tones that he interpreted as a softening of her feelings towards him. If he dared? Yes, he must follow his feelings, or his purpose, or both.

"Do you think, after all you have suffered on my account, if you really believed I had changed, and had become what you wished,—do you believe your feelings would change?—I don't speak of respect simply, for I mean to deserve that,—but to any warmer regard?"

"Roderick," she said, "in this moment, when you have so much to think of, don't you think it better to leave this,—to avoid what would pain us both?"

"But in this last moment I am selfish enough to want to speak of the one thing that is dearer to me than life."

"You are excited, Roderick. You are heartily

sorry, I can see. You wish to atone for your wrong, and your feelings carry you beyond.— Isn't it enough that I forgive you?"

"No, Phœbe, not enough. My conscience makes a coward of me, or I would follow this up, — yes, I would take your hand, and lead you to my father and mother. I would not let you go. As it is, I will prove my sincerity by my conduct. I will shed my blood to prove it. If I return, Phœbe, I shall return to claim you. You won't deny me? This thought will comfort me in tent, on the march, in the battle. Phœbe, my life belongs to you. I think more of the hope of being worthy of you than of my country or my God."

This vehemence almost overpowered her. She felt strangely perplexed. She did not doubt his repentance, although she could not in her heart thoroughly trust him. She did not wish to have him go away feeling that he had not been forgiven. She was quite sure, that, but for his remorse at her flight, he would have staid at home to comfort his mother. And how much she owed to that mother! Should she send him away in despair? Like most women, she temporized.

"This is very sudden, Roderick. I can't say that I am sure of my own mind. I don't know how I shall feel when this terrible struggle is over, and you are away. I sha'n't forget your generous words. I shall think of you, and pray for you. I grieve to think that it was — that I was the innocent cause. And you don't know how your mother's anguish touched me. It seems that I am your fate — and, if you should fall" — She could go on no farther.

"Let me hope that I shall live for you. You must pardon my mother. She is unreasoning, and to-day there is but one subject in her mind. But, Phœbe, don't let me go without hope. Pray return home with my mother and comfort her; be a daughter to her."

"If she asks me, I will return."

"Let me tell her something to make her cheerful, — tell her that you will be her dear daughter."

Phœbe shook her head. "These things must shape themselves: we can't control them."

They were now at the farthest part of the parade-ground. The men had been refreshed with a bountiful collation, and were getting on their knapsacks, and taking their guns. All about the large quadrangle the people waited, forming a dense background for the moving picture. The officers were coming out of the marquee, servants came up with the horses; and then the thrilling tantara of the trumpet called Roderick from his ideal world.

"God's will be done, Phœbe!" said he. "I can say no more. Let us walk rapidly back. Father and mother and Miss Thorpe are on the brow of the hill. I will leave you with them, and then" —

Phœbe was greatly agitated. Her eyes were misty, and she almost lost her footing as they pressed on. Roderick's servant followed him with his eyes; and, by the time the family met, the horse was waiting. He flung his arm about his mother's neck, and kissed her, bade farewell stoutly to his step-father, shook hands with Miss Thorpe, and, with a soul full of anguish, gave a parting hand-shake to Phœbe. Mounting his horse, he spurred to his place in the line.

Shouts arose from all sides of the quadrangle, tumultuous and incessant, like the sound of waves. The cannon thundered; the band played a lively melody. Flags streamed in the air, and white handkerchiefs fluttered on every side, looking in the distance like white blossoms shaken by the wind. Another cannon was heard; then all was still. The line was formed. The adjutant reported. The colonel shouted the order to forward. Then, amid roars of cheers, the drums and fifes struck up, — sounds once inspiring to us, but now associated with all that is terrible in war. The line broke into platoons; and with a steady step the —th regiment passed from the beautiful field to the wharf where the transport steamer lay. What the men felt, few returned to tell; but every spectator struggled with a lump in his throat, and from men and women alike there was a sudden gush of tears like rain.

They were black men going to fight for a country in which they had no part, — a country in which they were aliens and strangers.

CHAPTER XII.

The sound of the drums was dying away in the distance, and the crowd had mostly dispersed; but Mrs. Prescott remained in the marquee half unconscious, and sobbing hysterically. A consultation was had, and it was determined that Phœbe should for this day return with Miss Thorpe, but should shortly revisit her home when Mrs. Prescott was restored. By the help of a policeman, Mr. Prescott got a carriage for his wife. Miss Thorpe and Phœbe preferred to walk.

When they reached the house, they were admitted by Mrs. Maloney, who explained that she was keeping house while her sister Bridget was gone to see the soldiers. Mrs. Maloney was overjoyed to meet her darling Phœbe, whom she had seen but seldom since Mrs. Prescott took charge of her.

The scenes of the day had been very trying to Phœbe. Continually rang in her ears the agonized cry of Mrs. Prescott, " It is for you that I have lost my son ; " while in her fancy endless files of men in blue, with glittering arms, marched to the sound of drum and fife, and handsome officers led the way to death or glory.

Her whole being throbbed with the fierce excitement. She thought of Mr. Prescott's fatherly kindness, and of his wife's unaffected goodness towards her for so many years, and the debt of gratitude seemed beyond reckoning. In Roderick's repentance she had forgiven his fault. As fire burns out plague, she believed love had consumed the old lawless impulses. Roderick was a hero. He would come back as famous as his great-grandfather the admiral. And what then? That made her pause. For he was coming *for her :* so he said. Did she love him? She pitied him for his sufferings, for his self-abasement, and for his mother's sake : beyond this she did not consciously go.

Miss Thorpe asked no questions about her interview on the parade-ground with Roderick ; for she saw that the girl was sorely troubled. But Phœbe volunteered the remark that Major Prescott *had* been rude to her on an occasion, but that he had apologized, and she had forgiven him. To relate this was easier than to be cross-examined.

When supper was over, Miss Thorpe, desiring to change the current of thought, said, " Phœbe, I suppose Mrs. Maloney seems something like a mother to you, and perhaps you would like to have her come in for a while. Do you remember your own mother ? "

" I scarcely remember her. There is a faint recollection of a delicate woman with creamy complexion and great melancholy black eyes, not quite so tall as I am, looking quite ill and dejected. This is the way it comes to me; but the image is faint, and, as it were, distant. I should like to see Mrs. Maloney; though I have never got much from her. She doesn't even know my mother's full name. She thinks my father died while I was a babe."

"Then she had seen your father?"

"I think not, but am not sure. Certainly she had heard about him."

"You have no memento, or relic of them?"

"Nothing."

"It may not be very important to your future life, for that must lie much in the sphere of your own will; but it is a pardonable curiosity to know the source of one's being, the ancestral traits and tendencies. One of your parents was musical, I suppose."

"Oh, yes! my mother. There is a sound that comes to my ears when I think of her, — a low, sweet tremulous tone, a cradle-song that was worship and lullaby both. I imagine it a hymn to the Virgin, and a mother's blessing blended with it."

Mrs. Maloney came in, and went over the sad story she had so many times repeated to Phœbe. It was little she knew. A friendless woman with a young child — with a sweet and sorrowful face, and a slight foreign accent in her speech, with manners that belong only to a lady — had hired a room in a large tenement-house. She had a name which the good simple woman could not catch, and therefore could not now remember. The forlorn mother had picked out the stitched letters on her handkerchief: evidently she was covering her traces. No one came to see her, not one, until, as she fell sick, the city physician attended her. She left not a single letter. Her few clothes (only a small trunk full), Mrs. Maloney was fain to sell to get money to help support the child; for the good woman took the child as her own, and bestowed upon her all a mother's love. It was about all she had to bestow, except a share in the milk, bread, and potatoes she earned by washing. As time wore on, Mrs. Maloney began to think that the girl, who should have been a lady, ought to go to school, and ought, in fact, to have a "bring-ing up" beyond what a poor woman like herself could give her. Providence led Mrs. Prescott that way; and, as she proposed to take and educate the girl, the heroic woman gave her up, though it almost broke her heart to do it.

"You knew the child's name?" asked Miss Thorpe.

"Oh, yes! Her mother called her Phayba; and, besides, she had written out all her names some-where in a book."

"What was the book?"

"A mass-book."

"In English?"

"No: in such as the priest talks. They call it Latin, I b'lieve."

"And what became of that book?"

"It was sold with the mother's clothes, and I disremember who to."

Miss Thorpe took the woman into the library, and, pointing to various books, got her to designate the shape, size, and style of binding. It is needless to say that Mrs. Maloney was not a connoisseur; but Miss Thorpe finally got hints enough to make it probable that it was a prayer-book in Latin or Italian, eighteen mo, gilt-edged, though worn, bound in black morocco, with a clasp. Such a book, she meditated, would not probably have been destroyed. It was likely to be in existence. And in it was Phœbe's full name! Perhaps it was in some second-hand bookstore, or in the hands of some collector of curiosities.

Dismissing Mrs. Maloney with thanks, and something more, she said, "That book must be found."

"But I am afraid it is a hopeless task," said Phœbe."

"Nothing is hopeless. I will advertise it; offer a handsome reward, that will cause a search to be made."

Phœbe only looked gloomy and thoughtful.

"Your poor mother!" continued Miss Thorpe. "Do you know I think we shall find she was a singer, perhaps a great one, certainly beautiful and cultivated; that she married some man of fashion who mistreated her; that his friends cast them off; that, after he died, she was broken in spirit and in fortune? That is the way with sing-rs. Emotional beings, they surrender will, fortune, life itself, to a transient impulse. They marry badly: their husbands always live on their earnings, and love them only while flowers and diamonds are plenty, and the career of success continues. You have noticed the picture in your room? That is the portrait of my sister, — my half-sister I should say. The sketch I have drawn for your mother was substantially that sister's history. It is the common fate of those bright creatures. Her clothes are in your wardrobe; you have noticed their size. She was not a thin, insignificant creature like me. Her beautiful night-dresses you have worn; and this rich yellow tissue you are wearing was hers. But my poor sister, so we heard, was never blessed (or burdened) with a child. She went abroad, and died there. I don't know where her body rests. We have only her beautiful image here. At one time she was coming home, so it was said, and a trunk came with a portion of her clothes."

Phœbe heaved a deep sigh of sympathy. The story was full of pain to her; yet she could not keep her mind upon it, for every moment the thought of Mrs. Prescott's sharp cry returned, and she saw the writhing muscles that told of the mother's agony. Yes, she had driven the young man away: she had made her protectors wretched for life.

Miss Thorpe's face was a study while she touched lightly on these sacred topics. She seemed a being all nerve, resolve, and will, yet

the most delicate and womanly of women since
Eve. One could but wonder if she were utterly
cold on the physical side of her nature; if her
intellect were really built up of geometrical figures, like the architecture of the frost, in perfect
symmetry, capable of sustaining itself, and proving
its right to be, and finished with a Q. E. D. at the
pinnacle.

Phœbe, beside this statue of reasoning alabas-
ter, reminded one of a tropical plant in blossom.
But whoever looked at Phœbe *twice* saw that the
luxuriance of nature in her had no element of
weakness, none of the soft over-ripeness that belongs to the Helens and Cleopatras. The elderly
maiden received the homage due to pure intellect. Phœbe was indescribably attractive : every
one who saw her was her slave from the first.
But both equally commanded respect, and seemed
equally entitled to the most chivalrous service.

"I rather dread to meet Mrs. Prescott," said
Phœbe, "and I want you to go with me. Her
reproaches I cannot bear. I left her house —
because — because it was hard to keep self-respect.
I could not help it if her son wished to make himself unhappy about me, and did not wish to be
myself unhappy about him. But he seemed very
different when he went away. Truly, Miss
Thorpe, at the last, he was grand."

"I can imagine," said Miss Thorpe reflectively,
"as a gay young person, he has had no motives
but selfishness and vanity. There is a refined

cruelty in all that they call good-breeding. One grasp of a backwoodsman's hand such as I had when I left the Adirondacks is worth all the cool and polished civilities that we meet here in a whole season. But the simpering dandy face to face with terrible realities is coerced or frightened into downright sincerity. As the young men say, it drives the nonsense out, this preparing to meet, man to man, foot to foot, steel to steel. Yes, war is a terrible teacher; but useful lessons are taught. Perhaps it was worth while, even if that fop should be killed, to have lived a month of pure manliness. I am not hard. I know he is a sorrowing mother's son; but every one who takes the chances of battle is some mother's son. But I will go with you: we will see how she stands. If there is any thing, — the least 'if,' — you will return with me. And, my dear Phœbe, whatever she may say, I don't wish to give you up altogether. I am not so young as I was. I begin to feel that I want to sun myself, as old people do, in the light of some young face. I want you to stay with me as much as you can. We will make a compromise. You shall be the light of *two* sunless houses by turns."

"My dearest friend," said Phœbe, "I am grateful, believe me, not only for your kindness, but for the strength you give me. Your thoughts inspire me. I have learned much with you that I can never forget. I am not quick, like you, and I don't keep up with your thoughts; but I know you will forgive me. I must be myself—I can't pretend—and I *do* love music—and I love my grand old teacher—and I want to see him. I want to pour out my soul sometimes. How would the bird feel if he were shut up, and told not to sing? It is emotion, I know; but I *have* the emotion, although you think it is unworthy; and the emotion belongs to me, it *is* me. I wish I had a piano this moment. Isn't it better to sing than to cry? And I am so full of trouble—and I don't know how to bear it; and, if I could sing, my soul would rise on wings. Is it wrong? Then why did God give me a voice, and sympathy, and a soul to delight in music?"

"You are eloquent when your feelings prompt you, and I cannot blame you for insisting on being yourself. The Master, who forbade us to look for grapes from thorns, or figs from thistles, knew that I should love philosophy and you music. Be it so. But yet I would try to save you from the dreadful trials and temptations of a public. career. My dear Phœbe, sing, if you must (I see it is pleasure, worship, life itself, to you), but sing to me, to Mrs. Prescott, and your other friends. Shun the intoxication of public applause. It exhilarates, but maddens. It unfits one who has felt it for the repose of domestic life. Save your sweetest notes for him whom you are to love. A. song to your husband (provided he is worth singing to), or a lullaby to your first-born in a cradle, is something nobler than the greatest. efforts of the bejewelled prima donna."

Phœbe hardly felt able to grapple with this topic as she would. She thought that this was rather a stern repression. "Because I am a woman," she said, "am I to be silent when the Creator has given me power to sing? Will you say to the artist, 'Paint only for your wife'? Should Longfellow sing only to his children?"

"I know, my dear," said Miss Thorpe, "that my single life might be turned against me. I have never known the feeling that would make me desire to surrender my personality, or blend it with that of another. ·I have spoken of emotions before. This is one of them. If I had ever felt it, I would have trampled it out. But, for my sex in general, I see their duty and their destiny. They are to be wives and mothers. They are to create homes. Now, though there may be exceptions, I must take ground against any pursuit or aspiration that tends to disqualify woman for the great function of maternity. Of what a public career does in this respect we have unhappily too much evidence."

"But suppose one has the inspiration and the art?"

"Then she should consider whether she has the strength to renounce marriage and motherhood. If she can live for her art, she may be spotless. But, my dear, we know what temperaments and faculties are joined. Tell me, have you ever known a great singer that was not emotional,— greatly so? The voice that breathes the song of passion belongs to the heart that craves love. Philosophical people don't sing." Here Miss Thorpe turned over a volume of Buckle merrily, and read aloud some half-dozen abstruse sentences.

"Fancy a woman reading *that*, and then shrieking, '*Involami, t'amo, t'amo*'!"

But Phœbe said she was not fixed upon making singing a profession, nor did she feel sure she should ever marry. This with a rather innocently grave tone.

"Oh, yes! you will marry," said Miss Thorpe, looking with almost a lover's delight over the girl's sweet reserved face and eloquent eyes, and noting the whole atmosphere of attraction that surrounded her. "You will marry. It requires no witch or fortune-teller to predict that. If in no other way, some one will carry you off a Sabine captive. But we won't go on with this. You are fatigued, I see, and have much to think upon. I will read Spencer a while, and you can look in the evening paper for the roster of the —th regiment."

Miss Thorpe wheeled a chair to the centre-table and was soon buried in philosophy. Phœbe skimmed the newspaper, then walked about, noticing the stately rows of books in rich bindings, the busts on corner brackets, and the superb head of Pallas over the central bookcase, on which no boding raven nor Promethean vulture had ever perched. She was soon tired, and went to her room. The portrait, unchanging in its loveliness, looked down on the beautiful girl, and seemed to send a good-night across the darkening room.

The moment she closed her eyes, there were endless files of soldiers passing; officers spurred on with orders, drums beat, colors waved, and cannons roared. Then the scene was changed. There was a vast amphitheatre of hills enclosing a battle-ground. White specks of tents dotted the green slopes near the borders of the woods. White pufflets of smoke rose from the distant earth-works where the cannon were planted. Cavalry rode into the dense clouds of dust in the central plain. Long thin lines of infantry were posted on every vantage-ground, keeping up incessant fire. Over all rose an awful din, as if every sound of horror, rage, and pain, had blended. Phœbe looked and shivered, and could not look away. Mrs. Prescott was beside her, and evermore asked, "Was it for you that I have lost my son?" Then this vision faded. Untold leagues of country swept by; and she saw a man, in the rags of a uniform, sunburnt, torn by briers, now skulking among bushes, skirting water-courses, and now on a log drifting towards the sea. His face was averted from her, and he floated away. Then she walked through a hospital. Pale faces on every side, dying and dead, and still the line of white beds stretched interminably. Once or twice she saw Major Roderick, but at a distance, his arm in a sling. Before she got near where he had stood, there was a vacancy; and then, while her flesh crept with terror, she looked around only to see Mrs. Prescott following her, and again exclaiming, "Was it for you that I have lost my son?" Then came a transport of wounded men. A bright torch flashed at the landing to show the bearers of the stretchers where to step. At this new agony Phœbe could bear it no longer, and screamed.

Gentle Miss Thorpe stood at her bedside with a light; though it was some time before the frightened girl could collect her faculties, and be sure that she had been dreaming. "I heard you moaning, Phœbe," she said, "and guessed the cause. You have had a terrible strain to-day. I will give you these little pellets. You will soon be tranquil. Bridget shall draw a couch into your room, and sleep near you; and you can have a taper burning if you choose." Phœbe was too much exhausted by her ideal terrors to say more than a few words. Her face was pale, and her brow covered with perspiration. The hour of troubled sleep was an age of suffering. Bridget bathed her face, and rubbed her hands, and she was soon in a gentle, dreamless slumber.

Miss Thorpe concluded that she did not know all that was passing in Phœbe's mind, and she pondered how she might change the painful current of feeling.

CHAPTER XIII.

MISS THORPE waited anxiously to observe
Phœbe at breakfast; for it was evident that some
deep grief or burden rested on her mind. Phœbe
came down, looking rather pale, but cheerful, and
expressed regret that her haunting dreams had
caused so much disturbance; but she added, that,
as women could not fight, they. must have their
share of distress in some way. Miss Thorpe began
to see that the girl had something of the heroic
in her nature, that her imagination was active,
and that, more than all, there was something in
the recesses of thought as yet undeveloped.

But Miss Thorpe did not once allude to the
handsome young officer, nor to the interview of the
preceding day. She consented to go with Phœbe
to see Mrs. Prescott, but suggested that she
should afterwards take her music, and pay a visit
to her old teacher. This was the concession she
made in the hope that her coveted amusement
would be the means of bringing the high-spirited
girl nearer to the ordinary level of life.

They were received cheerfully, but with an
unusual earnestness, by Mr. Prescott, who had lingered that morning to console his wife. He was

in the back-parlor near to the conservatory, smoking fiercely, and chewing the end of his cigar, as was his habit when disturbed. The morning paper lay beside him unread. Seeing Miss Thorpe, and knowing her aversion to tobacco, he dropped his cigar, and made himself wretched for her sake. There was so much to be said about the late events that he did not know where to begin. He concluded to wait; and, learning that a call on Signor Belvedere was proposed, he invited both Miss Thorpe and Phœbe to return to dinner, and thought, that, in the evening, he could have his intended explanation with the runaway.

Presently Mrs. Prescott entered from her oratory, all in robes of white, and with her beautiful hair negligently disposed under a lace cap. But her grief was real, if her dress and manner were studied. She came forward slowly, with the port of Lady Macbeth in the sleep-walking scene, and extended coldly a white hand to Phœbe and to Miss Thorpe in silence. Her tears had been dried, and she wore the look of one who trusted to no earthly consolation.

"I have but one thing to live for now," she said, "and that is to pray for our dear sons in the field."

"Oh, pshaw!" said Mr. Prescott. "Better live to work for them, and to help their widows and sweethearts and children."

Mrs. Prescott looked unutterable things.

Miss Thorpe said she trusted Mrs. Prescott would now become interested in the Sanitary Commission.

"I have subscribed for tracts and Bibles to be sent to the army," said Mrs. Prescott solemnly.

"Tracts and Bibles are well enough," said her husband; "but the poor fellows in hospitals also need shirts and biscuit and tea and brandy."

"Yes," added Miss Thorpe; "and the best friends of the soldiers say they have better success in touching their hearts after carrying a supply of good food and clothing."

"'Seek ye first the kingdom of heaven and its righteousness,'" said Mrs. Prescott.

"Pooh, pooh!" said Mr. Prescott, "the people that Christ said that to hadn't been shot to pieces. They didn't need bandages and gruel and nursing. I can't believe he wouldn't do just what we do in the hospitals, and give a meal to the hungry soldiers, and a dressing for their wounds, before he plied them with tracts. The kingdom of heaven, with all due respect, wants a physical basis."

"But we won't make a discussion now," said Miss Thorpe. "When you are sufficiently recovered, Mrs. Prescott, we will go to the rooms of the society, and you will see what we are doing, and learn the results of our work."

"I have asked Miss Thorpe and Phœbe to dine with us," said Mr. Prescott, "and the protocol is signed. It waits for your approval, my dear."

Mrs. Prescott expressed her pleasure, and, having bowed courteously to Miss Thorpe, turned a half-searching, half-tender glance upon Phœbe.

The poor girl, who still shivered at the recollection of last night's dreams, looked as if she expected to hear once more the agonizing question, " Was it by you that I lost my son?"

Miss Thorpe saw that there was no prospect of much genial conversation, and soon rose to go, saying cheerily that her pensioners and constituents were doubtless wondering at her neglect.

As soon as she left the room, the reason of Mr. Prescott's disturbed state of mind became manifest. He took out a letter he had just received from his former clerk Amory, and glanced over it. The first pages referred to the repairs upon the house in Eaglemont, suggested in a conversation mentioned in a former chapter. That portion he did not read to his wife.

" I have a letter here from Amory," he said, — " a fine fellow, by the way, — written at our old home in the country. He is going West, but took Eaglemont on his way, — or out of his way. My niece, I fancy, was the magnet. The part that will interest you I will read." And he read, with occasional comments and shrugs and expressive but inarticulate sounds: " 'I have had a delightful time here, especially in going to various points on the hills to see the scenery' — yes, especially in the scenery. ' We see mountains in three States, — those on the north standing like walls of faint blue, and those on the south resting on the horizon's verge like masses of purple and gray. Your charming niece has been my guide and companion,'—of course!—'and has shared and doubled my pleasure. I have learned that her brother Robert has just made a flying visit here, and, from various scattered hints, I am sure he was a heart-broken man. It seems that he had a grand passion.' I did not know that clergymen were affected that way: I thought such desperate attacks were confined wholly to the laity. 'But the lady was unkind, and he is in despair. He bade his father and mother and sister farewell, told them they would hear of him in India, or China, or in some other heathen country.' This is quite extraordinary, unclerical, to be so put back for a woman. 'The family are in doleful dumps. They don't know who the lady is, and though I may *guess*, like a Yankee, still I shall hold my tongue. Your brother Solomon chews fearfully over this matter; and his wife (whom all the neighbors call aunt Zeruiah) knits and sews with the utmost resolution, both of them looking as if they had buried their first-born.

"'They will expect you'— Hm! no matter about that."

As he read, Phœbe's face underwent every possible change of expression. It was a terrible blow, and none the less painful that it was not unexpected.

"Well, Phœbe," said Mr. Prescott, "it seems as if you must soon have all the family at your feet. Two young Prescotts, as I conjecture, have been slain; and now, unless you come back to live with us, my wife and I will be your next victims."

"Pray don't jest," she replied: "I am broken down. I seem to carry nothing but sorrow with me, and am fated to make every one wretched who cares for me. But, if you and Mrs. Prescott want me to return, I will come, though I have promised Miss Thorpe that I will stay part of the time with her."

"Then come, Phœbe," said Mrs. Prescott. "We cannot alter what is past. It is a desolate heart that you will find. But I will try to be a mother to you still."

"Come," said Mr. Prescott. "You will cheer us up. I want you to sing to us in the evenings. I sha'n't be happy unless I see you about the house. Never mind the — the. And my wife won't be half so desolate as she thinks."

It was singular that both had instinctively avoided asking Phœbe any question about the cause of her going away. There are many recognized facts about which very little is said, and which people tacitly agree not to look at.

Insensibly the gloom began to wear off, and Mrs. Prescott was more serene. Still, Phœbe could not be wholly at ease. The loss of Roderick was too recent, the wound in the mother's heart was too new, and Phœbe was of a nature so sympathetic, that she felt the void and the anguish as if they had been her own. Time only would restore perfect harmony.

But the three sat by the window, through which came a fresh breeze laden with odors from the flowers, and enjoyed an hour of unruffled pleasure. Mr. Prescott had never known the delight of having children of his own, and he felt all his impulses moving towards this beautiful and noble girl. He determined now to be a father to her, and, with her consent, to adopt her by form of law. He did not mention it, however; for he thought it better to learn the state of her feelings in a private interview.

The postman rang, and a servant brought in a letter for Mrs. Prescott. It was a bulky letter with a foreign stamp and an old-fashioned, heavy seal of wax. Mrs. Prescott became agitated as if she feared to cut the envelope. With instinctive delicacy Phœbe rose, and said, —

"I intend this morning to call on Signor Belvedere, and perhaps sing a little. Will you excuse me if I go now? I may call on Miss Thorpe at lunch-time, and we will both come here in season for dinner."

Mr. Prescott assented cheerfully, while his wife still sat silent, holding the letter. Phœbe extended her hands to both, kissed Mrs. Prescott on her pale cheek, and took leave.

A walk of some ten minutes brought her to the apartments where we first saw her. Signor Belvedere was giving a lesson; and she remained in the adjacent room, while the ambitious pupil, like a tireless bird, soared and swooped, and beat against the wind, through the billowy variations of an operatic air. It was a brilliant specimen of execution, but Phœbe was not stirred. Her taste did not approve of ornament for ornament's sake. She thought of the amazing vocal difficulties, and that was fatal. The great singer not only overcomes difficulties, she does not let you perceive that there are any. Phœbe looked at the books, the casts, bronzes, and pictures, and chirruped at the mocking-bird, — the "intelligent feathered critic" that had given her the compliment of a rival song. In due time the lesson was ended; and the pupil, a full-blown rose of a woman, plump, radiant, and self-assured, passed out. Signor Belvedere entered with a grave but indescribably winning smile. He seemed to convey the idea that he had just been a bit of a hypocrite in commending the labored effort of his last pupil, though it would be difficult to say how he did it. His figure was erect, clothed all in black, and devoid of ornament; but his dome-like head was crowned with a small, closely-fitting purple velvet cap. He touched it uneasily as he came, as if it were an anomaly, but dropped his hand as if to say, "You have seen it, and I will wear it." His fine gray eyes sparkled as he spoke.

"My dear-a young lady, and so I see you again! You are welcome as the sun after rain. Come, tell me all about it. And-a so the young man has gone; and you don't-a leave Mistress Prescott? I was afraid you had run away, and had got yourself lost. What a loss it would be! But you don't-a speak!"

"How can I," said Phœbe, laughing, "when you are saying it all?"

"Ah! I am a garrulous old a-fool. But I am only bubbling over with joy. And so you will n̩t be triste any more? And you will singg,— of course you will sing?"

"Certainly! But let me recover my breath. I did intend to leave the Prescotts forever. I found a home with Miss Thorpe, and should have been content to stay with her, only I should have to escape sometimes. She doesn't like music, or rather thinks it belongs to an inferior order of minds. She is all spirit, a pure intelligence, and lives in the clear light of reason. Any emotion she thinks only clouds the soul."

"Ah, Miss Thorpe! Yes, I remember,—a diminish-ed copy of Pallas, just from the brain of Jove. A steady and bright woman,—I remember. I was once at the Plato Club. She was there, listening sharply. She might have been a type of mind, without mortal en-avironment, as she herself would say. And so 'emotion clouds the soul,' does it? Then-a the mother's soul is clouded by her love for her son? Christ's soul was-a clouded when he drove the money-changers in wrath from the temple? David's soul was-a clouded, both in his abject penitence and in his fervid psalms of praise? The souls of Augustine, Thomas à Kempis, Francis d'Assisi, John Bunyan—they were clouded also? And Handel was clouded when he wrote the Messiah, and so was the majestic Palestrini, whose litanies I hope to hear in-a heaven? And Beethoven too, his soul was-a clouded, when, retreating from external sense, he fashioned in the solitary chambers of his great soul those symphonies which seem to have existed from eternity, and will go sounding on *in sæcula sæculorum?* Ah, no! Miss Phaybe it is only intellectual pride that-a disdains emotion, and talks of the rule of reason. The race is in sexes. 'Male and female created he them.' And the nature of man, I will-a not call it either mind or soul, — the nature of man is complex. We perceive, we think, and-a we feel. That is all we know about it. The wisest of the philosophers, if he takes you through a do-zen volumes upon what he calls mental philosophy, which is all *scoria,* rubbish, will get no farther than when he started, namely, that we perceive, we think, and we feel. True, a person all feeling is pulpy, with no more backbone than a jelly-fish. That is a passionate child, a soft and good-for-nothing woman, a silly idiot. But a person with *no* feeling — Grand Dio, what a creature! Thought *and* feeling; and what-a God hath join-ed together, let-a not Miss Thorpe put asunder!"

Signor Belvedere looked like an ancient prophet in a vision: he had never made so long a speech before in his life. Phœbe listened in silent triumph. She had not felt convinced by Miss Thorpe's reasoning, and she could not share her contempt for emotional natures; but she had not

the power to confute her: and it was with a glowing, irrepressible joy that she saw the emotion connected with the reason, — the marriage of feeling
and thought. She was sure Signor Belvedere was
a great man, and need only write one small, eloquent treatise to demolish all the philosophers of
Miss Thorpe's school.

"As I love music, I like to feel that it is not
wrong, and that it is not unworthy. I have frequently wanted to ask Miss Thorpe why she
thought the angels were represented as singing
with harps."

"She would have-a told you that these thinggs
are symbols, — images adapted to the comprehension of children and-a the common people."

"But I like to believe in the singing and in the
real harps of gold. I have never felt so near
heaven as in listening to a great mass such as
Cherubini's."

"Ah, well! my dear Miss Phaybe, we shall-a
know a great deal better about heaven when-a we
get there. Let us come to mundane affairs."

They talked then of what had happened.
Phœbe extolled Miss Thorpe, and sympathized
with Mrs. Prescott, and declared that she could
not do without either of them. She did not refer
to her interview with the major on the parade-
ground. She remembered what she had said of
him to Signor Belvedere, and did not care to
explain the causes that had led her to forgive the
offence, and to a different view of his character.

She related artlessly the few reminiscences which Mrs. Maloney gave of her mother, and told of her faint recollection of a mother's lullaby. All the Italian in the master was aroused. He went to the piano, and touched the keys,

> " Beginning doubtfully and far away,
>   And let his fingers wander as they list,
>   To build a bridge from dreamland for his lay."

Then the music began to rock, and the master's head swayed with the rhythm ; and presently, with the rather husky tones of a voice that had once been fine, he looked at Phœbe, and began to sing, still as if rocking, and moving his head caressingly as if to a tired child : —

> Nel seno materno
> Riposa, cor mio,
> Ti salvi di Dio
> La somma pietà !
>
> La vergin ti guardi,
> Membrandosi il figlio,
> E piova dal ciglio
> Benigno fulgor.
>
> Ti cuoprin con l'ali
> Gli spirti celesti,
> Di cui tu rivesti
> L' imago quaggiù !
>
> Oh dormi, leggiadro,
> Bambino diletto !
> Vicina al tuo letto
> Vegliando starò.

Before many lines were gone over, Phœbe's eyes began to dilate, and her fine thin nostrils showed a delicate tension. Her breath came faster, and soon she found her eyelids weighted with tears. She seemed to be recalling from the far-off chambers of memory those sounds which were associated with helpless infancy and brooding maternal love. Though she could not before have repeated a line, nor hummed a note, of the simple melody, yet soon it was as familiar as her nightly prayer. She dropped her head, and sobbed.

"You have-a heard it, Miss Phaybe?"

"Oh, many times! It is the one thing that comes back to me, and I see my mother's beautiful sad face bending over me."

"It is a lullaby by Isabella Rossi. Said I not you were the daughter of an Italian mother? But I am sorry to have made you cry."

"No: they are sweet tears. Don't mind them."

"I will copy the little songg, and write out the music for you, as well as I can recollect."

Her tears soon dried, like the rain of an April day; and after a time she sang all her old songs, throwing a heart-felt pathos into the tones of her rich voice."

"This it is," said the master, "that rewards the toil and anxiety of years. I am a garden-er, and you are my rose, my lily, my mignonette."

If Phœbe had not felt a thrill of rapture, she would not have been a woman and an artist.

After making an appointment for the next lesson,
she was about to go, when Signor Belvedere
observed, " We have open-ed so successfully one
long-forgotten spring, that I have curiosity, I confess, to see that old prayer-book. Its cover, even
now, is perfum-ed by a mother's love. It was
a good thought of Miss Thorpe to advertise it.
We shall soon have the full name of the flower
I am so proud to have cultivated. Good-by, and
God-a bless you ! "

CHAPTER XIV.

THE dinner-hour came, and Phœbe and Miss Thorpe were seated at the table with Mr. and Mrs. Prescott. Though it was not dark, the blinds were closed, and the chandelier lighted. The table service was exquisite; and flowers, as usual, were in profusion. Mrs. Prescott had regained her composure, and her husband was in the happiest humor. He bowed to the elder and to the younger guest, and felicitated himself upon his position between music and philosophy, youth and maturity, wisdom and grace. He rallied Miss Thorpe upon Buckle's doctrine of averages, and asked her to compile a dictionary for beginners in Spencer. He would have turned his raillery upon Phœbe, only it occurred to him that her influence upon the fate of his nephew, or that of his stepson, would be hardly a delicate subject for jest.

Mrs. Prescott did not once mention the letter that had caused her so much agitation that morning; but it was evident she was thinking of it, for her conversation was mostly upon her old home and the members of her family. Phœbe was somewhat surprised at her reticence; for she knew that Mrs. Prescott had not heard from her English relatives for a long time.

"I have often thought," said Mrs. Prescott, "how much I should like to revisit England. You know I have not been there since my first marriage, and that was a long while ago. During Mr. Courtney's lifetime we often spoke of it, but the convenient time never came. Now, Mr. Prescott is even more devoted to business; but I think next year, 'when this cruel war is over,' as the ballad has it, we will make a little party and go." She was looking at Phœbe, and thinking at the same time of her absent son.

Mr. Prescott had good reasons for thinking the trip far from feasible; but he said nothing. Phœbe understood the look and the allusion, but gave no sign. Miss Thorpe remarked that she should enjoy going abroad, and especially to England; but she added, "The results of travel are what I chiefly enjoy; and those can be had at home. All of the art and architecture of the world are in books. You may speak of the associations of Westminster Abbey; but I follow an imaginary pilgrim among the tombs, and can recall all that is great in the lives of the dead that lie there. Emerson has distilled England as in an alembic. Story, the poet and sculptor, takes you through Rome: you see every thing on his vivid page, and especially if you have the Roman photographs; and you need not go there. Why, my friend, Mr. Q——, who was never in England, knows every noble family and the history of every house; knows who married whom: in short, he

is a living Burke's Peerage and an Itinerary of
the kingdom combined. He corrected a friend of
mine for an error in an account of his visit to
London, and showed him, that, upon leaving such
a street, he must have gone into *such* a one (giving the name), and that he could not have gone
by the street the narrator had mentioned. My
friend was astonished. 'Why, how long since
you went abroad?'—'I was never in London,' he
replied."

"That is very well," said Mr. Prescott: "and
so can a blind man study the plan of a city so as
to get about; but I had rather have my eyes, for
all that. A photograph of a Roman arch may be
fine and impressive; but I would much rather
look out through one into the Campagna or the
blue of an Italian sky. And I would give more
to see one Titian or a Rembrandt to my heart's
content than to look at all the engravings in
the universe. Our dinner here is only so much
carbon and nitrogen and other elements; yet I
don't want any one to come here and weigh me
out the chemical equivalents of a slice of beef: I
prefer the red and juicy article itself. Mr. Emerson may have distilled England, and Mr. Story
may have bottled up Rome; but I have my pref-
erences."

"I have seen some uneducated people," said
Mrs. Prescott, "who have made themselves quite
agreeable by travel. It seems to suppl'' the defi-
ciences of early training."

"Yes," said Miss Thorpe; "but it oftener supplies the ignorant with a few conventional phrases, and covers their ill-breeding with a thin varnish."

"Then let us be thankful for the varnish," said Mr. Prescott.

"Has Mr. Gibbs been abroad?" asked Phœbe innocently.

"No, my dear; and he needs to acquire both the polite phrases and the polish. By the way,"—and what the chain of association was to what he was about to say, no person could have guessed,—"I think I'll go up to Eaglemont shortly. Brother Solomon feels very blue about his son. I would like to see him, and to see the old town; and I have some notion of spending a month or two there this summer." He looked up cautiously to see the effect upon his wife. She remained placid, regarding him with her large, calm eyes.

"How would you like to go, my dear?—And you, Phœbe, just for a day or two?"

Mrs. Prescott replied that she would like to go, but would confer with him as to some matters, such as the care of the house in their absence, and providing for certain comforts not always to be had in the country.

Phœbe had but one regret, and that was to break her appointment with Signor Belvedere. Miss Thorpe said that a trip to the country would be enlivening both to Mrs. Prescott and Phœbe, though the town was still beautiful, and the heat not excessive.

After dinner Mr. Prescott went out to smoke a few whiffs of a cheroot, and then returned, and asked Phœbe to sing. Mrs. Prescott and Miss Thorpe meanwhile went into the library together, where they conversed for a long time.

Phœbe had recovered her elasticity of temper, and was in superb physical condition. A singer must have the fervid temperament in the strong body to produce the best effect. Few out of the profession know what a union of intellect, feeling, and will, as well as of throat, lungs, and muscle, is required.

Mr. Prescott was insatiable, and Phœbe was generous. She sang German songs and French chansons, English ballads and Italian cavatinas, not forgetting some of the touching African melodies, of which "Old Folks at Home" is a specimen. Mr. Prescott sat by her, sipping an occasional glass of Madeira, and chewing the end of his cheroot. His enjoyment was almost an ecstasy.

But now and then the thought of Gibbs intruded; and the bristly, repulsive face seemed to chuckle in triumph at the downfall which was not now far off; for Mr. Prescott had ceased to struggle, and was prepared to give up the business when the appointed time came. His only doubt was, whether, from the wreck of his fortune, he could save enough to support his wife and Phœbe in the old house at Eaglemont. He meant to make the visit there without delay, and when they were comfortably settled, and while the romance of country life was fresh, to break to them the evil news, and prepare them for giving up the luxury and society of the town. These were the thoughts that were running through his mind as he listened to Phœbe's singing. He was also making a mental inventory of the articles he would have carried up on the train; and the piano stood first in the list. He had fixed upon the day after to-morrow for the trip to Eaglemont.

The singing was done; and Mr. Prescott and Phœbe were in pleasant conversation for some time. As Mrs. Prescott and Miss Thorpe still lingered in the library, Mr. Prescott sauntered to the door, and saw both ladies writing. Discreetly he retired, but not without wonder. Something was going on: the secrets were not wholly on his side of the house. But nothing was said; and soon Miss Thorpe appeared, saying that it was time for her to go home. The carriage was ordered; and she was driven home, accompanied by Phœbe.

Mrs. Prescott proved that a woman can keep a secret; for she did not allude to the writing done by herself and Miss Thorpe, and next morning gave her husband, without comment, a stout letter to be mailed. It was addressed to her elder brother, Ralph Manning, Esq., Manning Park, Knutsbridge, Lancashire, England.

After breakfast Mr. Prescott, in glancing over the newspaper, chanced to see an odd advertisement offering a large reward for a prayer-book in

Latin or Italian. The description was written, he thought, by a practised hand; the phraseology was apt and terse: but the motive he could not divine. He showed it to his wife.

"Yes," she said, "I knew of it. Miss Thorpe last evening told me what she had done."

"Well, upon my soul, you are the *secretest* woman!"

"Do you always tell me every thing, my dear?"

"Why, of course I do," he plumply answered.

"You know, Miss Thorpe had a brilliant and unfortunate sister. I believe that she secretly cherishes the hope that Phœbe may turn out to be her niece. It is rather hoping against hope, for she had positive information that the sister died without children. The sister, I believe, was a half-sister, much taller and fuller in figure, and, being an artist, was of a different temperament. Now, there is a portrait of that sister in the house; and it certainly has some resemblance to Phœbe, especially in the far-away look of the eyes, and in the beautiful lips. It was always called an Italian face; and, as Phœbe probably had an Italian mother, the resemblance may not be so wonderful. But she has learned that Phœbe's mother had a Catholic prayer-book such as is described in the advertisement, and that Phœbe's full name was written upon a blank leaf, or was in the lining of the cover."

"Well, it is curious; but, for my part, I don't greatly care to trace Phœbe's history. I should

be afraid that some one with a legal right might
·come and take her away from us; and, if you are
willing, I propose to adopt her without delay."

" Well, yes, if Miss Thorpe does not find what
she hopes. Phœbe is a good child. That she is
lovely every one can see. It is possible, barely
possible, that another clew may be found to her
parentage."

Mr. Prescott gave a quick glance of interrogation; but his wife turned away to some indifferent
topic. He dropped the matter, knowing by experience that she would soon come to him to share
any trustworthy information.

CHAPTER XV.

Mr. and Mrs. Prescott and Phœbe were on their way to Eaglemont. Signor Belvedere had called the evening previous, and had given Phœbe a comic passport entitling her to protection in foreign parts; also some new music, including a manuscript copy of the cradle-song, with illuminations by his own hands. Miss Thorpe, being left alone, was devoting herself to the work of the Sanitary Commission.

As the train rolled on, Phœbe had an opportunity for reflection; and she began to think in what a trying position she was to be placed, between two mothers, each of whom believed her to have been the cause of her son's misery and exile. No one but herself knew how the matter stood with either suitor. Roderick had made no one a confidant; but she saw that his mother had observed closely, and had drawn her conclusions. Robert the preacher was no sentimental lover, and wasted no time in unmanly tears; but Amory's letter had shown that his deep disappointment was known at home; and, as he had left the country suddenly, there was a natural conclusion to be drawn in his case also.

Mrs. Hugh Prescott had been pacified in a measure, partly, perhaps, because she believed that Phœbe really loved her son, and that all would be well when he came back; but aunt Zeruiah, the wife of Solomon Prescott, was a person whom Phœbe dreaded to meet. The dilemma had not occurred to her until now, when she could not turn back. She had heard of the good lady's inflexible nature, her upright and downright speech, and she feared to come under her severe observation. Uncle Solomon, she knew, was quaint, and inclined to jollity, — such jollity as was possible in a puritan neighborhood; and Mary, whom she had seen a few times, was as fresh and charming as a clover-blossom. She thought she would temporize, make friends with the daughter, captivate the father if she could, and then face the solemn matron as best she might.

With such thoughts the time passed until the train reached the station. The town was located in a valley hemmed in by hills; and a swift river went winding through meadows, and turning corners by slopes of green pasture. The old Prescott place was two miles distant; and the road from the village led up a long hill, from which there was a magnificent prospect. Half-way up was the house which Mr. Prescott had ordered to be repaired; but he drove by without mentioning it, and drew up at his brother Solomon's door.

There was the usual surprise when the carriage neared the house, the quick putting-off of aprons and changing of calico dresses by aunt Zeruiah and Mary, the loud cackling of geese by the brook, the gathering of animals at the fence in the home lot to watch the coming of strangers, and finally the hearty welcome of uncle Solomon, who, in a long blue frock, came from the barn to the grassplat in front of the house, and held the horse while his visitors alighted.

Who shall describe the hospitality of a well-to-do farmer when his only brother comes from the great city to renew the old associations? The marvels of cookery, the almost oppressive attentions, the simplicity of rural manners, the freshness of feeling, combine to make the return a glad festival.

The brothers were strikingly alike; only the one had the sunburned face and heavy gait of a farmer, and the other the paler .complexion and alert movement of a man accustomed to city life. They soon walked off to look at the cattle, and inspect the garden and the adjacent fields in cultivation. The two matrons sat in rocking-chairs in the solemn retreat of the best room, and discussed their sons. Nothing was omitted in the experience of either. Mumps and measles were duly compared and chronicled, likewise the cutting of first teeth, and the dates of creeping and walking; and their accidents, tempers, and schooling, and all that concerns boyhood, were gone over with that fond attention to details which only mothers can bestow. They came back to two hard facts. One son had gone to the war: the other had gone to the heathen. And, without actually asserting it, each let the other know (in strict confidence), that the disdain of a certain young lady with beautiful black eyes had much to do with the sudden departure of her son.

The two girls meanwhile planned a little excursion for the afternoon; and uncle Solomon, as a special favor, harnessed his favorite colt to the elliptic-spring wagon, giving abundant caution to Mary to keep a sharp lookout, because the colt was spry. The "colt" was a tolerably lively but perfectly manageable animal of some six or seven years, and knew the hand of Mary as well as that of her father.

They drove down the hill at a rattling pace, laughing whenever the wagon tossed them over the "thank-ye-ma'ams," as the banks for turning water off the road were called; then whirled around the long bends of the river, where the water lay in tranquil pools, covered with lily-pads; then walked up a long acclivity under sweet-smelling birches and chestnuts; then dashed down across a sandy plain, beneath clusters of aromatic pines that were always whispering to each other across the narrow roadway; then skirted a lovely lake (which the country-people belittled by the name of a pond), and watched the inverted reflections of purple hills, white clouds, and blue sky in its glassy depths; then ascended more hills, until they reached a high ground that commanded the sweep of the whole horizon. Here they halted. Phœbe clapped her hands with delight. Northward stood the Old Sachem, a cloudy mass, with hues that seemed to waver from purple gray to chrysolite. Eastward were the lower blue ranges that sloped toward the sea-level. Southward were the billowy tops of hills, in an atmosphere of gold dust under the westering sun. Westward, and surprisingly near, were the picturesque mountains that hem in the Connecticut, — dark and gloomy shadows, with sharp-rimmed and irregularly serrated ridges. And over and beyond them were the faint lines of blue, scarcely discernible, which mark the mountain district that hangs over the valley of the Hudson. Truly it was wonderful, both in the grandeur of the whole and in the beauty of every detail. The eye was never weary of tracing out in the distance tender green meadows, clumps of maples, tall and feathery elms, pasture-slopes, white and red farmhouses, weather-stained barns, winding streams, ponds fringed with trees, and yellow-ochre roads. Every thing looked so *far!* It was a glance into Liliput, or a view of fairy-land through a reversed telescope. The air above them was a dome of absolute crystal purity. The nearer objects seemed almost within reach. As the vista receded, the blue and rosy and golden hues sifted in, until the remotest objects blended with the sky, and the pursuit became a pain. Phœbe, as we have said, clapped her hands at first; but, the longer she looked, the more serious she grew, the more rapt and exalted were her feelings. She experienced a sensation of awe, as if in the presence of Omnipotence.

"I could sit here forever!" she said. "Such distance, such magical color, such variety! Think of me at home, never seeing any thing but brick walls! How I envy you!"

Mary looked wonderingly upon her new friend.

"Yes, it is a high place up here. You can see very far. That mountain there is near fifty miles away: that ridge there is almost a hundred. I often drive up here."

"I don't speak of mere height and distance," said Phœbe. "I am dazzled by effects. Those clouds of gold, those western hills of yellow topaz, those tiny lakes of moonstone, the mountains of sapphire, — how gorgeous! I could fly, surely I could sing." And, without waiting for a suggestion, she poured forth a succession of thrilling notes. It is quite certain that the air of that serene hill-top had never been so disturbed before. It was a Tyrolean melody, with a wild yodel at the close. The distant cattle heard it, and came inquiringly towards the singer; the sheep gathered dubiously in clumps; distant farm-hands in the pastures dropped their bush-hoes and scythes: but, most wonderful of all, there came from the top of another hill somewhat lower, a series of lovely echoes, pure, clear, and far away, "like horns from Elfland blowing," — living illustrations of Tennyson's immortal song. Voices had been heard on the hill before, but never such a voice, nor one animated by such a soul.

Mary was greatly affected, though she hardly knew why. "What a voice you have! Oh, it is beautiful! It seemed as if you were calling the cows, where your voice went up and down so pretty."

Phœbe laughed in spite of herself. "Yes, Mary," she said, "that *yodel*, as they call it, does come from mountainous countries, like Switzerland; and it is an imitation of the notes of the shepherds calling their flocks while they listen to the echoes far above."

"But wait till we begin to go down the hill," said Mary: "there is a place at the bend of the road where a good voice can make three separate echoes, one coming back after another."

They began to descend, going westward, while the sun flooded the immense landscape with molten gold, and while amber and rose-gray shadows began to lurk behind the low hills near by.

"The last time I was here," said Mary, "was with a young city gentleman, Mr. Amory. Perhaps you know him?"

"Oh! Mr. Amory the poet, your uncle's clerk. Yes, I know him." She was about to utter some merry quip; but a sudden thought restrained her.

"He was greatly taken with this place. I had hard work to get him away. We got out of the wagon, and sat back there under a maple-tree; and how he talked! Oh, my! City people mostly go wild up here. We don't mind it so much, we see it so often." The little puritan talked in a sadly prosaic way; but she looked like a native blossom, tender and sweet, born to waste her beauty on unanointed eyes.

"You, you — like this Mr. Amory, don't you?" said Phœbe.

"Yes," said Mary simply. "He isn't handsome; but he is good, and he is so intelligent! Why, he got out for every blossom or weed that he took a notion to, and told all about it; and every bit of shining stone he picked up. And where the rocks seemed to have tipped over, and were standing up edgewise, he told how the earth heaved them up, and left them all out of order; and on the hill back there, the tip-top, he found long scratches on the broad rock, and said that icebergs had once lodged there, and scraped away into the stone until they melted. Oh, he knows a great deal! He is a superior man."

They were at the bend of the road that Mary spoke of, and Phœbe repeated the mountain-song with startling effect. The echo was a marvellous deception. One would think each repetition was surely by an answering voice. They kept on, the "colt" behaving admirably, and soon reached a glen, shut in by dark, high walls of rock, through which rushed a brook in a series of cascades, the spray and bubbles showing from the road like a piece of lace-work. The day was waning, and they could not delay; but they gathered some late columbines, a few of the lingering wild azaleas, which the country-people call swamp-pinks (the most gorgeous and the most fragrant of all the flowering shrubs), also some mosses and ferns, and then drove away down a level road, under lengthening shadows of pine-trees, towards the village.

On the way Phœbe mentioned that she had heard part of a letter from Mr. Amory read, and that she was interested to know more of him, and where he was, and how he was succeeding.

This opened a tender subject with Mary; for she knew that the letter was the one that gave the news of the sudden departure of her brother. This brother Robert was simply worshipped by Mary as well as by her father and mother; and his death would hardly have touched them more than his manner of leaving them. She feared she might say something to grate upon Phœbe's feelings, and had not intended to mention his name or his strange behavior during the brief visit. Mary urged on the horse, and after a time subdued her rising emotion. With delicate simplicity she went on to speak of Amory.

"I have a letter from him," she said; "or, rather, it is more like a journal; and, though it should be private, there are things in it I want uncle Hugh to see. I assure you Mr. Amory is a superior person."

"Is it a love-letter?" asked Phœbe merrily. "If it is, I want to read it. I never had one."

"Your lover," said Mary rather solemnly, "didn't trust to a letter, I suppose, but laid his love at your feet in person."

Phœbe felt the stroke. It was like the "Nathan said unto David."

"But, dear Phœbe, it is not a love-letter, though it has some lovely fringes and frills, — some dear little words put in here and there. Oh, no! it is a serious letter, and noble; and I think uncle Hugh ought to read it."

They passed through the village, — the fairest freight that any wagon ever bore. The piles of ferns, the bunches of many-colored blossoms, and especially the huge sheaf of gorgeous and odorous azaleas, attracted sufficient attention; and many a farmer-boy loitering by the stores wondered "why the city gals allers wanted to git such an all-fired lot of them swamp-pinks."

Supper was served at twilight. The affairs of the state and nation had been discussed by the brothers; the matrons had finished experiences; and the two girls had come home jubilant. Phœbe had never spent such a day in her life. Mary no longer wondered at her poor brother's fascination. The elder Prescotts looked on the two damsels, and each wondered if the earth could show another such a pair. The longer they looked, the stronger the conviction grew.

After a while the lights came in, and Mary proposed to read parts of a certain letter. There was the usual banter between the brothers as to why any parts should be omitted. There were the proper blushes by Mary, and the gay-humored suggestions by Phœbe, until the reading began.

CHAPTER XVI.

THE reader must supply what Mary called the preliminary "fringes and frills." Remembering Mr. Amory and his butterflies, we can imagine he had caught some particularly gorgeous specimens for his inamorata.

MY —— —— AND —— —— OF MY ——, — The passage of the St. Lawrence and the Great Lakes has been often described. I should weary you with the details, if I were to copy from my note-book. The majestic sheets of water deserve to be called oceans. I refer, of course, to Lakes Huron and Superior, as I have not seen Lake Michigan. The Greeks and Romans had no knowledge of inland seas so large, and never made any voyages so perilous as that from Lake St. Clair around into Lake Michigan. These immense distances, I find, do have an influence upon the habit of thinking. I find myself, so to speak, dilating, and have only begun to appreciate the immensity of the country we live in. When I have crossed the Rocky Mountains, I presume I shall have a still grander conception.

Well, here I am in the little village with an Indian name, and I propose to remain for some weeks. You probably know, my —— ——, that I gave some attention to mineralogy, among other branches of natural science. This is the region of copper-mines. Scores of fortunes have been made here, and hundreds of fortunes have been lost. It seems to be the general opinion here that a successful mine is a sheer piece of good luck. In a certain way I believe in luck; but in regard to matters depending on sharp observation, correct deduction, and intelligent action, there is very little of it.

What I am now writing embodies the experience of several days. I have been walking about the leaning derricks and crumbling furnaces of several abandoned mines. One is called the "Corinthian;" and my dear old governor, Hugh Prescott, was its chief owner and promoter. There is still a little office of one story, though not occupied; and there is a dwelling-house, in which a custodian lives, rent free, for keeping the property in order. In order! The task is not harder than disciplining a gallery of mummies. Every thing is as dead as Pompeii. From all I can see, the work done was as intelligent as the butting of a ram. Shafts were driven right into the hill on a venture. If they hit veins of copper, well; if not, just as well; for the company paid, all the same. The observation of scientific men, the experience of skilful miners, and the traditions of the aborigines, concur in the statement that there is copper here enough to supply the world. I propose to take a little time, and see what can be done.

The old custodian prefers to sit in the house, and smoke his pipe. I cannot tempt him out; but I have walked over the property, and have scaled hills, and inspected ravines, that I presume no one has trod for a long time before.

Some days ago I was looking at a steep acclivity in a remote position, on which there was an unusual growth of bushes and small trees. "Why," I asked myself, "is there this wealth of vegetation, these luxuriant bunches of shrubs?"—"Of course it is from some unusual fertilization of the soil."—"But why was this rocky place fertilized?"—"Because men have at some time haunted it, and the remains of their food or that of their animals have accumulated here." I determined to explore.

I went to the house, got an axe and a short, stout scythe, and made havoc among the brush. I grubbed up roots, and picked my way into crevices. By and by, when the bushes were cleared away, and the whole face of the spur of the hill could be observed, it was easy to see that a large central portion was composed of loam and sand that had fallen or settled there, while the ancient rocks stood out on either side. To remove that *detritus* of loam and sand was the next task. I dared not take any one into my confidence, for reasons that you will appreciate; and the whole work had to be done by my own hands. I stole a pick-axe, a hoe, and spade, and every day I worked steadily. In a week, I had dug away the alluvium, and come to the rocks. I was amply repaid. There were marks of tools on the sides of the opening I had made. Miners had wrought there. These were proofs of the correctness of my theory. Before long I had opened an *adit* that had been closed, perhaps for hundreds of years, by the earth sliding into and before it, blocking it up. It was an entrance that had been worked by intelligent miners: every thing showed that. Cautiously I kept at work, and soon came against *a solid wall of copper.*

I don't know as you know what this means; but my ——! I can tell you. It means unbounded wealth. It means trips to Europe, houses in upper-ten-dom, libraries, yachts, horses, and the gratification of every wish.

You have noticed that I mentioned the " *Corinthian.*" This mountain of copper, though unworked for centuries, is within the limits of that property. My best of friends, as I have said, is chief owner. The outstanding shares I will get hold of, and have sent to a shrewd broker to buy them for me, especially Gibbs's. I wouldn't miss seeing his rage for any thing on earth. I mean to buy them for about 1¼, and have them go up to 180. It will be a glorious spectacle to see him tear his hair.

"I am more glad than I can tell you, for the sake of my good friend, Hugh Prescott. Before this reaches you, you will have heard of his troubles. Gibbs has him tight as a vise. Gibbs will squeeze him, and pitch him out. This discovery is going to save him, if the news reaches him in season, and our projects can take firm root. The same mail that takes this letter will carry a similar one to him. If he bestirs himself, he can hoist that brute of a Gibbs, and make him retire, singing a popular melody.

You see, I can't leave here. I am keeping watch over the custodian, lest he behold, and blab. I have sent for two gallons of whiskey and two pounds of smoking-tobacco for him, and he is happy. I have also sent East for a trusty friend to come on instanter, and relieve me from keeping guard night and day. When I have bought all the loose certificates that are lying round, especially Gibbs's, I will take a nap. Hurrah for the "Corinthian"!

By the by, my —— —— ——, I am troubled to think about your brother Robert. He is a *splendid*, magnificent fellow, if he *is* a preacher; and I am sorry for his bad luck, as well as uneasy about him. Do you *know* where he has gone? I know he said he was going to foreign parts; but I have always heard, that, when a new batch of missionaries leaves, they meet on the wharf, and pray and sing, and give a solemn "send off." Now, I have looked at the New-York papers (and they are all mailed to me), under the head of "Religious Intelligence," but have seen no mention of the Reverend Robert. Of course he may have gone quietly. But I should like to be assured that he has kept his balance, and come to no harm. I wish he could be here with me. We two could run this machine.

With —— —— of my —— ——, and with a thousand ——, I am devotedly

Your —— —— ——,

G. P. AMORY.

Probably the innocent Mary, as she concluded reading, had not the least idea what a bomb-shell she had dropped in that quiet party. There was a missile in it for everybody. The revelation of

Hugh Prescott's affairs produced the utmost consternation. His plan of breaking the news gradually to his wife was frustrated. Solomon now saw why the old house was being repaired. Aunt Zeruiah had recourse to Scripture; and, between her sincere sorrow for Hugh's downfall and her renewed apprehensions for the fate of her son, she could hardly remember enough texts to meet the emergency. It was Phœbe's destiny to receive a fresh stab at every turn. The two Prescotts, her vehement lovers, had managed so ill as to leave her exposed to unjust censure, and make her relations with their families most unpleasant. The two mothers sat gazing at her, — the one looking like "a section of the day of judgment;" the other dissolved in tears, sobbing hysterically, now moaning for her lost son, and now for her ruined husband. It was noticeable that not one of the company appeared to place much confidence in Amory's discovery. Being a poet, he was considered as necessarily a flighty person, without sound judgment or discretion. Hugh Prescott, who was the one most vitally interested, had listened to the letter very earnestly, and was somewhat affected by the writer's enthusiasm; but he remembered that many similar "discoveries" had been made that afterwards turned out to be of no practical value. His ruin he knew was a certainty: the rescue by the rise of copper stock was exceedingly problematical. Besides, the time in which he would have to raise the money, if he attempted to pay off Gibbs, and save the business, was now very short ; and the value of the Corinthian stock could not be really established, except upon the evidence of a scientific expert.

Phœbe was at first overwhelmed solely with the thought of her protector's situation. While she had lived with him, she had never known a want. Money had been as natural and as plenty as Cochituate : it was only touching the knob of a faucet. The thought of living upon a narrow income, of counting the price of dresses, or of supplying such wants by the sale of eggs and chickens, had never occurred to her. Poverty, like death, was an ugly subject, to be kept in the background : now its grim visage was appallingly near. But her courage rose ; and she was ready to meet what was inevitable in a far nobler spirit than Mrs. Prescott could show. But the mother's laments for Roderick, and the solemn looks of the mother of Robert, were too much. How was she to explain to the one the unutterable things that had preceded Roderick's going away ? And what right had that stern Hebrew to assume that her preacher son had any claim upon a fresh young girl ? How could she unfold the intricacy of feeling with which she had regarded that religious enthusiast ? How could she explain that all the feeling of love which the glowing man might have inspired was quenched by the solemnity of the preacher ? She pitied the mother of Roderick, though she saw her weakness ; but she was rather indignant with the mother of Robert, who, with her implacable Old-Testament wrath, sat corruscating and frowning at her across the room. It was an unequal strife. Phœbe soon touched the arm of Mary, and the two girls retired to their chamber.

There a long conversation followed, in which Phœbe opened her heart to her friend; and, when at a very late hour sleep came, the two girls were locked in each other's arms.

Mrs. Prescott had sobbed herself into helplessness, and was persuaded to go to bed. Her large blue eyes seemed to have been made for weeping, and her soft and flexible lips were always under the dominion of some emotion.

The brothers walked out into the front-yard, and talked under the shade-trees till bed-time. Aunt Zeruiah was left to herself, a Nemesis whose retributions now fell chiefly on her own head.

It was a sorrowful group that met for breakfast next morning. The interval of rest had brought no healing to sore hearts. The visit of which so much was anticipated became dismal in reality. There was no way to restore harmony, still less to bring cheerfulness or gayety. Mr. Prescott proposed to return to the city to look after the expected letter from Amory, but persuaded his wife to stay until the servants could come with a portion of the furniture for the refitted house. Phœbe also determined to go. She could not bear to be the focus of those two pairs of eyes;

and she did not know which gave her the most pain. She would go to stay with Miss Thorpe until there was a calmer atmosphere on the old hill.

After their departure by the early train, uncle Solomon got his team, sent for some hands to help, and spent the day in putting the yard and garden of his brother's house in order. He transported corned beef, pork, and vegetables for his cellar, hay and grain for his barn, set up a cooking-stove in the kitchen in the lean-to, and got a stock of groceries from the store in the village; so that the house was ready for occupancy. Mary stole down the hill with bunches of azaleas and other flowers, and disposed them in vases and pitchers, opened the windows to air the rooms, and put away the articles in the closets.

The two disconsolate mothers meanwhile had a sorry time.

Mary, simple-hearted creature, had not understood why the letter that to her was so full of promise should have given every one such a shock.

CHAPTER XVII.

On the way to the city Phœbe had an opportunity to meditate. Her position was becoming very disagreeable. She could not take up her abode with Miss Thorpe without wounding the feelings of her old friends; and she was beginning to feel that she ought not to be a pensioner upon the bounty of any one. With the Prescotts she must be perpetually reminded of the double mischance; and she did not know which was the more painful to bear, — the somewhat ostentatious sorrow of the one bereaved mother, or the stern and unrelenting disfavor of the other. If she became wholly an inmate of her foster-father's house in Eaglemont, she would constantly encounter either the sighing Episcopalian, or the frowning Calvinistic dame. It was not to be borne. She had tried it; and, much as she loved her dear and fatherly protector, she shrunk from returning to the country with him, either in his prosperity or adversity. She pondered; and when she took a carriage at the station, after leaving Mr. Prescott, she ordered the coachman to drive to Signor Belvedere's rooms.

The master was voluble, as usual, and profuse in

compliment, as became a man of his race and culture. Phœbe carefully opened the matter, and asked him what she could do to support herself. "And you really, really, Meess Phaybe, wish to work, to teach?"

"I really, really do."

"It is a most serious thing. You are tender in feeling, and you are-a proud too. It will not be life in a rose-garden for you to teach the indifferents, the incapables, and the insolents. Many and hateful characters are group-ed in schools; "and the teachers get all the hatefulness."

"I am prepared, and will try."

"Well-a, then, I rejoice to tell you there is a chance. The new *collegium puellarum* needs a teacher of music. Who can play better? Who can sing so well? Yes, my dear-a Phaybe,— Meess Phaybe, I should say,—the head of the college has done me the honor to consult me. I will hasten to him and announce, that, after much persuasion, I have induced a very lovely and accomplish-ed youngg lady, moving in-a the selectest circles of the *haut ton*, to accept the situation in his-a college. I shall represent that the appointment will-a confer lustre upon the new and risingg institution, and that I am prepar-ed to receive his congratulations for the great favor I have-a done him."

Phœbe had gone to him in her grim mood, and had meant to be as resolute as one of the Fates; but his raillery conquered, and she laughed heartily.

"And do you think I can make good your magnificent commendations? You cover me with loads of roses."

" With rose-leaves, Meess Phaybe, to judge from the beautiful flush that-a covers your lovely cheeks."

" To be serious for a moment, let me say, that to know how to sing or play is one thing; to teach is quite another."

" Ah, instinct is a great matter, as your Shake-a-speare's Falstaff says. You will not-a have difficulty. Put yourself in the pupil's place. Remember your own trials. Besides, I will go over the method, not as before, but with a view to make you the instructor."

" So you think I can do it?"

" Certainly. It will be necessary, that, when the faculty see a white raven, you see one too; that is, a certain deference to the opinion of the people in power is to be commended. They may know nothing; but you must-a treat them as if they were Solomons and Lord-a Bacons. Perhaps you are orthodox (it is a hard word to say, and I don't-a know what it means); but, if you are not, it is not-a necessary that you publish it by sound of trumpet on the house-top. It is just as well to be in favor — and then to think *in petto* what you like."

With his usual celerity and good-fortune, Signor Belvedere went and obtained the place, and came in the evening to Miss Thorpe's to announce his success.   He had arranged that she was to pass Saturday and Sunday in the city; and that was some consolation to Miss Thorpe, who at first had been strongly against the project. Phœbe was firm, and chiefly because she felt she was right. Let come what would she was now independent, and would neither burden Mr. Prescott, nor humble herself by subsisting upon the bounty of a newly-found friend. She was to enter upon her duties at the beginning of the new term, now not far distant.

Mr. Prescott found no letter from Amory. There was no doubt that the letter had been written; but who can account for the mistakes of the post-office, and explain why a plainly directed epistle sometimes makes the round of half the States in the Union before it comes to its proper destination? He wrote to Amory, but knew, that, before an answer could be received, the time for his settlement with Gibbs would come. Daily he thought of the missing letter; but no tidings came. Still he thought best to get all the mining shares he could into his possession, and through a broker he secured all that could be found, including those which Gibbs had. They cost but a trifle, and would add but little to his losses, even if Amory's hopes were fallacious. He was ready to take advantage of fortune if the fickle goddess did not again elude him.

He sent up the furniture by rail in charge of two servants, dismissed the others, sold his horses, and shut up his town house. A fortnight remained, and he resolved to spend that interval in the country. Among the letters he carried to his wife was one that attracted his attention by its size and by the foreign stamps and seal. This he handed to her on his arrival, and waited for her to read it. He saw with pleasure how thoroughly his wishes had been carried out in the arrangements of the house, and thought, if the downfall came, he could scarcely desire a more comfortable home.

Mrs. Prescott was absent but a few minutes; but on her return her face was a miracle of surprise and joy.

"I never wanted to keep any secrets from you," she exclaimed; "but Miss Thorpe thought it prudent to keep this matter private for a time, as the interests involved were so near and dear, and we didn't wish to have any hopes raised until there was a sure ground for them. But this is too good news. I fear it can't be true. I always felt drawn to that darling. I didn't suspect she was my own flesh and blood."

Mrs. Prescott was so excited, that, in trying to read the letter, it dropped from her hand. "Read it, my dear," she said: "I can't command myself."

Mr. Prescott picked up the letter, and carefully read the first pages. When he had reached a certain point he was quite as excited as his wife. He lost his spectacles, found them on the top of his head, pulled out his handkerchief, laid it on the table, folded the letter instead, and crammed it in his pocket, all the time walking about, and plying his wife with questions. A happier couple was never seen. They embraced each other, cried, kissed, tried to look over the letter again; but neither could read a line: and at length they sat down, side by side, hand in hand, like two young lovers, and talked no end of nonsensical endearment.

The purport of the letter was this. Mrs. Prescott's brother, Roderick Manning, a year younger than herself, had many years ago married an Italian opera-singer, — a young widow with a title, still in her first bloom, and with an unblemished fame. But the marriage had cost the young man his father's favor. He was cast off, and left unprovided for. He fell into evil habits, especially gambling, and absorbed all his wife's earnings to gratify his fatal passion. A child was born to them; and the husband, for a time, gave up vice, and became a more thoughtful and provident man. But the wife lost her voice and her energy, and could appear no more in public; and, as nothing had been saved in the time of her success, the road to starvation and misery was very short. They disappeared, and it was believed they had gone to America.

The story told by Mrs. Maloney seemed to furnish the sequel. There was as yet no legal proof, but a high degree of probability. Mrs. Prescott then reminded her husband of Miss Thorpe's advertisement for the lost prayer-book. If that book could be found, the evidence would be complete.

"By George, I have it!" exclaimed Mr. Prescott. "Why didn't Miss Thorpe go to the antiquarian bookstore?—Benham, you know, who keeps those stacks of old books that you wonder what they are good for. Why, he knows every volume in the shop. Try him; and he will scratch his head a moment, then go up a ladder, and in ten seconds put his hand on the book you ask for. He buys every thing that offers: nothing comes amiss. Ten to one he has that prayer-book now."

"Then why don't you write to Miss Thorpe?"

"I will, at once. But let me look at that letter again."

He read it again, and this time to the end. It appeared that Phœbe would be entitled, when the necessary proof was furnished,—and this part was underscored,—to a legacy of ten thousand pounds, and that she with Mrs. Prescott were also heirs presumptive to the writer of the letter. Then were renewed the embraces of the pair of elderly lovers. When they became sober again, a letter was written and despatched to Miss Thorpe. It gave a brief epitome of Mr. Ralph Manning's letter, and recommended her to go to Benham's bookstore at once.

Miss Thorpe, upon reading the news, was as

much excited as her nature would allow; but she carefully concealed from Phœbe her feelings and the letter. It was mid-day; and upon some pretence she left the house, and with trembling steps went towards the bookstore. Much as Miss Thorpe repelled the idea of married life, she possessed a warm heart; and her feelings towards Phœbe were like those of a mother. Day by day the ties had grown stronger; and she had an almost feverish hope that the girl might prove to be her niece, the daughter of her unfortunate sister. In any event, the position of Phœbe was what the position of her sister's child would have been. That fact alone enlisted her sympathy; and who could say, from the little that was known, whether the report that her sister had died childless was not a conjecture? True, the mother of Phœbe had an Italian name; but did not the same report say that she was a widow, a widow with a title, when she married the young Englishman? Her sister in youth had greatly resembled Phœbe; she had lived for years in Italy, so as to become like an Italian in speech and manner; she had been in her day a prima donna, and had married a degenerate Italian noble. Phœbe might be her sister's child, after all. The thought almost took away her breath, and made her limbs tremble beneath her. Who shall blame the childless woman, now that the tendrils of her heart were twined about this girl, if she hoped and prayed that the whole story might prove to be a fiction, unless the part in which she was interested, the name of the mother, should be established as well as that of the father? She could not give her up.

It is not necessary to explain how the mind of a bookseller retains the thousands of titles: it is enough, that, upon being asked for the Italian prayer-book by Miss Thorpe, Mr. Benham went into a corner, and brought it out. Her prognostications as to its size and appearance were nearly correct; only the covers were limp, and fastened by a simple leathern strap; and in one side there was a receptacle just large enough to admit a visiting-card. Miss Thorpe turned away as she observed this, so that the bookseller might not see her emotion. She drew out a thin piece of paper, — so it seemed, — so thin as to have escaped notice. Her breath came quick as she took it.

It was a card, worn and soiled; but the inscription was still legible. There was a faint outline of a coronet at the top, and below were the words, "LA CONTESSA DELLA TORRE." Who was the countess? At that moment Miss Thorpe would have given her whole fortune to have read there, "*nata* Thorpe;" but there was nothing more to be seen. She turned the card. Lines seemed struggling into view; but the glazed and grimy surface made them indistinct, and the sorrowful lady's eyes were dim with tears. Yes, the high priestess of intellect had succumbed to an emotion: the serene, high head was bowed, and she wept like another woman. She put the card in her own case, intending to scan it more closely at home. She paid the bookseller the price charged. He had not noticed the advertised reward, and now refused to take the large sum offered.

While returning home, Miss Thorpe recovered her mental discipline ; but it was necessary to lave her hot face, and cool her inflamed eyes. After a time, she came into the library, where Phœbe was sitting, and chatted pleasantly about the books and periodicals.

Phœbe thought her singularly alert in feeling and manner. Her mental movements seemed like those of the needle when agitated by the neighborhood of the magnet,—trembling, aiming, swerving, poising, and still returning to its polar allegiance. Still Miss Thorpe thought herself calm, until, in preparing her microscope for use, she was compelled to see that her hands were quite unsteady. She stopped a moment to recover herself, and asked Bridget to go for Mrs. Maloney.

Phœbe wondered at the agitation ; but she had learned to control herself in Miss Thorpe's society, and never disturbed her friend by questions. After some meditation, Miss Thorpe said, " You remember, Phœbe, what I have told you about my beautiful sister. I told you she became a great singer, and married a man of rank, but a man unworthy of her, and that after a season of married life, full of pain and trouble, she died. You know I said she had no child (that was the report) ; but I have doubted it. You certainly look very much as she did, and her name was Phœbe."

The girl's eyes sparkled with a sudden animation.

"Do you know any thing more now? Have you any news? Oh, if it could be true!"

"Then you would like to have it true?"

"Of all things!" she answered eagerly. "You are like a mother to me; though, to be sure, Mrs. Prescott has been a mother too. But I hope you have something to tell me. If you were truly my aunt, how I should love you!"

"And don't you love me now?"

"I love you with all my heart; but if you were my aunt, you know, my poor mother's sister, my own blood, why I should have a better *right* to love you. Now, while I am not your relative, your love to me is a little like a charity, and I feel I don't deserve it; and though I am grateful, and I know how good you are, yet — yet I am not entitled to the least thing. It makes a difference, doesn't it? I know I shouldn't be *entitled* to any thing, even as your niece; but it wouldn't be so unusual. No one likes always to take favors and kindness that can never be returned."

"I hope your heart will be always where it is now. I want you to love me, whether it turns out that I am your aunt or not. Tell me that you will."

"I always shall."

"Even if your father's relatives claim you?"

"No one shall ever come between us. Of course, if I find my father's people, I shall owe something to them. But I can never forget you, never."

She seized Miss Thorpe's hand to kiss it ; but the nervous little woman drew the unresisting girl down to her side upon the sofa, and, putting her arm round her waist, drew her to her bosom, and kissed her fondly. It had been many a year since Miss Thorpe had kissed any one, even of her own sex. Miss Thorpe now brought out the missal and the card, but held them in her own hands.

" Before I tell you about these, will you please read this card ? "

Phœbe took it, and read aloud, " LA CONTESSA DELLA TORRE." Miss Thorpe, by a great effort, then asked her to look at the reverse. The writing was not clear, even to Phœbe's fine vision : so the card was put under the microscope. " Tell me what you see. Begin at the top, and give it in order."

Phœbe read hesitatingly these names : —

" Febe —— Ludovico.

Febe Maria Isabella, rosabella.

Roderick Manning.

Febe della T. Manning, nata " —

But great currents of blood were surging through Phœbe's heart, dizzying her brain, and flushing scarlet her cheeks. She could be restrained no longer.

" And this was my mother's ! " She kissed the soiled paper. The rush of emotion choked her.

Then tears came. Then she grew paler, and sat down overcome.

Miss Thorpe wished she had not been so abrupt; but she soothed her, and soon had the delight of seeing her natural color return.

"You have not asked me about these names, and I have no certain information to give you; but I think this is the explanation: The names 'Febe' and 'Ludovico' are coupled, showing the first marriage, — Febe (somebody) and Ludovico, Count della Torre; for your mother was a countess and a widow when she married your father. That is his name, as I believe, — 'Roderick Manning.' We know at least that Mrs. Prescott had a brother Roderick (for whom her son was named), who married an Italian countess, formerly a public singer, and was cast off by his family. 'Febe Maria Isabella' of course is your own name. 'Rosabella' may have been a transient word of affection for you — beautiful rose — as she wrote your name."

Then she set Phœbe at a little distance, to look at her. It was a perpetual pleasure to observe the "pure and eloquent blood" in her checks, the delicate play of emotion about her beautiful lips, and the lively but humid brilliancy of her eyes. She was a being formed to love.

"Phœbe," she said, "I suppose there is now very little doubt that your father's name and family have been ascertained."

"That is what Signor Belvedere said," she

replied, with a kindling interest, — "an English father and an Italian mother."

"He was of a good family; and the head of it, who is now an elderly man without children, has lately written in answer to a letter of inquiry. Some legal formalities have to be gone through with; but, if the truth prevails, you will soon come into possession of a sum sufficient for your support. I fear they will want you to go over there."

"And leave you? Never! The family probably cast my parents off, and left my mother to die. I owe them nothing. You and Mrs. Prescott have been like mothers to me. I will never leave you, not even for a fortune."

"I don't know — I trust you won't. But a fortune and position are very tempting."

"Well, if I have·a fortune, I shall be my own mistress in a year, and I can do as I like. And, if I have to go over, I'll take you and Mr. and Mrs. Prescott with me."

"Mrs. Prescott, I have no doubt, would like to visit her old home."

"Yes!" said the girl, with a sudden burst of enthusiasm; "and they shall go. Mr. Prescott has lost all, only his house and books and furniture. He is too old to begin business again. Oh, if I could now take care of him, and make him comfortable! Shall I have enough?"

"I hope so. And you would find your visit with them very pleasant. You would go to the same neighborhood, to the same house; for, do you comprehend? you are a Manning, a descendant of the great admiral, Mrs. Prescott's niece."

"And Roderick is my cousin; and Robert — no, Robert is not."

"Yes, Roderick is your cousin; and cousins should not marry."

Phœbe answered only by an untranslatable glance; but in a moment she returned in thought to the card. "After all, I don't know any more about my mother. Who was the Countess della Torre?"

"I cannot answer you," said Miss Thorpe sadly. "Only she was young, a singer, and a widow when she married your father. I could never trace my poor sister."

Phœbe looked at the face of the woman who was hungering for affection, and thought with a great throb what a joy it would be if her mother should really have been that lost sister.

But now came Mrs. Maloney, and looked at the book. "O Blissed Virgin!" she exclaimed; "and that is the same! Oh, truly, Miss Phayba, that was your mother's! Niver paert with it; and say your prayers out uv it, my daerlin', as your mother did. They made her soul aisy, anyhow. An' she told me she was born a Protestant."

Then, looking with glistening eyes on the card, 'Ah! An' there is the name that my poor head couldn't remember." She was turning it over, and looking at it upside down mostly, having deciphered nothing but the coronet.

"An' *that's* to show she was to be a saint in heaven. The holy mother and the angels in the pictures always has thim gold hoops over their heads."

Phœbe and Miss Thorpe exchanged faint smiles, but did not enlighten her upon the difference between the coronet and an angelic halo.

"An' to think that I couldn't rmembcer the name!" Miss Thorpe gave a signal of silence to Phœbe. Mrs. Maloney might become garrulous, if she knew the story.

"Never mind," said Phœbe: "it is no matter now. And when I have a home of my own, — and that will not be long, — I shall have a place in it for you as long as you live. I have been so sorry that I could do no more for you while I was with Mrs. Prescott; but I had nothing of my own. It will soon be different; and then, Mrs. Maloney, you good soul! then you will know that I remember my friends."

This was something of an effort for Phœbe; but she spoke with an earnestness that showed the depth of her feelings. Mrs. Maloney was profuse in her thanks and her blessings; and it was with considerable delay and friction that she took her departure.

"Now," said Miss Thorpe, "we must reply to Mr. Prescott's letter, and inform them of the discovery; but, for many reasons, I would advise you to keep this a secret from your other friends, for the present. Perhaps you might make an exception in favor of Signor Belvedere, first binding him to silence. As he must have known most of the famous singers of twenty years ago, he may be able to tell us who the Countess della Torre was."

Phœbe saw the wisdom of the advice; but she almost fluttered like a bird in her impatience, until she could see her teacher, and impart to him the wonderful news. Her mother a countess! Surely an educated Italian gentleman must know the family names of the nobility.

But Signor Belvedere was strangely cool or non-committal. "Yes, Meess Phaybe," he said, "I have-a heard of the Della Torres,—an old and respectable family. But that any one of its countesses should be a singer, and should drift across the Atlantic to die alone in a tenement-house, is, at the least, very surprising. Do not a-believe it, my dear youngg lady, until it is prov-ed. We will inquire. Be calm. The heart of youth should reache forward more than backward. I think, however, you will yet know your parents."

Phœbe was silent, meditative: evidently she had something more to say. The master saw, but shrugged his shoulders. "It will a-come out," he might have said.

"It is some time since you were in Italy, is it not?"

"Oh, yes! A do-zen years and more."

"Do you never think of going back?"

"Of course, some time. My parents are dead

some years; but I have a sister and brother, and I don't know how many nephews and nieces."

" And you say you knew the Della Torres ? "

" And-a what does all this mean, Meess Phaybe ? "

Phœbe was not in the least confused, but looked at him with a soft and steady gaze, as if her eyes had been two stars.

" I would not put my burdens on others; but think how a girl must feel who has not a mother! How I should adore the man who found her for me, although I am never to see her! The gleam of light from that prayer-book, — it is like a ray from heaven. Can't I trace that book? Its worn and soiled leather is fragrant to me. It was my mother's, you know, — my mother's. I must follow the trace. I have thought that some time you would make a visit to your native land, and " —

" And — and, my dear Phaybe, in the God's good time I will. We will find out the truth about La Contessa."

" You will not forget? You will write perhaps; some time you will go. It is a great thing to ask. You see, I presume on your generosity. You seem all nobleness to me. You rise always higher with each occasion."

" And you grow always the lovelier."

Phœbe was beginning to weep, from sheer excess of sensibility.

" Come, come, dear Meess Phaybe, let us not have the April rain at this time of the year. Good-by. The thought-seed you have planted will-a sprout."

CHAPTER XVIII.

THE good news was duly sent to Eaglemont by Phœbe in a letter full of unaffected tenderness and of lively gratitude to her benefactors. They replied, asking her to come and pass the remainder of the pleasant season, and to bring Miss Thorpe. But Phœbe's new engagement rendered it impracticable to make any but a short visit away from the city. As Mr. Prescott was soon to come down on business, Phœbe promised to return with him, and pass a Sunday.

Meantime Phœbe continued the course of reading she had begun with Miss Thorpe, practised singing with her master an hour daily, and renewed her acquaintance with French and German. Idleness was impossible with Miss Thorpe, and her mental activity was stimulating and contagious. Phœbe had been fairly educated, after the prevailing mode; but she found she had got more of the results of learning under her friend's direction than in all her life before. Nothing more was said about fitting herself for the stage. The calm good sense of her friend had checked the incipient desire, and the terrible lesson of the lost sister's career had not been without effect. Miss

Thorpe, on her part, yielded somewhat, and made no objection to the girl's giving lessons, or singing for practice.

The time came for Mr. Prescott to meet his late partner. Mr. Gibbs had been growing stouter; though, with his increasing prosperity, he affected juvenile costumes. He carried a slender cane, and had a habit, while talking or listening, of tapping his patent-leather boots with it. His watch-chains were massive and gorgeous, and he wore a broad seal-ring. But nothing could take the attention of the beholder from his increasing corpulence, and from the deepening colors in his full cheeks and extraordinary nose.

When the partners met, there was little said. Mr. Prescott observed that the unusual balance against him was, in a measure, factitious, being largely made up of advances to corporations which the firm had not been obliged to make, and for which it appeared that Mr. Gibbs had furnished the funds, probably in anticipation of this very result. Mr. Gibbs replied that there were corporations that had to be carried, and it was well for the reputation of the house of Prescott & Co. that he had had the necessary funds. Mr. Prescott said the object was evident, which was to place the junior in a position to use his capital as a lever to push the senior out. His exterior manner was calm; but who can tell the sufferings of such a man on the verge of his ruin? It did not console him to think that by his own neglect, and by leaving all affairs to the trusted junior, he had brought this destruction upon himself. Even at that late minute he looked for the sign of some relenting, some touch of feeling in the face of Gibbs. It was as bare of any remorseful expression as a vessel's wooden figure-head. In fact, Mr. Gibbs was almost in a good-humor, — almost as complaisant as if he were at a wedding or christening. He felt grateful, if at all, that Mr. Prescott had accepted the situation, and was going to leave gracefully, instead of making a scene.

The papers were brought out and signed. Mr. Gibbs handed his old partner a check for an insignificant amount, and bowed politely.

Mr. Prescott took the check, and, walking slowly through the open space, paused, and gave a cordial good-by to each clerk in turn. There is a melancholy feeling, as Henry Crabb Robinson says, when we think of doing *any thing* for the last time. It was done. The house of Prescott & Co. was no longer. Full of tumult within, and with an almost broken heart, but with all the old stately manner, Mr. Prescott left the warehouse.

The check was sufficient to pay his small bills. He had his dwelling-house, the little property in the country, and a lot of dubious copper stock.

But Mr. Gibbs had in a measure reckoned without his host. The news of the senior's forced retirement had got abroad: in fact, Gibbs had boasted of the transaction at the club. "Business," however, was not quite what Amory had defined it. There were some old-fashioned people in the street who respected honor and the golden rule, and who even had notions of gratitude; and among these the conduct of Gibbs was vigorously denounced. A bank director came and talked to Gibbs pointedly about it, to that great man's extreme disgust. Even his set at the club gave him more room than formerly. The clerks gathered in knots, and whispered. The very porters and the sweeper looked sidelong at him. The preacher next Sunday, so Gibbs thought, was aiming at him in a sermon he preached upon commercial morality. And he remembered that the lawyer who drew up the papers had asked him impertinent questions. Gibbs was pachydermatous; but in time missiles will go through even the hide of an elephant.

But all this would have been nothing, if his plans had been successful. It was with the utmost astonishment and rage, that, shortly after the change, he read letters from treasurers of some of the largest corporations, announcing, that as their arrangements had been made with Prescott & Co., without privilege of transfer, and that house had ceased to exist, their goods would now go to a rival selling-agent. More of the same kind of letters came, until but two companies remained, each of which was largely indebted to Gibbs for money advanced on acceptances, and was therefore unable to change the account. Truly it was a barren victory he had won.

Mr. Prescott thought somewhat upon his purchase of Corinthian stock, and queried whether an absolute morality would justify the gaining possession of shares while the seller had no information, as he himself had, affecting their prospective value. It was not a time for a ruined man to be too nice, however; and, as he truly observed, if every man is to disclose all he knows in making a purchase, and to unfold his plans for making a profit out of the transaction, where will business go to? So he reasoned, somewhat obscuring the clear communism of primitive Christianity, but not guilty to himself of any falsehood or misrepresentation. The time has not come when Christianity — the abnegation of self — can thrive in Wall Street or State Street. Nor can any merchant yet stand and prosper on the high moral plane of Cicero's *De Officiis*.

The next day after Mr. Prescott had relinquished business, and while he was thinking what he should do to escape stagnation and paralysis, the long-expected letter from Amory came. Where it had been straying it was useless to inquire. It fully confirmed all he had heard, and added many particulars. He sought out the former secretary of the company, and got a list of the stockholders. Calling upon some of these, he found they had all disposed of their stock, and to the same broker. He guessed immediately what this meant. Amory had written on, and taken up all that could be got; so that he and

Amory now held the whole, except, perhaps, some fifty straggling shares. To manage the affairs of an incorporated company under these circumstances would not be difficult. He engaged a skilful mining engineer and chemist, and sent him West without delay. He could now sit down and wait for results. Letters came every few days. The custodian of the mine had followed Amory, and learned the results of his labors. Interlopers had come with surveying instruments, and hoped to find that some part of the coveted copper mountain was outside the limits of the Corinthian property, but in vain. The whole peninsula was in a fever. Capitalists came, and made tempting offers; miners proffered their services: but as Amory with shocking taste wrote —

> " I am monarch of all I survey,
>   My right there is none to dispute,
>   From the centre all round to the *say*
>   I am lord of the derrick and shute."

"This is better than rhyming advertisements for Shaver's furniture or Macgregor's carpets: I am even content to let the finishing of my poem on the sparrows go till slack times."

" A wise little fool," said Mr. Prescott, with a hearty laugh. " Now, when these shares go up to 180, I would like to meet Gibbs. I think I'll take an office opposite to the old warehouse, and have ' Corinthian' on a sign, in plain sight of his window, with letters two feet high."

Such a secret could not be kept long. Letters from the upper lake region came to the newspapers; and the luck of the Corinthian was in every paragraph. Mr. Prescott held off till the fever ran high, and until the reports of experts settled the value of the mine. Then he sold for himself and Amory enough shares to raise a working capital, and the operations began. The company was re-organized on a solid basis. Mr. Prescott was president, and Amory superintendent, of the mine. Leaving a clerk in charge of the office, Mr. Prescott determined to return to Eaglemont for a visit, taking Phœbe with him. During the time he had been in the city he had been so absorbed in business, — first with regard to his settlement with Gibbs, and afterwards while the company was being re-organized, — that he had scarcely a moment to give to his darling Phœbe. He had staid at a hotel, and given his undivided attention to affairs. Now he was free : now he would see her, and tell her of his good-fortune.

Should he? It might turn her head. He concluded to wait. It was Friday afternoon, and there were two leisure days. Phœbe meanwhile, on their way in the cars, was meditating how to carry out a simple little plot of her own without giving offence. After a variety of observations upon matters of no consequence, this profound dissembler began to ask her companion about his business affairs.

" Aha ! " thought the old gentleman, " she thinks I am poor. I will be sly."

"You know," said the girl, "that Mr. Amory wrote quite confidently — rudely, perhaps — about the business with Mr. Gibbs. Is it really so? Was he such an ungrateful creature?"

"The firm is dissolved," he replied.

"And did he really get all your money?"

"He has the business, my dear, — the business that gave me my money."

"And you have no business now?"

"None — to speak of."

"But you haven't lost all?"

"Oh, no!   I haven't lost you."

"But I should be only a burden — I couldn't be what you would call part of the assets.   Oh, no! I am — let me see — yes — I am a liability, am I not?"

"You are liable to be curious, like all women, big and little.   I have my house in Boston, and the little place on the hill; and I am a young man, young and active, open for an engagement, with good recommendations from my last employer."

"I declare, it is a shame!" said Phœbe, still thinking of Gibbs.   "But you sha'n't talk about engagements, at your age.   I am not going to have you accept a salary."

"Oh, you aren't!   A proud puss you are; but I can work yet.   And I'll not· put up with any remarks upon my age."

"I will engage you."

Mr. Prescott laughed hilariously.

She was blushing deeply, but, after a time, turned a face towards him full of affection, but with a look of embarrassment also.

" I mean it."

" *You* give me a salary ? "

" Perhaps we won't put it that way. Miss Thorpe says I have a large legacy waiting for me, — as much as ten thousand pounds."

" Well ? "

" And somebody has to prove who I am, and to get the money, and manage it for me. And I don't want any, — at least, I don't want much, — as I am teaching this year, and earn my own living. I couldn't spend but little of the income. And I mean to give you all the rest of it, for taking care of me."

"Confound the girl!" he. thought. " She's fairly got ahead of me." He had some Corinthian shares then in his pocket, made out in her name.

" So you will give me your income for taking care of it? Trustees and agents do sometimes manage in that way ; but I shouldn't know how."

" But I want it so, and I will have it so."

" You have the right to be peremptory — all beautiful young women have ; and we men always submit."

" You ought to think how I feel to see you losing your business, and knowing all you have done for me for so many years. And it isn't right nor generous of you to deny me, and to make fun. I don't want the legacy, unless I can do as I choose with it. And sha'n't we all share together? And it won't be that you are under any obligation: each one puts in what he has, that is all."

"What a glorious partner you would be — for some fine fellow! But that kind of business wouldn't be safe with Gibbs."

"We aren't talking of selfish people without souls."

"No, my dear girl, evidently not. Your soul is in your eyes, in your voice, and in your actions; and I should be a brute to make you unhappy for a moment. I will drop nonsense. Your generosity is not any surprise to me: I have seen it from the time of your pinafores and bibs. You are just a lump of goodness, and a pretty substantial lump too. If I need any money, and you have more income than you want, I sha'n't hesitate to accept your offer. By the Lord, what a noble girl!" he added involuntarily, and half aloud.

Phœbe placed her hand in his, but said nothing further.

"And now," said Mr. Prescott, taking out of his pocket the stock certificates on which her name was written in his own clear and beautiful hand, "as you have shown your hand, — or heart I should say — I will show mine. It isn't yet positively sure; but I presume these shares are worth a great deal of money, and will yield you twice as much income as your legacy. You see your name. I was planning a little surprise; but you got the start of me, and now I have to come in second."

" Then you are not poor!"

"I hope not: in fact, it looks quite otherwise."

" Then I care for nothing more. Of course I am a thousand times obliged for your goodness; but for myself I don't care a pin. That you and aunt Prescott are comfortable is enough — more than enough. It is glorious!"

" But you needn't despise the shares. Some fine fellow will be glad to get the income on them. I wonder who it will be. I am selfish enough to hope that he will not come along just yet. I don't want to part with you, not even for your happiness."

" That is past," said Phœbe solemnly. "I shall teach, and shall remain in Boston."

" The deuse!" thought he. "What a sigh that was!—from the very bottom of her heart. I wonder which of the two runaways it is, — my stepson, or my nephew? Roderick may live to come back; and, if he does win her, he is a lucky dog. But Robert, away in some country of fevers and cannibals, or cholera and earthquakes — that is a bourn from which no missionary ever returns."

CHAPTER XIX

MRS. PRESCOTT with Mary, in a basket phaeton, had been taking the circuit of the mountain, a pleasant drive of some five or six miles, when the train arrived. She saw her husband and Phœbe get off, and waited for them. Mr. Prescott gave up Phœbe to his wife's charge, and got a conveyance for himself and Mary.

The manner in which the aunt and niece met was characteristic. Phœbe came impetuously up to the phaeton, and offered to kiss her aunt; while the latter calmly bent over, and received the salute on her cheek. "To think that you are my aunt, after all! It seems like a story. You couldn't have been kinder, though, if .you had known it from the beginning." This was uttered in short little sallies and with touching emotion.

"I might have known you were brother Roderick's child, you are *so* impulsive!" was the reply. "Come, step in, my dear. You will disarrange my collar."

Phœbe was hurt. It was incredible to her that her aunt could be so composed, if not actually cool. She did not know, that, with her aunt, the weather-gauge was connected with her absent son. Whenever she was anxious about him, then Phœbe was remembered as the cause of his going into danger. She had just received a letter from him, dated from the vicinity of a great battle-field. His regiment had suffered terribly, both in officers and men, and he was now promoted to the rank of lieutenant-colonel. He had been slightly wounded, a flesh wound he said, a mere scratch. Mrs. Prescott told Phœbe of this as they rode up the long hill; and it seemed to the girl that she took a pleasure in dwelling upon all the painful aspects of the situation, and kept making observations that stung her like brushes from a bunch of nettles. She did not offer to read the letter, but said that Roderick wished to be affectionately remembered to a certain young lady; that, if he lived, he should return to claim her; and, if he died, it would be with her name on his lips. Even the ideal picture was too much for the mother. She sobbed before she finished the sentence, and of course Phœbe sobbed too; and they reached the house both crying, while Mr. Prescott and Mary were waiting for them in blank surprise.

Phœbe began to see, that, while Roderick was away, she could have no peace with her aunt. Often she had thought, when bearing these implied or open reproaches, that in self-defence she would let the mother know what she had experienced from this darling son of hers. But then she reflected that he might fall, and she did not wish to leave a stain on his memory in the mother's heart. Besides, he had repented, as she believed, in sincerity. So she could not show to the mother what were her feelings towards him. The time and circumstances had not come to show even to herself what her feelings were.

Mary was persuaded by her uncle to stay to tea. In such stormy weather he wanted to see one sunshiny face. Uncle and niece set themselves to cheer up the sorrowing ones, and before long the tears were dried.

Mr. Prescott had been talking with Mary about Amory's operations, and after tea the subject was resumed. This brought to mind Mrs. Prescott's *other* great grief, the loss of property and position. She inquired about the settlement with Mr. Gibbs, and commented upon it with an asperity that Phœbe had never observed before. The tone of her mind was sombre. Every object took a shade from the prevailing gloom. The eclipse of cheerfulness continued until Mr. Prescott became desperate.

"Why, Eleanor!" he exclaimed "I am sorry for you, and more sorry for these young girls, whom you are making wretched with your glum looks. You will give Phœbe a fine specimen of the delights of home: you will make her sorry for the new-found relationship."

"I don't see much to be cheerful about," she answered. "With Roderick away, and in danger all the time, and with poverty before us in our old age, I can't pretend to be light-hearted."

" Have you heard from Roderick ? "

She repeated in a melancholy tone the news she had just told Phœbe, omitting the little message.

" A lieutenant-colonel, is he ? I don't see any thing very sad about that. And as for our poverty — I have had an offer of salary." (Here he gave a sly glance at Phœbe.)

" A salary, indeed ! I should think that was a fine thing for a merchant, and the head of an old house, to boast of."

" Oh ! but I haven't accepted the salary yet. I am taking it under consideration. Something better may turn up."

" Don't talk of things 'turning up,' Mr. Prescott. That person Micawber, if that was his name, in Dickens's vulgar story, has made the expression odious. I hope you don't mean that you are looking out for the air-castles that Amory is building ! He is an enthusiast, a silly — I forget, Mary : I don't wish to underrate your friend, who, I presume, is honest and sincere, but so flighty and unpractical, you know, like all persons with a poetical turn."

" Come, now, don't be disagreeable. Amory has given practical proof of his good sense. The mine is a fact, a gigantic fact.

" I am sure Mr. Amory is entirely too generous," said Mary, " to make ill-natured observations about others in their absence, and I should think that he might be spared, especially as he is so devoted to his friends."

"Well done!" said Mr. Prescott, "I like that. Nothing is so common as to sit and listen to detraction of the absent. I admire your courage, Mary. — But now, Eleanor, can't we drive away that black cloud? I won't boast, and I don't want a word repeated; but I consider I am worth more to-day than I ever was, and certainly my income will be double. If poverty is your bugbear, you can smile at your fears. You will have every thing you want."

"Then we can go back to town?"

"Yes, when the season is over. I want to enjoy the country a while, now we are here."

Mrs. Prescott's spirits rose momently. She would have seriously preferred death to banishment from her fashionable society, from her church, and from the Plato Club. Visions of future glories came with the thought of re-established fortune.

"Don't you think, my dear," she said, after a moment's reflection, "that, now we have our old faded furniture up here, we should get new things for our house in town? The house itself has needed some touches a good while. I should hope we might have new carpets, sofas, chairs, and fauteuils, some larger mirrors, some electric bells to call the servants, some new bookcases. The books, too, ought to be rebound: the leather is worn, and the gilding faded. And our conservatory is so small! — just room for about two dozen plants. I would like a stately dome of glass, and some rare tropical plants with long feathery leaves. It would give such a vista to the drawing-room!"

Mr. Prescott was exchanging amused glances with Phœbe. She went on:—

"And our carriage is quite old and musty. The horses, too, have lost the step. They should be exchanged for a younger pair with a more pronounced gait. The oratory should be repainted, and a picture or two put in it: some saint or madonna would be so pretty in the recess back of the candles! I am tired of those old servants: they are getting stupid. I should like an English coachman, in a handsome livery, and an indoor man that is *au fait* with modern usages. Of course, we will have a new door and doorway in black walnut, made from an original design. The old black door, and the great silver plate, and the staring number, are old-fashioned and common. I haven't spoken of dress; but I haven't had a new costume for a twelvemonth; and Phœbe, there, is dressed like a nun. We shall have to receive on a stated day, and must have a list of our callers in the 'Reporter.' The Plato Club receptions are always printed, you know; and it looks well to see the names of poets and judges and clergymen, and other *beaux esprits*, as your friends."

"Is there any thing more, Eleanor? Haven't you forgotten something?"

"I haven't asked for any thing unreasonable, have I? In a certain position in life we have certain duties. I feel that we owe something to society, and I don't wish to shrink from any sacrifice."

The sacrifices that society demands are always made heroically.

"What do you think, Phœbe?" asked Mr. Prescott.

"I don't think, uncle. I am not to pass judgment on aunt's plans. It all sounds very fine. If aunt wants it, and you can afford it, I should be glad for her sake. The house as it is, is very dear to me. It has a look of comfort, and seems to fit you both, as if it had been made for you."

Phœbe was fated that day to ruffle her aunt's temper at every turn. It was a perfectly honest reply she had made, but, like most honest speeches, it was not guarded and discreet: it conveyed a censure, and the lady was wroth. Then she thought of Roderick again; and, between the two causes of irritation, she managed to keep herself pretty constantly unhappy.

After tea Phœbe took the phaeton, and drove Mary home. She at first hoped Mary would ask her to stay; but then she reflected that she might have to endure a solemn woman in place of an irritable one, and she wisely returned to her uncle's, after chatting a while with Mary and her father at the door. She began to sigh for the serene atmosphere of Miss Thorpe's home, and wished she had a pretext for returning there. Her aunt had developed traits unsuspected before.

In prosperity she had been often gracious, suave, and delightful; but she could not bear adversity. She had no power to adapt herself to circumstances. Self-denial in regard to luxuries was something she had never contemplated. Phœbe, like all fresh young people, enjoyed society, music, and dancing, and could take her share of Fortune's favors equably; but she could also have resigned herself to the seclusion of a farmhouse, if it had been necessary, and would have been happy there with the uncle in whose feelings and tastes she sympathized.

The next day rose clear and bright. Once more, by the favor of uncle Solomon, the colt was harnessed to the elliptic-spring wagon, and the two girls made the tour of the country. The glory of the summer was gone, but Phœbe thought the russet-brown of the pastures even finer in tone than the green had been. The highest prospect, too, was more soft and alluring. The summits of the far hills, seen through long stretches of valleys, seemed to be sparkling with powdered gold. The blue smokes rose straight upwards from the farmhouses, — mere specks of white or red, recognized chiefly by the checker-board lines of orchards near them and by the long-backed roofs of the ash-colored barns.

Then returning, when they had descended half way, they hitched the horse by the roadside, and plunged into the woods, following the course of a stream that went tinkling over the ledges, and freshening a series of pools that kept the autumn grass green. At length they came to the place for which the experienced country-girl had been seeking,— the beds of those exquisite ferns which rustics and poets call maiden's-hair. With arms full of the long and tangled vines, they returned to the wagon, and went on their way again.

When quite near the town, a figure came into the middle of the road as if to stop their horse. Phœbe gave a sharp scream; but Mary only breathed shorter, and exclaimed, "*Percival Amory!* where *have* you come from? and why *do* you scare us to death? and we driving the colt too!"

It was the sturdy and happy little man surely.

"Aren't you going to get out?" he asked cheerily, "or shall I get in?— Miss — Miss Phœbe, I am delighted to see you."

Reaching his hand to Mary, she stepped on the wheel, whereupon he caught and landed her by the road-side in some way, although the particuulars of the descent are difficult to describe in set phrase. This being accomplished, not heeding the presence of the other, he bestowed a rousing kiss upon Mary's pretty mouth. She resisted, to be sure, and said, " For shame!" which Amory did not seem to hear. He only observed that now he had fulfilled a solemn vow that he had made when he left Ontonagon. He had vowed, he said, to kiss the first girl who gave him her hand to descend from a wagon. Then it occurred to him that the whole affair was a little absurd; and he proposed that Mary should get in again, where-upon all three laughed helplessly. "Ride with us," said Mary.

"On one seat? Three of us? Oh, no!"

"But father rides with us. See!" And she pulled a drawer from under the seat, that afforded a small resting-place for the driver. Behold now the happy Amory, between two of the handsomest women in the world, driving through the curious village, and up to the old hill. He was not, on this occasion,

> " A sweetly unobtrusive third."

In fact, he was a dominating presence, full of spirits and of no end of talk, and he entirely frustrated the plans of Mary. That artful girl had been endeavoring to learn what were Phœbe's real feelings towards her brother, the absent Robert. At the very moment when Amory appeared in the road, she had been leading to a test question with great care. She was just going to ask Phœbe plumply, "Would you have loved and married Robert if he had not been a minister and a missionary?" Phœbe divined the approaches of the good and simple-hearted sister, and was unutterably pained. The road she had travelled with Robert was full of thorns, and not to be passed over again. Amory was now her welcome shield. She plied him with questions, and he was only too happy to talk. The Corinthian was a fixed fact. Cheops wasn't more solid; nor was Cyprus or Corinth more — more coppery. The mine would supply the universe. For himself, he should never be happy until he had done *two* things, — first, kicked Gibbs; second, ridden down State Street in a coach, with a foot out of each window. Then looking at Mary, and recollecting that there was no mention of her in the two things he most desired, he added, "These are the things I wish to do *after* a certain auspicious event."

As to his poetic effusions, Amory was not very hopeful. The Western air had not stimulated his genius as he expected. The projected poem upon the sparrows was still "on the stocks."

The coming of Amory was a surprise to the two families on the hill; but all were glad to see the brave and cheerful man who had accomplished so much. With the one Prescott he had long and satisfactory talks about the mine: with the other, we may fairly suppose that a matter no less important was discussed, and with a similar pleasing result.

As our story is about to pass over a considerable interval, it may be proper to make a summary of lesser events.

Amory was soon announced as the accepted lover of Mary Prescott, and, having left a substitute at the mine, proposed to spend the winter at the East.

The city residence of Mr. and Mrs. Hugh Prescott was improved and beautified, though not upon the magnificent scale proposed by its ambitious mistress. They returned to the city in the early autumn.

The scanty evidence bearing upon the parentage of Phœbe was put in due form, and forwarded; but it was agreed that the affair should be kept secret until the claim was acknowledged by Ralph Manning, the head of the family.

Roderick was heard from less frequently; but it was announced that he was acting colonel of the regiment.

Phœbe returned to the city on the next Monday, and thenceforth kept steadily on her course, teaching and reading, spending only her Sundays in town.

Robert Prescott made no sign. Whether he was among Afric's sunny fountains, or on India's coral strand, no one knew. Aunt Zeruiah's rigid sternness gave way: she softened and wept, — a pitiable sight, at which uncle Solomon was accustomed to take refuge with his cattle in the barn, finding some consolation in their mute faces.

CHAPTER XX.

THIS was the summer of battles. The awful struggle of Gettysburg, protracted for three days, with varying fortunes, had sent new thrills through the land. Almost as vast as a war of the elements, the commotion spread through the air, and the cannon seemed to reverberate from prairie to ocean. The fierce engagement at Chancellorsville, the siege of Charleston, the terrible carnage at Chattanooga, the capture of Vicksburg, and scores of less famous conflicts, filled all the dreary year. Men's hearts began to fail them; and the future had nothing but gloom.

Winter was coming; and the pressing needs of the soldiers in camps and hospitals were uppermost in the thoughts of all generous minds.

The patriotic women belonging to the society auxiliary to the Sanitary Commission had projected a concert to raise funds. It was to be given in a large hall, but was to be in a manner private, as the tickets were to be disposed of by the members and their friends; and there was to be no publicity given to the performances. It was expected in this way to secure the aid of many brilliant amateur players and singers, and to sell the tickets at high prices.

Naturally they waited upon Signor Belvedere to obtain his co-operation. He cheerfully assented, and promised to use his influence with his pupils. He made out a list of names, of which Phœbe's was first, and, at the request of the ladies, went to see Miss Thorpe and Mrs. Prescott, to get their consent for her appearance. Miss Thorpe was an active member of the society, and, in fact, was giving her whole time to its interests. For almost any other purpose she would have refused her consent for Phœbe to appear in public, even in this semi-private fashion. She hated the stage, especially the opera. She dreaded the influence of excitement and applause upon Phœbe's susceptible soul. She was determined that Phœbe should have no incitement to follow a public career. It was only after repeated conversations that she gave a reluctant consent. Phœbe, who had begun her career as teacher, was overjoyed, and on Saturdays made preparations for the concert. She was to sing an elaborate cavatina and a ballad in the first part of the programme. The second part was to consist of an operatic burlesque in Italian: its authorship was an open secret. It was printed anonymously, but was known to be written by a well-known professor, and was adapted with exquisite skill to the most striking musical selections from a number of famous operas. There was a chorus of students, and three or four characters in costume; and the grandiose music, joined to the elaborate nonsense of the libretto, made it one of the most amusing trifles ever presented on the stage. The nature of Phœbe was wholly averse to burlesque. She could have made nothing of it; and her feelings had become so serious that any trifling was a pain to her. As the weeks went by, Miss Thorpe noticed with ever-increasing anxiety how Phœbe's expression was changing. Her cheeks lost their rosy flush; lines of thought began to be apparent; and, above all, her eyes were no longer sparkling and changing in hue and expression as she spoke. She looked like one gazing into distance, even into another sphere. There was a fixedness in her looks that was almost like the beginning of insanity. Miss Thorpe would then have dissuaded her from taking any part in the concert, but it was too late: Phœbe was immovable. So she went weekly to Signor Belvedere's rooms, and practised her exercises and songs, singing with an undreamed-of power and intensity, but looking the picture of settled melancholy.

The time wore away, and the day for the concert came. The hall was completely filled by an audience distinguished for wealth and social eminence. Signor Belvedere was conspicuous in the front row, seated with a party of his country men and women, members of an opera troupe temporarily in Boston on a vacation. He looked around the house with an air of triumph, as if to say, "This is my pupil you have come to hear. The voice is one I have formed. The grand manner of Pasta and Malibran lives again in a girl whose ancestry not one of you knows. The beauty you are to dote upon, however, belongs to my country." He could not sit still, but chatted and gestured with unceasing vivacity, returning the bows of pupils and musical friends.

At length the curtain was raised. The concert began with a piano solo by a professional artist; then followed one of Signor Belvedere's pupils, whose brilliant performance of Rode's Variations Phœbe had once heard while waiting for her lesson. A fine bass singer with a slight German accent next came, with a dramatic rendering of Schumann's "Two Grenadiers." It was now Phœbe's turn. As she came forward, there was a sudden stir throughout the hall. She was known to but few persons, even by sight, and had never sung except in Mrs. Prescott's parlor, or when taking a lesson. But her youth and resplendent beauty, her dignified, statuesque attitude, the simplicity of her costume, and the sweet, melancholy expression of her eyes, captivated every one. Women, as well as men, felt the fascination of her presence, and applauded, almost with tears of admiration, as she came forward. "See!" whispered Signor Belvedere, in Italian, to the prima donna beside him. "What a figure! Grand Dio! what a soul in those eyes! What a presence for the lyric stage! Observe that beautiful hand; not a ring to mar the symmetry of those lovely fingers! Not a barbaric hoop, either, in those ears of pink shell! All in white, rich as silk can be, but pure white, only those tea-rose buds at her neck. Corpo di Bacco! what a neck! An ivory column for the queenly head! And those glossy masses of hair, worthy to shade the brows of alma Venus herself!"

Mrs. Prescott was present, surrounded by a large party.

Miss Thorpe, who never attended concerts, naturally made an exception in this case, and sat near the front, but at one side, near the entrance to the stage.

The chords were given, and the cavatina began. Knowing how her severe master had been affected by her singing, it would be useless to attempt any description of the impression made upon this musically cultivated audience. Critics listened in vain to find the least point of objection. The voice was melody itself. The expression was dictated by the purest taste, and enlivened by dramatic power; and, as if by instinct, her slightest movements were in harmony with the sentiment. It was her first venture, and yet it was as if she had trod the stage all her life. So it seemed to the audience; but the case was far different in the heart of the singer. As she recalled her sensations afterwards, she felt like the somnambulist walking over the perilous mill-race, while the tones of her voice sounded as if made by another, and heard afar in a dream. Her smiles were the automatic expression of the feel-

ings that possessed her. Her artistic style of singing had become a second nature, so that she had
but to open her mouth. It was a magnificent
success; but she felt that it was the result of
causes wholly apart from her volition.

As she ceased, the applause was long and loud,
and a repetition seemed to be imperatively demanded. But Phœbe felt unequal to the task,
and, after bowing her acknowledgments, was retir-
ing, when the recall arose in louder tones, and she
hesitated. She beckoned to the accompanist, and
prepared to sing the ballad. She could not wait
and appear again: it must be done on the instant
for she felt the strain on her nerves was too
intense to be borne. The audience cheered as she
came forward, and she took her place at the side
of the piano.

The ballad was the well-known "Robin Adair,"
a piece of genuine poetic merit, set to one of
the finest of old Celtic melodies:—

Welcome on shore again,
Robin Adair!
Welcome once more again,
Robin Adair!
I feel thy trembling hand:
Tears in thy eyelids stand,
To greet thy native land,
Robin Adair!

Come to my heart again,
Robin Adair!
Never to part again,
Robin Adair!

> And, if thou still art true,
> I will be constant too,
> And will wed none but you,
>   Robin Adair!

Now a strange scene was enacted. The expression of Phœbe's face became wonderfully pathetic. Her voice alternately melted and thrilled the heart. The story of the ballad became a living reality, as when Rachel revived a classic tragedy. The tones became like a pain, and the action rose to the sublime. Before the last line was concluded, the audience rose half way, and leaned forward, and some stood on their feet, a tempestuous crowd, excited almost to frenzy. With the final note the curtain fell, and it was some minutes before quiet was restored. It was then announced that the singer must be excused, being too much indisposed to appear again.

The burlesque was then performed with immense success, and the performance ended.

But the first part of the performance had another and unexpected issue. When the curtain fell upon Phœbe's song, she had stepped back, deadly pale, and with a strange look, as if beholding some sight of horror. The next moment she was prostrate on the floor, without sense or motion. Luckily the performers that were to take part in the burlesque were in a room apart. The manager for the evening, with singular presence of mind, called the accompanist, and they two carried her away to a side-room without a word. A carriage was procured, Miss Thorpe was cautiously beckoned out, and the still unconscious girl was carried home. A physician was summoned, and every expedient was resorted to for her restoration. By midnight she moved and moaned, although her eyes remained closed. At daybreak she looked about, and spoke; but her utterances were "like sweet bells jangled out of tune." A slow nervous fever was predicted,—a disease that would test the strength of her constitution, and would require the utmost patience of nurses and attendants.

Miss Thorpe had not anticipated such a result; but she had long observed Phœbe's increasing susceptibility, her eager movements and smileless looks. She had drawn certain conclusions as to the girl's feelings towards the absent Roderick and to his unhappy mother, and she believed she saw in the irritation that had been produced by that mother's reproaches constantly acting upon a sensitive nature a sufficient cause for the attack; for Phœbe professed that her labors as a teacher were not beyond her strength. Miss Thorpe meditated upon this, and determined to acquaint Mrs. Prescott in as delicate a way as possible with the facts, and to beg her not to come into Phœbe's presence until the morbid excitement had subsided.

She reasoned well, but did not act promptly enough. "Ill news," they say, "flies fast." Mrs.

Prescott was not long in hearing of Phœbe's sudden and alarming illness, and came at once to see her. Miss Thorpe was absent for the moment; and the visitor brushed past the servant, and entered the chamber where Phœbe lay. Mrs. Prescott came towards the bedside, and reached out her hand. The poor girl beheld her with wildly staring eyes, and exclaimed, "I did not do it; ask him. He is not dead; no, only he limps. His head is bound up, his arm in a sling. But he was good to me at last — not always. Any young man may love his mother; the mother doesn't know — nor Polonius. But he is good now. He wants me to love him: perhaps I shall. I am Ophelia; but I can't find any flowers for a garland, so I must wait here. I have no brother to fight for me."

Mrs. Prescott was so shocked, that she could neither speak nor move. Phœbe would not take her hand, and by every tone and gesture repelled her advances.

At this point Miss Thorpe entered, and comprehended what was passing. She stepped lightly between her visitor and the bed; and, while she smoothed Phœbe's brow with one hand, she made a warning sign to the visitor with the other. Still covering Mrs. Prescott from Phœbe's sight, she pointed towards the door, and then followed the astonished woman out. As they talked in low tones in the passage-way, Phœbe's voice came in plaintive, fragmentary sentences, — fragments of speech and wild strains of song, with merry little laughs and melancholy interjections. Mrs. Prescott wept as she listened. Miss Thorpe was kind enough to suppress much of what she thought, and only suggested, that, in certain states of aberration of mind, the nearest friends are objects of the strongest dislike.

Mrs. Prescott was greatly overcome, but soon, remembering that the girl needed Miss Thorpe's constant attention, she reluctantly went home. She had a glimpse of the truth, and it was sad enough: to have known the whole would have been more than she could bear. She saw that she must resign Phœbe wholly to Miss Thorpe's care.

Imagine the thrill she experienced, with Phœbe's incoherent sentences still sounding in her ears, when, on reaching home, she opened a letter just come from her Roderick, in which he mentioned that he had been injured by the explosion of a shell, and was suffering from a bruise on his foot, a contusion on his head, and a sprained wrist. There was reason, then, for his limp, for his bandaged head, and his suspended arm.

CHAPTER XXI.

THE physician was a wise and observant man, — a phenomenon by no means so rare in our day as formerly. When Miss Thorpe described Phœbe's conduct on seeing her aunt, and told of her half droll, half pathetic sayings during the night, he only advised perfect quiet and seclusion. Opiates or nerve-soothing medicines, he said, might, in the end, reduce her strength enough to counterbalance all that was gained. If she wished to talk, she must not be prevented, only gently led, like a child, to pleasant views of things. So during the long day the poor girl uttered disconnected phrases, mingling her varied experiences till all the threads of the warp and woof of her life were inwoven into the strangest though often the most affecting figures.

It was a case of exaltation, of strong nervous excitement, not of dementia. In many respects she was at intervals almost perfectly sensible. The chief peculiarity was the presence of visions of the absent. She mentioned no names, but related adventures as if she were actually beholding them. She narrated an officer's escape one day with wonderful spirit : —

"It is a deep-chested, powerful horse; his head is held low, and thrust forward; the nostrils are distended; and I see the muscles of his thighs play under the glossy skin. The rider does not spur: no, the noble animal needs no spur. The rider leans forward, pats his neck lovingly, and the horse makes leaps like a flying creature. The rider is one: the pursuers are many, and are clattering close behind. There! *there!* THERE! Their pistols flash; but the horseman does not stop, nor look back. Oh, how the horse pants along the white dusty road up that long hill! How the enemy come yelling on behind!

"Now there is an open stretch. A few miles more, good horse! The distance from the pursuers increases. They feel it, and again, flash, flash! go their pistols, while their baffled rage is heard in their despairing cries. Still on goes the noble horse, and now he dashes past the friendly pickets. How they cheer! Glory to God! He is safe. The squadron of cavalry posted near now rides forward. The order is to charge. Away they gallop. The pursuing enemy wheel, and ride back, but not till some saddles are empty. Friends welcome the brave man, and they praise the noble and enduring horse. The horse shall never be put in peril again. He shall feed in green pastures henceforth."

At another time her mind was far away, fixed upon a strange scene. The scene grew into an act, and the act was protracted into a drama that lasted many days. This may serve for a summary of the sentences and ejaculations that came at intervals : —

"Immense, gloomy forests, hung with mossy beards filled with thick undergrowth and tangled vines, spread on every side. The ground is damp, and the stagnant pools are mantled with green. Strange bright birds are in the boughs. At night there are whippoorwills; mocking-birds sing all day; while serpents, lizards, and lazy alligators lurk among the dark bushes, or glide along the dull water-courses."

" Pressing through briers and bushes, I see a man in the wretched fragments of a uniform. His face is sunburned and anxious; his hands are scratched; there are blood-stains showing through the torn clothes. The man reaches the bank of a large river. Screened from view, he waits till the sun goes down and the stars rise: and now he looks that he may know the points of the compass. He is so hungry that he could even eat a reptile if he could catch one. But he finds a log, and he rolls it into the water: he takes a smaller piece of wood that is to serve him for a paddle, and, if necessary, for a weapon. Astride the log, he floats mid-stream, holding his course with the rude paddle, and keeping watch for alligators. All night he floats, until now the stars begin to fade. Further progress is dangerous. How he watches the banks ! He sees a faint blue smoke: it rises from a cabin, a mere heap of blackened logs on the bank. He reconnoitres. A negro comes out. How the lonely voyager blesses God for the sight of that black face! The negro has a gun; he raises it, and stands in position. ·A friend!' cries the wretched and famished soldier, showing some remains of his uniform. The gun is dropped, and the soldier is welcomed. His log is shoved ashore. A few sweet-potatoes roasted in the embers make the most delicious breakfast the soldier ever ate. But the cabin is a dangerous place for a loiterer. Up in a full-topped tree, out of sight of his friend, the soldier climbs, and passes the long day, longing for the night. With a few potatoes, he sets out again under cover of darkness, floating towards the sea. The next day he finds another cabin; he espies another black man: they are always friendly to his colors. But does he *trust* his friends? No, I see he does not: the risk is too great. He eats the potatoes, or, it may be the bit of hard corn-bread, and, having given his thanks, withdraws to his fastness, his watch-tower in a tree-top, unseen of any. Only God looks down upon him, and the angels pity him.

"The river flows on; the days go by. The soldier on his log floats past earth-mounds, and great guns, and scattered pickets: he is sometimes challenged and fired at, but never hit. He begins, so he hopes, to smell the grateful odor of the sea. It is quite time. The sun has roasted him; insects have bitten him; thorns have lacerated him; his hair and his nails are like those of a beast; his feet are swollen, — alternately softened in water, and then bruised on shore. His mother would not know him; but any mother would cry over such a pitiable object.

"Coming down from his perch in a tree, he hears a horrible sound. He has never heard it before: it is a strange sound. His heart fails him, — it must be the bark of a bloodhound. He sees a fierce dog approaching; he must despatch this one before his fellows come. The paddle-club does its work well, and the fugitive takes to the river again. Ah, yes; the water will break the scent. On he floats, for he prefers death from a bullet to a grapple with the ferocious hounds. All day he hears their distant baying. Luckily no eyes observe him; none, at least, but the eyes of skulkers like himself. Now, as he thinks of the distance, he must leave the river. There must be danger ahead, for the river's mouth is closely watched. Guided by the power that guides the far-flying bird, he strikes into the forest. Oh the labor, the pain, hunger, wounds, and heart-ache! At length the white sands are near: he hears the billows come wallowing upon the smooth white beach. He is naked, — oh, horror! and a map of his bruises would be such a wretched sight —

"There lie the giant ships out on the tumbling plain; the bright ensigns float from the mast-heads. On that blue plain is heaven; in the forest behind is " —

The narrator could go no further; the picture was too horrible; the suspense could not be borne. From mere faintness she ceased, closed her eyes in a blessed swoon, and afterwards slept.

From this time gentle opiates were given daily, and the startling visions came no more. Brief glimpses of battle, of flight, of wounds and captivity came, but only at rare intervals.

Signor Belvedere had been present while Phœbe's fevered brain had conjured up some of these terrible visions, although out of her sight. He sat with Miss Thorpe in a recess near by, and when, at length, she slept, her condition was discussed. He was naturally sympathetic, although his instinct would have led him to avoid such painful scenes.

"Ah, Miss Thorpe, but this is dreadful! It is not a malady of body, but of soul. To the doctor I would say, 'Canst thou minister to a *mind* diseas-ed? pluck up the memory of a rooted sorrow?'"

"Something to turn the current of her thought is needed," said Miss Thorpe.

"But what can do it? Bring her lover back? Impossible. Take her to him? Impossible."

"What do you suggest, then?"

"A change of scene. A voyage to Europe."

"She could not survive it."

"But how long will she survive *this?*"

"True. Something must be risked. But she must gain somewhat in strength first. And mean-

time we may interest her in her English relatives."
A long conversation ensued upon the question of
Phœbe's parentage, which, as we have seen, had
been taken for granted, but had not been legally
established. The marriage of Roderick Manning
to the countess, and the birth of Phœbe as an
issue of that marriage rather than of the former
one, were not yet fully proven. Signor Belvedere thought that Phœbe should not risk a rejec-
tion of her claim, but should go to England armed
with full proof, if she went at all. An unsuccess-
ful attempt might overthrow her reason altogether. As the matter now stood, Mrs. Prescott
could not be consulted, at least in Phœbe's presence. Mr. Prescott would not be likely to under-
take the voyage, because he was of an age to make
it appear a serious undertaking, because he would
be too proud to act vigorously to secure a legacy
for his wife's niece under such circumstances, and
because he would take no step that might result
in his losing her.

The fact remained that no reply had come from
Ralph Manning, and the proof as it was sent over
was undoubtedly insufficient in law in several
particulars. Signor Belvedere meditated, and
went home — to meditate more at his leisure.

Phœbe remained an invalid. While under the
influence of her imagination in trances, her intellect showed all its original force, though sadly
unbalanced; but, when these visions ended, she
was silent, as if mind and body were in slow

decay together. She was after a time able to sit up; but she rarely uttered a word, only now and then with a sigh she half whispered, " For you I have lost my son." So the weeks passed. It seemed as if nature could not long hold out without a mental change. "Something must be done to rouse her," thought Miss Thorpe.

But a thought and a purpose had been maturing in Phœbe's mind which they little guessed. In her dreams she had been journeying through the seat of war. She wondered if she were ever to be strong enough to go there. *Could* she be allowed to go? Were there means for women to live in camps or in fortified towns? Who would go with her? Signor Belvedere? No; for she hoped he would go to Europe in the spring. Mr. Hugh Prescott? Yes, probably. Catching at this, her soul climbed as to a serene hope, and the nervous discord within began to subside.

With as much tranquillity as she could command, Phœbe said, "Could we not go South to meet the spring? It comes late here. I should like to be out of doors, in a softer air."

It was a voice as sweet as a silver bell, and its undulations trembled in the heart.

" Perhaps so, my dear," answered Miss Thorpe, " when you are able to bear such a journey."

Miss Thorpe herself was worn by her constant care; and a cough that had haunted her before began to be troublesome. Had it been in time of peace, she would have desired to go to some South-

ern city so as to breathe a softer air for the remainder of the season. Some of the Southern
ports were occupied by our troops; and Miss
Thorpe conceived that permission might be obtained from the secretary of war for a small party
to sail there in a government vessel. She broached
the matter to the physician the same day, and,
rather to her surprise, found him decidedly in
favor of the project. Still she feared the difficulties would be great.

She consulted Mr. Prescott. She reasoned that
Phœbe's aversion to that family would vanish as
soon as sanity returned, and that, if she could be
made to take an interest in such a trip, the new
circumstances would tend to dispel the illusions
that had clouded her mind.

Mr. Prescott was doubtful about the ability of
delicate women to bear the hardship of a winter
voyage on our stormy coast, and he feared they
would also miss many comforts while living in
towns occupied by troops; but for himself he was
ready to bear them company. He suggested that
Amory, who had returned for the winter, should
go also. "We want a spry young man to wait
upon us," he said; "and we may have something
new from him upon the sublimity of the sea, or
upon the grandeur of a battle.

"As for Mrs. Prescott," he continued, "I don't
think it is best for her to go. She is in a terrible
state about Roderick. She has not heard from
him personally for some little time, although the

papers have been mentioning his name almost every day, and with great praise. It really seems he has turned out a hero. I knew he was brave; but I did not give him credit for so much capacity. It is said he has planned and carried out some brilliant movements."

"Probably your judgment is right about Mrs. Prescott's going. She is a fond mother, and her heart is sore. Has she seen — have you seen the telegrams of to-day? Pardon me, if I am abrupt."

"Oh, yes! I have seen them; but she has not. Nothing can be certain when such conflicting reports are sent. Now it is that Col. Prescott received thanks for his gallant conduct. Now it is Col. Prescott who was taken prisoner, and sent to the pen at Florence. Now it is Col. Prescott that escaped to the fleet. Now the news comes that the same officer was left for dead on the field. I have faith in Roderick's luck. The Southern bullets are not to kill him. He will come back. He will come back."

"Does his mother read the papers?"

"Yes, I am sorry to say. I can't keep them from her. But this last report, left for dead, she has not seen."

"But I should think that the authorities would know about some of these reports. Are not the places given? And, if Col. Prescott had been taken prisoner at one place, he couldn't be leading his regiment at another."

"Every thing appears to be mixed up. I don't know the geography very well; and lots of the names are not on the maps. It is hard to say what the truth is. Time will show."

It was agreed then that Mr. Prescott and Mr. Amory would accompany Miss Thorpe and Phœbe, provided the permits could be got from the war department, as soon as the conditions were favorable.

Phœbe appeared to be only dreaming. She was slowly recuperating, however, and her half sad smiles and faintly moving lips told of sweet and tender thoughts.

CHAPTER XXII.

In the early part of January, one fine bright day, Phœbe was sitting in an easy-chair, looking out of an upper window, when she saw Signor Belvedere approaching the house. The delusions that had so long enthralled her faculties seemed to have vanished, like frost-pictures from the window-panes, leaving the outlook clear. In a few moments he was in the room, attended by Miss Thorpe. Phœbe looked at them with clear and loving eyes. She was still pale and wan; but the wild lights and dark shadows had gone from her eyes, and the old trustful look had come back. The master was greatly affected, though he strove to mask his feeling under a show of gayety. Gently taking her hand, he said, —

"Bless your eyes, Miss Phaybe, this is a miracle! You are so lovely to-day! How I envy Miss Thorpe the pleasure of sitting before you! And now you are to grow strongg and rosy and joyous, and to sing again! Ah, yes! when I see you again, you will sing to me a cavatina."

Phœbe smiled; but a look of melancholy followed, as she replied, "I fear you will wait some time." Tears came to her eyes for mere weakness.

Miss Thorpe soothed her, and said, "The signor has come with his p. p. c. He is going on a little trip, and expects you to be well on his return."

Phœbe for an instant looked inquiringly, but quickly turned on him her beautiful eyes with a look of the deepest gratitude.

"It is a little trip," he said, "in one point of view. It is but a little part of the earth's circle. But, my dear pupil, it is for you that I am going away."

"For me?" and she looked radiant.

"Yes," said Miss Thorpe. "The signor is good enough to interest himself in a matter that is very near to us all. You know, we wish to know more about your father and mother; and it seems to be necessary for some one to make the journey. We won't weary you by talking to-day, but will explain more fully when you are stronger."

"All the way over the stormy and dreadful sea — and for poor me. It is too much."

"I wish you could go with me, Meess Phaybe. You would come back as hearty as the first mate. And you would see all about your fortune for yourself."

Phœbe looked at him a moment steadfastly. "Not for the fortune, no: I would not make the passage to Europe — for the fortune. If I live, I can teach. How long have I been here, — in this room, I mean?"

"Don't agitate yourself, dear," interposed Miss Thorpe. "You have been here for some time."

" And what month is it?"

" January."

She mused a while, and then murmured to her-self, — " three months, and yet only a dream."

" Do you think you could be moved by and by, and venture out?" asked Miss Thorpe.

" Perhaps so," said Phœbe in a faint tone. Then in a louder voice she added, " If I could, I know where I would. I have been humming ' Oh that I had wings!' I should fly to sunny weather."

" And would you really go South in this dreadful war-time?"

" Yes," she answered with an excited look. " I am not afraid. I think I must have been there: I think I should know the landscapes. And I do know the faces that I have seen. I should find friends, protectors."

" Pray, be calmer," said Miss Thorpe. " Think, please, that we want you tranquil, so that you may become able to go. For if you can improve for a few weeks, and get some strength and appetite and color, we will endeavor to gratify your wishes."

Phœbe's eyes closed; her hands were crossed upon her breast, her lips moved, and a faint approach to a smile spread over her features. She could not speak; but, as soon as she unclosed the lids, her eyes beamed with an expression so grateful, so touching, so eloquent, that her friends were thrilled, and by the same impulse moved nearer, and gently caressed her thin hands.

A moment later Signor Belvedere arose, and

having, by some feat of prestidigitation, cleared the rheum from his eyes, with his silk handkerchief blew a sonorous nasal blast that set Phœbe to laughing in spite of herself.

"Farewell!" he said. "*Cras ingens iterabimus æquor.* I have not-a seen Italy for many years. I wish to settle the affairs between Papa Pius and Victor Emmanuel, and abridge the un-a-constitutional spread of his warlike mustachios. There are other persons I would see, notably a family in Florence, for whose name Belvedere has been a pleasant substitute. 'Noblesse' obliges in many ways; and if a chevalier with a longg pedigree at his-a back insists on giving music lessons, even in a foreign land, he will not con-a-taminate the name of his noble kinsmen. It is not Delle Torre — the name — but it is well enough. It cannot have happen-ed that a Delle Torre contracted marriage that is not-a recorded. Then for England, and, when the roses come, back to this pleasant and drowsy little city. Farewell!"

He was gone. Phœbe had listened to his gay but suggestive sentences, first amused, then interested, then excited. But it was marvellous to see how she bore it. Her mind had rapidly regained its equilibrium. Though her nerves were still tremulous, and her strength almost a negative quantity, she had clear vision and the natural sensations. Miss Thorpe had watched her anxiously, and was rejoiced when the strain of the interview was ended.

The parting words of the music-master gave both Miss Thorpe and Phœbe enough to reflect upon. For many days the person and character of this brilliant and eccentric man were discussed. Phœbe recalled his fencing-foils, and his habitual military port, the perfection of details in dress, — impossible for any but men of the highest *ton*, — the rare intaglio in his signet-ring and the priceless work upon his scarf-pin, and above all his manners, in which a commanding air of superiority was blended with the most subtile, flattering attention and deference. These things were evidently part of the history of a man once in high station.

It was as good as a play to notice the bland courtesy of the fine aristocrat. His professional income must have been ample; but it was not wholly for money that he taught. He would instruct whom he chose, and no others. The best houses in the city had always been open to him. The foreign residents apparently avoided him. He did not much dissemble towards the uneducated and vulgar, but moved before them with a calm dignity that made him as distant as Mont Blanc from the Italian plains. He was a splendid mystery while near, and not less so now that he had gone.

It will be readily believed that the recovery of the invalid was thenceforth rapid. There seemed to have arisen for her new objects in life. How much had been done for her, and by how many persons of mark! — the noble Italian was crossing the wintry seas for her; and now, for her sake, her friends were going to sail far southward, and venture into the midst of armies in constant activity, and surrounded by vigilant foes. Her spirits rose with the occasion, and all the native timidity of the maiden was forgotten. She longed for the time to come. The huge hulk of a ship is steered by a small rudder. A girl's will, apparently so feeble and so yielding, had brought about two great purposes. A sagacious and zealous agent had started to ascertain her parentage; and now the friends who were nearest were constrained to accompany her to the region she had dreamed of, — perhaps to her destiny. Yet the influences had not been obvious to the persons she had moved. Her inmost wishes had been fulfilled as if by spirit acting upon obedient matter. The time of visions had passed: the realities were now to come.

Preparations for the voyage were rapidly made. Mr. Prescott obtained the necessary permission from the authorities at Washington, and passes, for his party to sail in the steamer "Leverrier," from New York. Only the physician and a few intimate friends knew of the project. Mary Prescott was sent for from the country to stay with her aunt; and without a farewell call, or the least ripple of excitement, the adventurers set out. Phœbe appeared the cheerful and calm leader of the party. They reached New York without any incident, and without fatigue. The "Leverrier," a steamer of over three thousand tons, carrying provisions, arms, army stores, and a large number of recruits, was to sail as soon as she could be got ready. When a steamer sets out for Europe with a crowd of happy tourists, while friends on the dock are waving white handkerchiefs, and smiles are chasing tears, and pleasant words and airy farewells are flung, — that is a joyous scene. The sailing of the "Leverrier" furnished a very different spectacle. It was at the time of the lowest ebb in the fortunes of the nation. Soldiers no longer went away humming *La donna è mobile:* it was a serious business. The sailors had seen such incessant labor, that they snapped out every word with oaths, and with the expression of mastiffs. The petty officers, mates and the like, were fiercer than the sailors. They howled their orders like demons; and, amidst a babel that could only be paralleled by the New-York Gold Board on the memorable Black Friday, the work of loading the great vessel went on. To a landsman it seemed as if every thing was pitched pell-mell into the hold. The captain had his eye upon the scene probably; but he was invisible until steam was up and the hawser was cast off. The other superior officers looked as if they had been brought up under Charon, and acquired their civility in ferrying huddles of damned souls across the Styx. Whoever was upon the ship, in their view, was an inferior being, except the military officer of highest rank on board: *he* was the "king pin;"

and every one, even the captain, had to render him implicit obedience. It was for him to say when meals should be served, and who might sit at table; whether any one might smoke, and, if so, where. But over the civil passengers the ship's officers had full sway, and every civilian was a dog. It was a rash man, who, without epaulets, dared ask an officer which way was the wind, or how the ship was heading, or how many knots an hour were made. The questioner was pulling a plug, and he could not tell what scalding or filthy gush would come upon him.

Into this scene, where hundreds of men were exerting every energy to do the work of many days in one; where turmoil was incessant, and cursing only a common mode of breathing; where frantic beings, unwashed and uncombed, rushed about, rolling barrels, tilting boxes, and propelling trucks; where drays jammed in with endless loads; and where stern men in blue overcoats, with guns and bayonets, kept off the ill-looking crowd of loungers, — into this scene, preceded by a friendly young lieutenant, came the delicate Miss Thorpe (a diminutive Minerva) and Miss Phœbe (a slender but stately Diana) and the two gentlemen.

At sight of the women a lane was made without remark: only the under officers swore; for them it was a state-room less. The ladies were shown at once to a large room well astern, in which were two wide berths, a sofa, and a lounge. Two ladies, wives of officers, were to be their room-mates.

Mr. Prescott and Amory were to have berths nearer amidships. Only one cabin was saved for the use of the passengers: the others were filled with stores or hammocks. All prudent passengers, male and female, brought their own wraps and bed-clothing.

It was in February, and the cold was intense. The air seemed to be full of ice-needles. No one could walk the deck in comfort, least of all a woman in shawls and skirts. A steam pipe kept the ladies' state-room comfortable; but most of the accessible parts of the ship were cold, dark, and cheerless, and bare of the most ordinary comforts.

Some time passed, and the turmoil on the wharf suddenly lessened, then ceased. Then loud and decisive orders were heard from the deck. The steam sang its tremendous monotone in the great pipe, and now and then gave a *pish* of impatience through a stop-cock. The speaking-trumpets renewed their discord. "LET GO THERE!" There was a heavy splash of a hawser; the gangway-plank was shoved off; the pilot touched the bell; the engine groaned; the great paddle-wheels began to turn; and the "Leverrier" was off. Slowly churning the half-frozen water and the floating masses of ice and refuse, the vessel swung round into the stream.

Much of this was seen by Phœbe and Miss Thorpe through the glazed port-hole of their state-room. Then, as the majestic vessel slowly

moved on, a pert little tug-boat came alongside,
puffing with importance, and bringing the end of
an enormous cable. When the cable was fastened,
and pulled taut, a superbly-rigged bark appeared
in tow, and thenceforth followed the steamer.
The bark was loaded with live cattle, to furnish
beef for the Southern army.

About this time the ladies thought they would
inquire for their friends; but neither Mr. Prescott nor Mr. Amory could be found on board.
Miss Thorpe had the pass from the government,
and she had sufficient money; but the thought
of making the voyage alone, and of arriving at
a military post unfriended, was appalling. It was
now Phœbe's turn to be brave, and to sustain
the drooping spirits of·her convoy. They were
assured by fellow-passengers that steamers sailed
every few days, and of course the gentlemen
would follow them by the first vessel that offered.

The steamer, before many hours, was rolling
and struggling in the terrible winter sea. Squalls
of snow darkened the air: every wave that was
shipped left more and more ice, until the vessel
was armor-plated. But of this the hapless women
knew nothing. The violence of the storm obliged
them to keep their berths; and neither had a look
at sea or sky until when, three or four days later,
they were running in smooth water, and tracing
out a fringe of feathery palmettos on the edge of
the horizon.

CHAPTER XXIII.

It was remarkably imprudent in Mr. Prescott; but he yielded to the suggestion of Amory that they should go on shore to get some newspapers, fruit, cigars, and a few other indispensable articles. He had put the all-important *pass* in Miss Thorpe's keeping. The two went up the wharf, walked a square or two, made their purchases with what speed they might, and then returned. The gate of the lower wharf was chained, and a sentinel stood by with his musket. "No one admitted without a pass." — "But I have a pass." — "Show it." — "It is in the hands of my friend aboard ship." — "The worse for you." — "I can get it, and show you." — "No; for you can't go by here." — "But I just passed out." — "Well, you had a right to." — "But not to go back?" — "Not without a pass." — "Why was the gate open when I went out, and shut now?" — "Gate is allus shut before steamer starts." — "Do you say I can't get aboard that vessel?" — "I say so. That's what I'm here for." The wheels were already revolving. Amory and Prescott both redoubled their entreaties with the obdurate sentinel, until he finally ordered them away, with a threat of arrest. The steamer was off. Amory, with wild eyes, and fingers clawing at his hair, was swearing like a stevedore [truth demands the statement]; but Mr. Prescott sat down on a bale, and sobbed.

It was a sorrowful pair that·went up to the Astor House.

Luckily the next day there was another steamer in berth. Another pass was procured by telegraph; new personal supplies were obtained; and the impatient voyagers embarked.

The ship soon ran into the same storm in which the "Leverrier" had started. It blew what sailors call a fresh breeze; that is to say, no human being could stand on deck without holding on to something. The sea precipitated itself, came head first upon the deck; and the water froze as it fell. The ice on the lower rigging, bulwarks, and wheelhouse, was nearly a foot thick; and gangs of men, held by ropes around their waists, were set to cut it off, because its vast weight made the vessel topheavy. Such was the penalty of passing Hatteras in a north-easter. Prescott and Amory had found a friend in office, and got a comfortable stateroom; only the animals (horses and cows) on deck were directly over head; and as often as a dash of the icy spray came over the creatures, or as, sometimes, a ton of water thundered down upon them, they kicked and groaned in such a way as to make sleep impossible. The waves, too, came with a rush and a roar, and at times with a series of crushing blows as though the ship's ribs were struck by some gigantic hammer; then the vessel would sway and twist and creak like a willow basket. After the stormy point was passed, though the wind continued cold, the water was about sixty degrees; and a light mist rose from the waves, so that their curling, whitening edges seemed to smoke.

Afterwards came two delightful days, with clear skies, bland airs, and a distant line of gleaming white sand on the starboard. Still southward they went on an even keel, with glimpses of sandy shore, and tufts of palmetto, in the golden west. How beautiful every thing looked to eyes that had seen only angry waves so long!

Soon the unmistakable signs of a military post appeared. Long, low buildings of immense extent were seen; and piers jutted into the harbor, at which were lying hundreds of vessels of all classes, from sutler's schooners up to ocean steamers and men-of-war. In the rear were fortifications; and flags, mere glancing specks of red and white, floated above.

It was Sunday; and the pier was crowded with an eighth of a mile of soldiers, laborers, and teamsters. Making their way through the throng with some difficulty, our friends traversed the long pier, and across the dazzling white sand (up to the ankles at every step), to the office of the provost-marshal.

They had sought for information on board their

vessel in vain : the Ancient Mariner might just as well have made the same inquiries of his spectre crew. Up to this moment, the voyagers had not the least idea where they should find Col. Prescott, nor upon what service he was bound. Not a soldier nor officer on the wharf would answer any sort of a question with regard to the location of regiments or commanders. There was wisdom and necessity in this; but our two civilians did not then know that publicity had been such a damage to the government as to make silence imperative.

Their passes were *viséd*, and they went to the only hotel. Its claims to distinction lay in the fact that the price was five dollars a day, and that "native wine" (so called, but in fact a very fair champagne without any label) could be obtained at four dollars a bottle. The lodging-rooms were a series of boxes much like those provided for cattle in ocean steamers, and the beds, —

Infandum! . . . jubes renovare dolorem.

At the table bets were daily made, so it was said, as to whether the particular piece of flesh offered for mastication was beef, pork, or mutton. As for poultry and eggs, not a hen had been heard to cackle at the island for a year. Wild fowl were plenty, but no one was allowed to fire a gun. The tin can was the only horn of plenty.

To return to our travellers. Miss Thorpe and Phœbe were not at the hotel. The inference was, that they must have gone to Beaufort, where they would have better accommodations, and society of their own sex. The steamer for Beaufort was to sail in a few hours; and Mr. Prescott and Amory, having had their passes *viséd* by the quartermaster at the pier, obtained permission to go.

They spent the few hours of leisure on the long pier. preferring to observe that scene of activity than to lounge about the hotel. They soon espied a tall and familiar form in a colonel's uniform. Neither of them could remember his name or belongings, but Amory felt sure he had seen him in a pulpit. Mr. Prescott accosted the officer; and, receiving a civil and even friendly reply, the conversation was continued. The officer was stationed near Beaufort, and, by singular good-fortune, had met Miss Thorpe and Phœbe on their arrival, — the former being an old friend and fellow-member of the Plato Club, — and had obtained for them a temporary home with some noble women at the well-known Smith plantation. This was an inexpressible relief.

Now came up the matter of Roderick. The colonel was discreet: the movements of the army were not to be discussed, not even the where-abouts of an officer. Events were in the air. The colonel parleyed, admitted that Roderick had been wounded, but said he was now on duty, and in an important position. This extreme caution was new to Mr. Prescott; and his curiosity, not to say his anxiety, was momently on the increase.

At length the colonel said, in a string of vague but suggestive sentences, that a despatch steamer was going at once to Jacksonville. He had no advice to offer, no permission to give. Mr. Prescott must decide for himself. The ladies were well cared for, and with genial companions: so much was certain. Mr. Prescott need have no fears about their safety and comforts. If he wished to see his son, the colonel, why, the despatch steamer would take him to the St. John in a few hours; and then Mr. Prescott would learn more than the colonel was now at liberty to communicate, and he would learn what he could not learn at the present station. Probably he could return in a few days; but a pass must be got from Gen. Gillmore, the fort-crusher.

If Col. Hunt had known what was going to happen, he would have hesitated before advising two peaceable non-combatants to go to Jacksonville. But he had said just enough to pique curiosity to the utmost; and Mr. Prescott, having heard how delightfully the ladies were situated, and finding that he could go by boat so quickly, and probably could return at any time, proposed to Amory to accompany him. The plan was not so attractive to the young man, but he consented cheerfully. Col. Hunt succeeded in getting passes in the face of strong opposition.

The steamer that took our travellers from Port Royal to the coast of Florida seemed to be a thing of mystery. Its captain was a severe-looking person, who scowled on the first officer, who scowled on the second, who transmitted the scowl to the third, and so on down. What the vessel was going for, what had happened or was going to happen, was beyond any one's knowledge. There was a singular absence of conveniences on board, except in the matter of implements of war.

The weather continued fine. After a very swift passage, the steamer went at half-speed, and presently a sound was heard like the roaring of surf. All rushed on deck to behold the entrance of St. John's River. There was a long line of breakers on the bar stretching north-east, a deserted lighthouse on the left bank, and, just inside, a field of tumultuous eddies, formed by the rising tide in its struggles with the current of the river.

When the steamer had passed the tide-rips, the stillness of death brooded over the broad and sluggish stream. Trees hung with moss lined the banks; and withered reeds leaned in the black ooze by the shore. Here and there stood a planter's house or a negro's cabin, and around them a scarcely perceptible bloom showed the coming of early spring to the peach-trees; but not a human being was to be seen, white or black. The steamer moved cautiously on. Its two Parrott guns were shotted and manned, and in the place of the steamer's captain the senior military officer gave the noiseless orders as she steamed up the stream. Not a word was spoken, but even the silence was appalling.

The reason of all this was soon apparent. The town of Jacksonville, or what remained of it, came into view; and there at the wharf our travellers saw a fleet of transport-steamers, and in the stream a gunboat commanding the approaches. The town had a wofully battered look. Chimneys had been overturned, roofs burned, gardens trampled, and fences demolished, mostly by the Southern troops on their retreat.

This was war. It was as far from a holiday excursion as possible. Now came on the first of the waves of that "sea of troubles" with which our civilians were to contend. There were no residents, except a few troops, servants, and stragglers. It was an armed camp under rigid discipline. They showed their passports to a beardless impertinence in shoulder-straps, who demanded names and business, and who only allowed them to go ashore after an exciting and not very courteous examination of nearly fifteen minutes. It was incredible to officers in the service that any man would actually come to the front, unless he were a renegade, a spy, or a prospective sutler. The story would have been called *thin*, if that slang had then existed. So Mr. Prescott answered again and again why he had started, who came with him, and where he had left his company. And the officer then condescended to inform him that the army had come to Florida "on business;" that there would be a movement soon, naturally, but when or where he could not say. There might be a chance to return to Port Royal soon, or there might not. They could live on shore, under surveillance, of course, if they could find a mess that would admit strangers; or they might live on the steamer by agreeing with the commissary's deputy. If the army should move, there might be a few companies left to protect the place, or there might not. If not, they (our travellers) might have their choice, — to remain on the steamer with a chance of being sent back to New York, or to follow the army on foot in its forced marches inland.

During the interview briefly sketched, Amory was inflamed with wrath visibly. His cheeks were scarlet, and his eyes glaring. But Mr. Prescott, though fully as angry, gave his arm a gripe, and insisted on silence.

"Lieutenant," said our elder traveller gravely, "as you have *viséed* our passports, I believe we have a right to go on shore. For your information as to how and where we can live, and for your warnings in regard to the future, we are deeply grateful. We are properly sorry we came, but that cannot be helped now. We will endeavor to bestow ourselves where we shall burden no one, nor intrude in any exclusive mess; and for that purpose we shall try to see your superior officer. He will be glad to hear, doubtless, with what zeal you use the authority in which you are clothed, also with what delicate and considerate kindness you have cheered and aided us."

The lieutenant, if he still lives, probably remembers the tingling emphasis, and the signs of the vehement emotion that *would* have surged up like lava, if an enforced, icy courtesy had not covered the hidden fire.

The three formed a striking group. The strutting officer had half a mind to be angry and resentful; yet he was awed involuntarily by the steady gaze of Mr. Prescott, and perhaps was half afraid that it was the Secretary of War or some senator whom he had been bullying. Amory was swollen, bulbous, and high-shouldered. His pulpy lips had hardened to sealing-wax. For all his supposed softness and poetic sensibility, he was as pugnacious a fellow as one often meets. He drew deep, wheezy breaths while the senior was returning thanks, and watched the color come and go in the young cock's face. Mr. Prescott, with his resolute countenance and his large and luminous eyes, looked the master of the situation, as he was. Touching their hats to the officer with an excessive politeness, they walked up the river-bank.

Only a small regiment of colored troops was found at the town. The expedition was already in motion.

These were facts that our friends ascertained a little later. On their way they were repeatedly stopped by the guard; and at last, approaching a house that retained some vestiges of its former credit, they were desired to enter, and show their papers to the provost-marshal.

The provost was represented by a deputy; and our travellers were asked anew all the questions they had answered at the wharf, and a hundred more besides. This was a ruddy, good-natured fellow, however, and in the end he gave some hints of the reasons why strangers were so sharply questioned and watched. In justice to the much-tried officers, it must be said that civilians were out of place "at the front."

The prospects of our travellers indeed appeared dubious. The rebel general Finnegan was known as a wily and restless enemy. If he could elude the vigilance of Seymour, he might turn and annihilate the few troops in Jacksonville, destroy the transport-steamers, or even capture the gunboat. The freedom of our civilians, and their hope of returning to Port Royal, appeared to hang on the success of the expedition; and it was impossible to say whether they would be in greater personal danger on their steamer, in the town, or with the rear guard of the army in pursuit of Finnegan.

Soon the provost-marshal in person appeared. Amory gave one look at him, and sprang forward to seize the hand of an old and intimate friend. It was a hearty, generous meeting on both sides. Red tape was forgotten: passports were useless scrawls. The party withdrew to an inner room, where army hospitalities were duly tendered, and the "assurances" exchanged over tin dippers (gills only) of the regulation whiskey known as "commissary [D]." It was not nectar, but was the best the gallant provost had to offer.

Their immediate wants being provided for, the baggage was brought ashore, and a "shake-down" was spread in a chamber that was fragrant with yellow jessamine flowers peeping in through open windows; and then the evening passed in cheerful talk, and with the incense of reed-stemmed Powhatan pipes.

CHAPTER XXIV.

Mr. Prescott slept as soundly on the hard pallet as if he had been accustomed to it; but while he was dreaming of seeing Phœbe perpetually near, yet always eluding him, he suddenly woke. The provost-marshal was at his bedside, also an orderly with a lantern. A small party with letters and orders was going forward at once. It was two o'clock in the morning. There was an opportunity, if Mr. Prescott wished, to accompany the party. Due emphasis was laid upon Mr. Prescott's *wish;* the means of conveyance was an ambulance. Amory was already dressed, and held his hand bag. Mr. Prescott brushed the sleep from his eyes, hurriedly laved them in cool water, put on his surtout, and followed the party.

The troops moved promptly and without sound, except from the hoofs of horses and the rumbling of wheels. Vedettes preceded, and scoured the woods on either hand, while the small column steadily followed. All was still. Not a human being was seen.

Late in the evening of the same day the rear of the main body of the advancing forces was reached. For the first time Mr, Prescott and

Amory comprehended their position. They were following a small army of less than six thousand men — four thousand four hundred actual combatants — into the heart of Florida, advancing to meet an unknown enemy posted no one knew where, and, being perfectly acquainted with the country, ready to take prompt advantage of any error on the part of the invaders.

Mr. Prescott was struck with the grim and fixed expression of countenance of both officers and men. It was as far as possible from a holiday parade. Officers were vigorous and curt: the men were alert and resolute. When the column encamped at St. Mary's Ford, and the preparations for the night-watch were made, our friends, under guidance of the friendly sergeant, went through the darkness to visit Col. Prescott. An orderly lifted the fold of the tent; and there, in a colonel's uniform, on his knees in prayer, was Robert Prescott.

Both stepped back, and raised their hats, their surprise and reverence mingling in an overpowering emotion, until the preacher-colonel rose.

How they rushed together! What embraces and hand-shakings! what exclamations of delight! "My dear Robert," at length Mr. Prescott found breath to say, "and so this is the field? Not India or Africa, but your own land! God in heaven bless you! How could I doubt my brother's son? We have a land worth fighting for, and what could be nobler than to die for her! Oh the old blood tells! My grandfather spent that dreadful winter at Valley Forge. Your grandfather was out in the war of 1812. Now you are here! Whenever the country needs her sons, there will always be a Prescott in arms. But tell us, how did you come here?"

"I know," said Col. Robert modestly, "that this is strange for a man of my chosen profession; but it was no fickleness that led me to volunteer. When I came to reflect upon it, as I was about leaving Boston, the peril of the country was immediate, and my first duty was to defend her. If this country were to go down, the hope of liberty and Christianity everywhere would be darkened. I went to Albany, and offered my services. What moved the governor to trust me, a stranger, a student without military training, I can't say; but he gave me a second lieutenant's commission in a regiment just setting out. We have been in constant service; and so many men have been killed and disabled and captured, that the force is wholly changed. The present officers are mostly new men, risen from the ranks. I am to-day the senior. The ordinary experience of years has been crowded into months. I have been taken prisoner, and have escaped. I have been two or three times hit, just grazed by bullets, but have not had a serious wound. The severest ordeal I have had was in escaping by way of the Edisto River to the sea, when I lay hid in tree-tops by day, and paddled on a log by night, when I lived on a sweet-potato a day, raw or roasted as it might happen, given me by some skulking negro."

Light was breaking in upon Mr. Prescott's mind. He began to understand the reason for the conflicting reports.   There were *two* Col. Prescotts.

" And where is Roderick?" asked Mr. Prescott eagerly.

" Close at hand.   I will send for him."

While the orderly went to the camp of the negro regiment, Mr. Prescott gave a rapid account of the journey.   Robert's surprise was now redoubled.   That Phœbe should have chosen to come to the seat of war, and should have succeeded in bringing the fragile and shrinking Miss Thorpe as her companion, was beyond his comprehension.   His cheeks colored with pleasure; and then he thought of a leave of absence and the delight of meeting the only woman he had ever loved.   Then the imminent struggle came to mind, and he shuddered to think what fatal mischances might come between him and his hopes. Then, too, he wondered if Roderick had not been the attraction.   Unless Phœbe had some hidden source of information as to himself — could this be possible? — she must have been impelled by curiosity, or sympathy for the rival.

His meditations were cut short by the arrival of Col. Roderick.   Behold a young man with closely cropped hair, a thin and brown face, so brown that his blue eyes showed like turquoises in leather, with a sharp and rather disagreeable, dare-devil expression, and with a lithe movement of body like that of a trained athlete. The silken dandy had been thoroughly broken in and hardened to his work.

The greetings were hearty, and the surprise on Roderick's part, perhaps, even greater than with Robert. That his step-father and Amory, and the ladies, should come to the seat of war through so much of difficulty and danger was beyond belief. First he inquired affectionately with regard to his mother, and then paused.

The two colonels looked at each other meaningly, and then Robert slowly spoke.

"I suppose you didn't come over here without knowing that you come straight into danger?"

"Well, no," replied Mr. Prescott. "We knew fighting was going on."

"But we are liable to be attacked any moment. We are prepared for that risk,—Roderick and I, —but you must be cared for. Roderick and I will see that you have quarters with the surgeons and commissaries in the rear."

"Then you expect a battle?"

"I only know we are marching into an unknown country, and that we have one of the craftiest of foes watching our movements. Finnegan, the rebel leader, they say, was once a private in the regular army under Seymour, and he vows he will beat his old captain. We may fall into an ambuscade like Braddock, or we may sweep across the country to the gulf; but I think we shall have hot work within twenty-four hours."

"Sure of that!" said Roderick.

Amory looked admiringly upon the two heroes, and began actually to regret he had not volunteered. His ideas were rising to the high level; and he burned for leisure, a table, pen, ink, and paper, that he might record the glorious thrills he felt, before their impression faded. Mary should read a description of this scene in the tented field the night before battle.

"It is surmised," said Robert cautiously, "that Seymour is advancing on his own responsibility, and contrary to Gillmore's orders. If he succeeds, the fault will be atoned for: if he fails, he will have a double load to bear."

"But don't let us talk politics," said Roderick. "Here are we four. Not far away are two women. What new throw of the dice may happen to-morrow, who can say? Now, let us talk practical sense, just as if to-morrow was going to" — He looked at his step-father, checked himself, and then went on more cheerily, —

"Now, here is my parson, my pet preacher. You can't be more surprised to find him here than I was. We have only met within three months. Before that, I think I hated him about as thoroughly as a man could hate another. · I didn't know him."

Robert listened with a half-amused expression, and wondered if "Commissary [D]" had any thing to do with this frankness.

"I've been thinking I ought to speak," continued Roderick. "Most men think they are good enough for any woman; but I am an exception. Now this parson-colonel here thinks he keeps his secret; but it is hidden like the red-bordered handkerchief peeping out of a swell's breast-pocket. There are about three things this singular man worships, — God, his country, and a certain young lady. Perhaps we should reverse the order; but let it stand."

Mr. Prescott thought Roderick unsettled in mind, perhaps by premonitions of the morrow, perhaps by the thoughts of home which had been awakened by this visit. He endeavored to turn the conversation.

"Your mother has pleasant news from England. She thinks of making her brother a visit next season, or as soon as you can go with us."

"Oh, yes! 'when this cruel war is over,' of course we will go. I hope I'll get a star or two on my shoulders first. I understand the copper stock has come up booming. Mother must be happy now. And how does Gibbs like it?"

"Your mother can bear a great deal of prosperity, and I am glad she has her share of it. Gibbs, I think, is really cut. He looks at me as if I had been his enemy."

"That is according to the old poetical adage, said Robert: —

> "'Forgiveness to the injured does belong;
> But they ne'er pardon who have done the wrong.'"

"Sometimes they *do*," said Roderick. "I was in the wrong and did the wrong. I forgive. This Col. Robert here, father, is the *best* man (oh! I go for religion after this); he has saved my life, and much more than that. — Keep quiet, will you, colonel? I have something to say in view of certain contingencies."

"Come, Roderick," said his step-father, "don't distress yourself. The rebels haven't a shot that is to hit you."

"Well, maybe so; but they've hit me some half-dozen times before now. But you don't know all I have been thinking of — do they, colonel?"

"Scarcely. But you are in an odd humor."

"Let me have my way. I see that my friend goes in such a bee-line in regard to his affection, that he could die for a man, — or a woman. And I have asked myself, 'Now could you, would you, Roderick, die for any woman?' And, when I reflect upon it, I find the everlasting truth is, I wouldn't: besides, mother has written to me about Phœbe's visions. They fit this man's case better than mine. *He* has escaped to the sea. *His* fortune has interested her. Now, here we are in this treacherous country, and we don't know — well, the fact is, if a man has no property to dispose of, he ought to make a will and testament *for something*. And things have been a little mixed. And while the young lady is splendid, and all that, I believe she really ought to love — or might love

—this solemn, but awfully good fellow. Am I to be the selfish, naughty boy? No, I'll go away and sulk; or rather I'll beat the bush for new game. So here, Robert Prescott, rise up, give me your hand! This is a nuncupative will (I think that's the phrase). I read law once,—about two months. You know what I would say. Go ahead. I'm not in your way."

How much of this strange jumble was due to gratitude, how much to a fickle nature, how much to a flaunting generosity, and how much to the lingering fumes of " Commissary [D]," can hardly be told. Were the beautiful Phœbe present, or within reach, it would never have been uttered. For Roderick, as the reader has seen, was much under the influence of the moment; and now, in camp, with certain grateful impulses in mind, and some lugubrious prospects ahead, he could be heroic in self-denial. But the speech lifted a load off the mind of his rival, and caused his step-father and Amory not a little surprise.

Robert simply said, " I appreciate your intended kindness. But it is not for us to dispose of the young lady. She is to decide the momentous question for herself." Mr. Prescott gravely assented to Robert's remark, and added that such a matter should be deferred to a more fitting season. Many subjects came up,—the departure of Belvedere, the prayer-book, and the probability of Phœbe's relationship to the Mannings. Amory came in for his share of credit in discovering the rich deposits of copper, and related his experiences. It seemed that the young colonels could never be satisfied with asking questions about the people they had known. The current of talk ran freely; and probably in all the field there were not four men whose hearts were so knit together, so thoroughly in sympathy, so prepared to meet the inevitable for themselves, and so eager to aid each other.

The hour was late. All were in need of sleep. With the exchange of fervent good-nights, good wishes, and sweet messages, they separated, and Mr. Prescott and Amory were conducted to the tent where they were to lie down; but of actual sleep they had little. The situation was novel, the events of the day had been exciting, and the future was too full of contingencies to allow their minds to rest.

Amory looked out at the stars on the northern part of the horizon, and wondered if Mary Prescott could be looking at them too. Mr. Prescott closed his eyes, but could not still the pounding of his heart and the answering throbs in his brain.

CHAPTER XXV.

THE events of this chapter belong to history. It is to be hoped that the historic Muse will in due time bestir herself to gather and put them in order. The heroes who acted their parts in the momentous scene are soon to pass away. The best accounts thus far published are in news-papers; and they are inadequate, often conflict-ing, and perhaps partial. They are yet to be compared, sifted, and harmonized. Compared with battles like those of Gettysburg, Antietam, and the Wilderness, this action in Florida appears very small; yet to each man who faced the foe, the ordeal was as terrible, and the stake as great, as when the line of fire was measured by miles.

As our friends Prescott and Amory were far in the rear, we shall endeavor by and by to look at the battle with the eyes of some, still living, who were among the prominent actors.

The camp was in motion at an early hour. Ra-tions had been served, and animals fed, and the forces began to move in three lines, parallel with a railroad-track, across a level country. The cavalry started half an hour in advance. Col. Robert's regiment was near the centre of the little army,

and Col. Roderick's in the rear. Mr. Prescott
and Mr. Amory had made the acquaintance of
members of the Commissions, those Good Samari-
tans whose generous efforts did so much to alle-
viate the sufferings of the wounded in battle, and
who have given a far higher than any military
renown to the American name. These camp-fol-
lowers, so unlike the dregs of armies of other
days, rode in ambulances and walked by turns.
But one short halt was called during the morning. About noon, while the troops were resting
and taking a hurried meal, there was heard the
solid thunder of brass field-pieces, and then the
distant, clattering sound of musketry. The troops
were urged forward with all speed; yet, as the
regiments were generally a mile apart, it was
some hours before the last came into the action.

The brigade of cavalry was very small in numbers, but composed of veteran troops, and was
commanded by Col. Guy V. Henry of the Fortieth Massachusetts Regiment of Mounted Infantry.
Major Stevens of the First Battalion of Massachusetts Cavalry led the advance. The skirmishers
were under Capt. W. A. Smith of the Fortieth,
whose company was the first to open fire, and the
last to leave the field. The behavior of the cavalry
was worthy of the highest praise throughout the
day. They were eating their hard-bread, and feed-
ing their horses when they were fired upon by a
company of mounted skirmishers. The fire was
returned, and our cavalry pressed forward, driv-

ing back the enemy for nearly two miles to the place where the railroad crosses the sand road, and where two or three poor houses form what is called Olustee. It was at this crossing that the trap had been set; and the company of rebel cavalry had been sent forward to skirmish and to retreat, with a view of drawing our regiments, one after another, under the fire of their whole line.

The forces under Gen. Finnegan, from nine thousand to twelve thousand in number, were disposed on each side of the railroad-track in an eccentric curve, one wing resting upon the shore of a pond, while the other stretched around, under cover of bushes, to a heavily-wooded cypress swamp. Earthworks were thrown up on the exposed parts of the line, and batteries were planted to sweep the roads. Perfectly sheltered from musketry, and inaccessible to cavalry, the enemy's converging fire was awfully destructive.

The Seventh Connecticut Regiment of Gen. Hawley's brigade had come up with the cavalry, and moved on towards the enemy's impregnable position. Elder's and Hamilton's batteries of light artillery followed. At the outset, not much effect was produced, except by our field-pieces. More batteries were sent for, and the remaining regiments ordered up. The Seventh Connecticut was a splendid regiment, armed with Spencer rifles, and behaved with gallantry. The Seventh New-Hampshire, Col. Abbott, which had had a high reputation in previous actions, was not so fortunate this day, and began to waver. At this moment the Eighth United-States Regiment of colored troops came forward, under Col. Fribley. These men had never been under fire; but they held their ground with determined bravery for considerably more than an hour, until the colonel and more than half the men were killed and disabled, when the remnant fell back in disorder.

The battle was now waged in terrible earnest. Langdon's battery had come up to the front with the Eighth (colored troops), and had been partially covered by them. The confusion and retreat of the Eighth left the batteries of Langdon and Hamilton uncovered; and the fire of the enemy, especially of the sharpshooters, was directed upon the artillerists and horses with deadly effect. In a quarter of an hour there were not horses enough left to draw the guns; and later, when our troops fell back upon a new line, four or five guns had to be left in the possession of the enemy.

The New-York brigade, under Gen. Barton, which included Col. Robert's regiment, next came on, and fought with resolute bravery. The disheartening thing was to be under an incessant and withering fire, which could not be silenced nor effectively returned while the enemy kept in its well-protected line.

Gen. Seymour, who had the responsibility of the expedition, arrived at the front soon after

Gen. Hawley. He saw too late that the army had been decoyed and led to slaughter, and he made superhuman exertions to save it from total defeat. He made the best possible disposition of his limited forces, as each new occasion required. The batteries were managed with consummate skill. When the lines of battle were thinned, he sent forward new troops, until there were no more. He was on foot with the New-York regiments while they were at the front, in the very hottest of the fire, and exposed himself with heroic unconcern.

At this time the cavalry and mounted infantry were stationed behind some bushes on the enemy's flank, out of the action. They desired and expected an order to charge, and were especially chagrined not to receive it when, later, the enemy came out of their line of defence, and made a forward movement. Capt. Smith of the Fortieth went to Gen. Seymour while he was dismounted and in the thick of the fight, and asked that the order to charge might be given; but the general was unwilling to risk it. He probably had become convinced that it was impossible to change the fate of the day against an enemy whose effective forces were more than double his own.

The losses of the New-York brigade were severe. The ammunition was giving out, and the lines were wavering, when the two remaining regiments of colored troops, including Col. Robert's, were ordered to move. These defiled in front of the white regiments, and received, for a time, the whole fire of the enemy.

At this moment a grand stroke was planned by the rebel commander, and that was to break our line by a furious assault. His cavalry first attempted to move (perhaps as a feint), but was immediately confronted by ours. There was no advance on either side, and the forces sat facing each other in silence for a time. But the rebel infantry rushed forward with a shout, formed in solid column by *échelon*, and came towards the centre of our line at double-quick. The black men stood their ground; and meanwhile Elder's battery, which was planted so as to give a volley on a diagonal line at the column, opened a terrific fire with canister at short range. It was the only opportunity our side had during the day to give the enemy as good as he had sent. The column did not hold together to deal the decisive blow: it was frightfully cut up, and its advance checked. The rebel general had expected to turn the defeat into a rout and a massacre; but the unexpected fire of the battery at such an angle as to enfilade the advancing column, and the determined bravery of the black men, saved our troops from any worse disaster. The negroes charged back, and even recaptured some of the guns which had been left on the field. They fought like demons, and even believed for a time they were to retrieve our fortunes. It was too late. Their officers were all killed or disabled, and their numbers too small to continue the fight.

Three times during the battle the lines of our troops were re-formed, and each time a little farther back. While this last and most desperate fighting was going on, Gen. Seymour was collecting his few shattered forces in the rear in order to save his transportation, to care for his wounded, and to retreat still farther. At sundown the enemy ceased firing suddenly. Another rally and another charge were expected, but none came.

The negro regiments were recalled, and fell back without a single mounted officer. One brave young fellow whom Mr. Prescott had known from a boy, and for whom he had brought a new uniform from his father, was among the fallen. The uniform was at Hilton Head; and the gallant youth was left on the field, to recover afterwards, as best he could, under the tender care of the military nurses of Andersonville.

A parting volley was sent into the woods from our batteries. The Seventh Connecticut, alert, and resolute to the end, formed last of the infantry; the cavalry closed in the rear; and the broken and dispirited army began its march back towards Jacksonville. The enemy's cavalry made some dashes occasionally, but no effective pursuit. Such is the brief outline of the disastrous battle of Olustee. Finnegan had been as good as his word.

When the first surprise of the attack was over, and the wounded began to be brought to the rear,

Mr. Prescott and Amory naturally and eagerly volunteered their help; and for those three terrible hours, which seemed an eternity of pain and apprehension, they gave refreshments, bandaged wounds, cheered the drooping, and soothed the dying. More and more wounded were brought in, until all the resources of the camp were insufficient for their relief. If there had not been something for these non-combatants to do, the suspense would have been insupportable. Where was Robert now?—and Roderick? Perhaps they were stretched on that sandy plain, trampled by hurrying feet of men and horses.

More than once the hospital tents had to be moved back; for the missiles of the enemy, as they came nearer, whistled among the surgeons, and wounded some of the volunteer helpers. Neither Mr. Prescott nor Amory flinched. They toiled the harder, pulling off their coats, and laboring until they were dissolved in perspiration. News came momently from the front by those who brought in the wounded. First it was Henry's cavalry that was swept away like chaff; and here was a trooper, shot through the neck and shoulder, whose face was strangely familiar. They remembered him as a hostler at the little tavern in Eaglemont. He opened his eyes at the sound of familiar voices. "Tell mother," he said with faltering voice, then took off his watch, or tried to, and closed his eyes forever. He lies on the fatal field with hundreds more. Both the friends wept over the fate of the bright and cheerful boy.

Every messenger brought fresh tidings of disaster. It was all one way. All was darkness and death.

When the repulse of the New-York brigade was announced, with what eager eyes did the friends scan the faces on the stretchers! It was with perpetual shudders that they looked, every moment fearing that the noble features of Robert would be disclosed. They eagerly questioned all who came, but to little purpose. No one had any certain knowledge, except that half of all the regiments were struck, and that nothing could be known as to the survivors until the fight was over. It is not easy to account for all the names on the roll of a demoralized and retreating troop. However, they knew Robert had not been *known* to be wounded, and they trusted that " no news " might be " good news." So they redoubled their efforts. Water was the great need, and there was none except in the stagnant pond covered by the Confederate fire. This made the sufferings of the wounded insupportable.

After a while the wounded of the Eighth United-States Colored Regiment were carried by to the place assigned for their own division. Many of them were singing strains from spiritual songs, as if only music and religion could lessen their pangs.

At last, when the colored regiments with terrible loss had withstood the rebel charge, and the main body of the army was re-formed, and ready to march, Amory rushed out to learn the fate of Roderick. A straggler said that the negro regiments had come back without their officers; that there was not a horse left; all were bowled down.

"The colonel too?" inquired Amory.

"Yes," said the informant, — "dead on the field."

"Are you sure?"

"Sure. And two of his men who tried to carry him off were shot dead, and fell upon him where he lay."

Still Amory could not fully believe it, although the news seemed so direct. He met a reporter for a New-York journal, — one who had been exposed to fire for the whole time. He was an Englishman, short in stature, and planted in a pair of immensely tall leather boots. It was not an heroic figure, and Amory could hardly help smiling in spite of the terrible situation.

"Have you seen Col. Prescott of the colored regiment?" Amory inquired.

The little man looked up. To the honor of human nature, two large tears bubbled out of his blue eyes, and with a faltering voice he answered,

"Yes, I have seen him, on the field — dead. All the officers of the —th are killed, including my young friend Major Melrose."

It was with a heavy heart that Amory went back to the hospital tent to carry the fatal news to Mr. Prescott. A very few words sufficed. The tears of women and children fall easily, one might sometimes say naturally; but the anguish of a mature and reserved man is terrible to behold.

There was little time for mourning. The well, and all who could keep on their feet, must march; for the army was in full retreat. Stores and officers' baggage were burned, so that the wounded might be carried; for their number was so great that there were not enough ambulances. The heavy army-wagons jolted and tortured the wretched beings they carried; and, with every vehicle in use, large numbers of the dying had to be left to breathe their last where they lay.

Before it was quite dark, Mr. Prescott met an officer who knew Roderick, and he had the melancholy satisfaction of finding that his portmanteau was saved, and in the care of the acting quartermaster. But the brave young man was struck down beyond a doubt. It was hard to realize it: he had been so full of life in the morning. Did he not have a premonition? Was it not this that inspired his affectionate reference to his mother, his singular and oppressive generosity to Col. Robert, and his thoughtful care of his stepfather? And now he lay upon his last field! How could the news be told to his mother?

Part of the army marched nine miles, and then halted. Other regiments reached Barber's Station, on the South Fork of St. Mary's River, accomplishing thirty-four miles in going and returning, besides having had three hours and a half of stubborn fighting. But the track of the army was marked by the knapsacks, guns, and blankets thrown away. After a time, a train of cars and a locomotive were found, and the wounded were put aboard. But the locomotive broke down; and the men of a Massachusetts colored regiment, wearied and suffering as they were, volunteered to push the train on to Jacksonville.

What a dismal retreat! — the army had been beaten, and was bleeding at every pore, its stores and most of its guns captured or abandoned, its dead left on the sandy plain or by the roadside, and its dying hurried on without water, without rest, without medical care. The whole night passed before all the scattered men found their places, and the losses could be known. Men continually came in who had crawled off the battle-field during the night. The negroes especially exhibited the stoicism of old 'campaigners, and made light of their wounds, even when frightfully mangled.

Shortly after dark, Mr. Prescott and Amory, while trying to eat their " hard-tack " without the aid of coffee, had the unspeakable satisfaction of seeing Col. Robert come into camp on foot. His horse had been killed, and he was near being captured; but he lay motionless a while, and then escaped unhurt, and found his way back with other stragglers.

We will not attempt to describe the weary night, nor the comfortless march of the day that followed.

CHAPTER XXVI.

As the reader remembers, Miss Thorpe and Phœbe, on landing at Hilton Head, were so fortunate as to meet an old friend, Col. Hunt, an officer who was stationed at Beaufort. By his advice they determined to go with him to that place, where he assured them they would find pleasant society, and more comfortable living than at the great military and naval depot. He attended to all their wants, and accompanied them to the provost-marshal's for the purpose of having their passports *viséed.* Then the party went on board "The Croton," an ancient and dilapidated river steamer from New York.

It was a sail of about fifteen miles, occupying an hour and a half. The landscape was full of strange beauty to Northern eyes. A soft and dreamy haze overhung the estuary. Live-oak groves with their outstretched arms stood in picturesque clumps on either hand. Avenues of magnolias were seen leading to the old plantations from the water-side. Here and there a few feathery and twisted palmettos, looking as if they had the worst of it in some tussle with the wind, and larger groups of the straight and towering pines, relieved the monotonous level. The scenery was neither that of winter nor of summer; for the foliage was heavy, dark green, and glossy. The trees were hung with abundant drapery of moss: it swung in festoons, it hung in tatters, it was packed in crows' nests.

The town of Beaufort, with its white houses and fine trees, looked charming from the water, though it was less attractive to our travellers upon a nearer view. But jonquils, hyacinths, and tulips in bloom, were in all the yards; and the windows under wide verandas were open to admit the delicious air. That was paradise after the pitiless storms of the north Atlantic coast.

Col. Hunt went to the quartermaster, and procured two confiscated "secesh" horses; and for the first time in their lives the two ladies enjoyed the surprise of being on horseback. As the jaded animals did not go out of a walk, there were no adventures by the way. It was about six miles to the famous Smith plantation. Their ride was mostly on the beach, sweeping around a long curve, over a firm, white surface of sea-beaten sand. The tide had just receded, and the marks of the horses' hoofs were like sculpture. They had the fresh sea-air on one side, and were protected on the other from the sun by a superb belt of pine-trees standing on the bluff above. On their way they stopped for a moment at the remains of the old fort built by the Huguenots under Jean Ribaut, in 1562, which readers of our romantic historian,

Parkman, will remember. The foundation-walls
of concrete shells were in good preservation. At
the Smith plantation are the grandest live-oaks
known, those in the Bonaventure Cemetery at
Savannah alone excepted. Miss Thorpe remarked
that she did not wonder the Druids worshipped
under oaks. Col. Hunt said the effect was so
solemn under the enormous spread of living green,
with moss hanging like tattered historic banners
from the roof, that he always instinctively took off
his hat, as if he were entering a cathedral.

They alighted at the gate, and saw a house much
like the home of a wealthy farmer in the Middle
States. The negroes within the enclosure, the
same all over the world, — happy, red-turbaned,
gay-shawled, chattering creatures, — came out to
look, and then rushed into the house with the
news.

Col. Hunt and the ladies were met by the occupants, — educated and noble women who had
come to teach the "contrabands." There were
hearty introductions and hospitable welcomes. In
a very few minutes Miss Thorpe and Phœbe were
at home with congenial people.

Promising to attend to forwarding their baggage, Col. Hunt rode back to Beaufort. No de-
tention had occurred on their journey: their
progress had been as steady and frictionless as the
launching of a ship. "To him who is shod, it is
the same as if the earth were covered with leather;" and the two shy and delicate women had

passed through camps as if they had been driven through a park.

Phœbe looked radiant. She was somewhat thinner than in her best estate; but her color had returned, and her hair was so loosely confined, that wavy tresses fell over her shoulders. Here it was possible for her to be in the open air all day. Here came the sense of freedom, the joy of motion, the delight in new flowers and in the boundless opulence of nature. This and much more was evident in her sparkling eyes and in her extravagant speech. It seemed as if she enjoyed every sight with an intensity of satisfaction like that of a person suddenly brought out of blindness into a garden.

Here Miss Thorpe and Phœbe found a charming home. They were surrounded with comforts. They were overwhelmed in hospitality. Their windows let in the fragrance of spring. The skies above and the earth beneath seemed to belong to another world. Their walks were bordered with lovely and fragrant but (to them) unnamed shrubs. They loitered by ponds whose edges were bristling with Spanish-bayonet. Huge cactus-plants, with lobes as large as shoulders of mutton, sprawled around. Enormous Mexican aloes bent their graceful leaves. A few steps took them to the beach to see the sandpipers, and to hear the melancholy plaint of the curlew and the ceaseless clatter of the water-hens.

Ah, what a rest for an invalid! What an ecstasy for an enthusiast like Phœbe!

But in intervals of repose Miss Thorpe felt that something unspoken rested upon Phœbe's mind. She could see the forerunners of thought and feeling in her looks; and the girl's lips seemed moving as if to utter something. But she did not speak. A singular change would come; and she would remain silent, or else refer to some unimportant matter.

"Why do you not say what you are thinking?" said Miss Thorpe, when they were together. "How much we talked of the awful news before we sailed! Is that what you are brooding over?"

"I seem to have been led here," Phœbe replied. "I have dreamed things I cannot relate in order. They are confusing. But I think Roderick is not dead, as we heard; and I hope we shall see him. I have seen him in dreams. I have seen also other friends and many strange things."

Except for the absence of Mr. Prescott, Phœbe appeared perfectly happy. The teachers with whom she was living were women of energy and character, refined and accomplished. They had all come from comfortable Northern homes, and had devoted themselves to the wants of the soldiers in hospitals, and to the education of the colored people, with unselfish zeal.

Miss Thorpe recovered from her cough, and was as joyous and demonstrative as was possible for one so instinctively serene.

There were nearly fifty ladies at the post in and around Beaufort, including the wives and daughters of officers, and the teachers and guests. Tea-parties were given, excursions were planned, and there were often rambles by the river-side. The officers were from nearly all sections of the country; but Col. Hunt was easily superior in manners, in intellect, and knowledge. Miss Thorpe said he had the brow of Sir Walter Raleigh and the bearing of Sir Philip Sidney. But then she had met him at the Plato Club; and it has been thought barely possible that the members of that Olympian circle may see each other looming up to miraculous stature. Certainly no more accomplished or more agreeable gentleman ever buckled on a sword. He was a tower of strength to our two ladies, and almost made them think that the war had no excuse for being, except as it furnished them a perfect sanitarium in the midst of the most vivid scenery in nature.

The 22d of February was approaching, and it was proposed that the birthday of Washington should be celebrated in such splendor as was possible. Upon a strong appeal to the great functionaries, an immense storehouse was cleared of its stock of hay and straw, and put in a state of cleanliness. Some tin-workers were found among the soldiers, who made from tomato-cans a set of gorgeous chandeliers, fitted to hold kerosene-lamps. Foraging parties daily went out into the woods, — vast numbers of them, — and were on the lookout for what was beautiful or strange. Ladies came daily to combine the harvest of evergreens into

striking and artistic forms. The post band practised music for quadrilles and waltzes. When all
was ready, this hastily-built pine structure, adorned
as it was, became the most magnificent ball-room
ever seen. A profusion of evergreens, oak-leaves,
magnolias, and bearded moss, hung in festoons from
the rafters, and coiled about the beams, braces,
and supports. Clusters of Spanish-bayonet imi-
tated the display in an armory. The music-stand
became a green bower. Leaves of palmetto waved
like gigantic ostrich-feathers. And through all
the rich, deep, and dense green, were set points of
color, where some jessamine, or tulip, or peach-bud
showed that the sun's call to the spring blossoms
was beginning to be felt. This enormous mass of
greenery so arranged, so alive with gold and rose-
color, and illuminated with such splendor, made
an impression that no beholder will ever forget.

The triumphs of dressmaking were hardly to be
looked for in a remote military post, to which it
was not allowed for each lady to carry a wagon-
load of Saratoga trunks. But clever and ingenious women will hardly ever be seen at a disad-
tage, if there is only a little time for preparation.
Very few of those who were present at that ball
probably thought of such a contingency, certainly
our Phœbe did not. But as a few wild blossoms
gave the grace of contrast to the masses of green
upholstery, so a bit of rich lace, a bright ribbon,
a Roman scarf, or wrought collar, made even plain
costumes attractive ; and few except those expe-

rienced in such matters would have said that the whole party had not brought their richest attire along with them.

Phœbe had been so depressed in mind, that, at starting, she had packed few except the most necessary clothes. Miss Thorpe, who did not dance, was more thoughtful; and as she foresaw that Phœbe's gloom would wear away, and that some fit occasion might arise, she had brought along for her a superb dress of corn-colored silk with black velvet trimmings, the appropriate laces, and the coral ornaments.

All the ladies came to the ball in ambulances. The *ensemble* was unexpectedly brilliant. The general commanding led off the dance with his lady. As Miss Thorpe declined to go upon the floor except as a spectator, Col. Hunt offered his arm to Phœbe. There was a general murmur of admiration as she moved across the hall. Her stature, her brilliant eyes, exquisite color, perfect carriage, and magnificent costume, would have attracted attention in any court.

During the evening the officers, for there were but few civilians present, flocked about for introductions; and our Phœbe conducted herself with her usual sweet discretion.

> " Favors to none, to all she smiles extends ;
> Oft she rejects, but never once offends."

Later, while sipping coffee with Col. Hunt, Miss Thorpe noticed Phœbe going forward, with a tall and athletic officer as her partner, in the "Lancers." That showy quadrille had not then been put under ban. The lively music struck up, and the large hall resounded with martial steps. Some jar occurred. Was there a tipsy musician? a dancer out of step? No: there was a little flurry about the music-stand. Miss Thorpe looked eagerly. Col. Hunt raised his stately head also. Both felt a simultaneous shock. Miss Thorpe's heart stood still; and she trembled violently, as the general commanding, emerging from the flurried group, mounted the stand and spoke in a dismal tone. It took several — seconds, shall we say? — for the musicians and the surging crowd on the floor to stop, and to concentrate their attention upon the general. They were like persons suddenly roused from sleep. In those few seconds many thoughts flitted by. The first notion was, that the town was attacked, although the gunboats kept up their steady patrol day and night, moving through dull creeks and lagoons, and entirely surrounding the town. But the gloomy voice of the general at length pierced the distracted air, and the gayety of the scene was dead. The purport of his message was, that our forces in Florida had met with a great disaster; that the steamer "Cosmopolitan" had just arrived at the wharf, bringing a large number of wounded and dying; that the help of every man was needed at once; that the ambulances were required at the wharf, and the ladies must walk home; that the wounded men would be carried past the ball-room on their way to the hospital, and the general thought they ought not to hear the sound of dancing music.

It was a wild, agitated throng. Ladies whose husbands were away on the fatal expedition shrieked and fainted. Officers hurried to get the ladies' wraps, and to arrange for their going home in squads. The ambulances were hurriedly hitched up, and rattled away. Musicians picked up their horns, and ran to help. The chaplain looked as if he thought it a fit time to offer prayer; but he was disregarded, and hustled about like an old woman. In less time than these sentences can be read, the whole company had dispersed. Women hurried home, satin-slippered, weeping and moaning; and every able-bodied man was on his way to the wharf.

When Miss Thorpe first observed Phœbe in the "Lancers," dancing with the athletic officer, and saw her at that dreadful moment pause with her partner, she noticed her face becoming luminously pale, and her eyes fixed, as if on an apparition of the dead. The next minute she had disappeared. With a strong grasp on her partner's arm, she said, "Come! my wraps, — the ambulance, quick! to be first at the wharf, — first!"

Like lightning, they flew to the shawls. Her own was flung about her, and out they rushed to an ambulance. The driver did not spare the mules, but lashed and swore, and they flew all the way as if they were winged with curses. The officer did not question Phœbe at first, so fierce and sudden was her approach ; but now he begged her to desist. He assured her she did not know what she was going to see; that she could not bear it ; that it would utterly overcome her ; that she was insufficiently clothed for the night air, and that her slippers were no protection against the damp ground. He begged, implored her to turn back.

" I am going to that steamboat," she said more calmly.

The great white side of the steamer was against the wharf. Men stood with iron jacks of pitch-pine, burning fiercely, and giving a lurid light on the scene. At the gangways, inclined planks were placed, and on the deck and by the stairs stood soldiers with spectral lanterns. As the wounded were seen under the wild and glancing lights, it was like searching out the outlines of some dying figure that seems to be writhing in a dusky picture painted centuries ago. The work of removal had barely begun when Phœbe and the officer reached the wharf. The crowd gathered momently, the soldiers, sutlers, and negro servants full of curiosity and of dread. But Phœbe would not yield : so the officer got a box and placed her on it, that she might see. A sharp groan was heard ; and the officer renewed his entreaty : " Leave, I pray you, leave this horrible place !" She was silent. The voice of the sufferer, by one of those modulations unknown to musical art, and acquired only by divine grace, seemed to change itself, and to escape from the burden of pain it was bearing, and to turn its wild anguish into the sweetest note, the prelude of a melodious strain of praise to the Redeemer. It was a sudden and instant appeal to the heart. The pulsations of that tone must have stirred the air of heaven.

"O Phœbe," exclaimed Miss Thorpe, who with Col. Hunt had now arrived, "why have you come here? Do you wish to die? Will you break my heart? Come, let us go. There are men enough to help, — *men.* It is no place for you, so lately an invalid."

Col. Hunt added his earnest admonitions. But she was inflexible.

So the ghastly sufferers were brought ashore on stretchers, — men with every form of injury: some were dying; some were dead; some were happily insensible.

As new groups appeared, bringing some new horror, Phœbe looked at each for one instant only, and then turned her face away.

Col. Hunt, Miss Thorpe, and the officer were thinking of carrying her off by force. The number of the wounded was very large, and their removal would take hours. It was now near one o'clock. A couple of men emerged from the darkness; one elderly, and rather stout, the other short, and brisk in movement. The light flashed on them, and Phœbe exclaimed with delight. Mr. Prescott heard her cry, then rushed towards her, and embraced her with tears and kisses.

"But, my darling," he said, "here this awful night!—O Miss Thorpe, and my good friend Col. Hunt, let us leave here! Let us go to the nearest house: I am sick of wounds; I am dying with the pain I cannot help. My flesh is quivering as I see those gashes. Oh, my God!"

"First tell me," said Phœbe, "is Roderick living?"

"Yes: I hope he is."

"Then he is not on board. But who came in charge of this boat?"

"Col. Prescott."

"Did you not say he was not on board?

"Col. Roderick Prescott is not: this Col. Prescott is another person."

Here Amory disappeared in the shadow, but presently came within hearing.

"Come, my darling," said Mr. Prescott, "let us go to the general's house and have our talk. I will have the other Col. Prescott follow us."

She made him no answer; but, looking steadily beyond him, she exclaimed, —

"Mr. Amory, come, let me shake your hand. You are a good and a brave man. Who is there behind you?"

The group of faces was strangely lighted up as Amory with manly pride stepped forward and took the proffered hand.

"Dear Miss Phœbe, be strong; for here is a surprise. — Colonel, please step forward."

A colonel's cap was raised, a brown-haired, sun-burned man appeared. Hardship and suffering had left their marks upon him; but there was no mistaking the noble features and the wonderful steel-blue eyes of Robert Prescott.

Mr. Hugh Prescott and Percival Amory, who had come on the boat with the newly-found colo-nel, had a sympathetic delight in the surprise of Phœbe and Miss Thorpe; and as the vivid signs of feeling trembled over the women's faces, their joy growing intense, until its ecstasy was like a pain, the men looked on with answering emo-tion, their sterner features at play with smiles, and then struggling in more rigid lines, until tears welled out of their eyes Under the fitful light of the torches, Phœbe was pale as marble. She held to Mr. Prescott with a spasmodic grasp; while Miss Thorpe, who feared a return of insan-ity, supported her on the other side.

After the first shock was over, Col. Robert was the only one who made any pretence to composure. Swift questions flew. Answers followed in brief words interpreted by quick glances. But not a moment had passed before the elder of the party saw the necessity of removing Phœbe from a scene that was making such a strain upon her sensibili-ties. Both he and Miss Thorpe interposed, and insisted upon her going to the house. Col. Robert was invited to accompany them; but, pointing to

the ghastly procession that was still slowly coming
up from the cabin, he said, " You would all despise
me if I left my post. I must stay here until the
last man is put into the ambulance. I shall see
you at breakfast."

" You are right," said Mr. Prescott proudly.
" But come and breakfast with us."

" Still faithful to duty," thought Phœbe; " always duty. Before, it was preaching to the heathen; now it is care of the wounded. Is there
place left for love? If his love and duty should
be one, what a noble lover he might be!" Something like this, not in set words, perhaps, flashed
through her mind as Col. Robert raised his hat,
and in a grave, sweet tone said, " Until morning,
then."

The fate of Roderick was not made known to
the women. It was thought not best to distress
them until there was a certainty.

The ladies were lodged at the house used for
the general's headquarters. The two men were
entertained by the post ordnance officer, — a great
hearted and enthusiastic young man from a Western State. He accompanied the whole party, so
as to give the countersign to the black sentinels,
whose rapid challenges and quickly levelled guns
were sometimes terrifying, even to their superior
officers.

As for Robert, his watch lasted until the stars
began to pale in the east; when, going below, he
flung himself into his berth, wrapped in his blan-
ket, for a few hours' repose.

CHAPTER XXVII.

IT was under a wide veranda on the sunny side,
looking out upon a spacious but neglected garden
surrounded by an overgrown and ragged hedge,
that our re-united friends sat the morning after
the ball. The great gate on the line with the
street, with flanking pillars surmounted by glossy,
black eight-inch shells, showed that this was the
headquarters of the ordnance department. Few
flowers grow where war sets its iron hoof; yet
through the decayed vegetation of the old year,
the timid white and pink and yellow blossoms were
putting out their pretty heads, and the chattering
birds were building nests in the garden trees.

Miss Thorpe and Phœbe, for whom a supply
of clothing had been brought from their lodgings,
were reposing in huge rustic chairs. They had
come over from the general's house to meet their
long-lost friends. Mr. Prescott was perched on a
stool that had once been a chair: he was still sad-
eyed but silent. Amory, seated on the floor of the
veranda, was swinging his legs over the edge, at
a safe distance above the flower-beds. Steps were
heard approaching the house. Phœbe's hand
rested in Miss Thorpe's palm, and at the sound

Miss Thorpe almost heard the bound of the girl's heart. An instant later, through the pale translucency of her face and neck were seen the fine reticulations in which the crimson flush was spreading and mingling, until the whole ivory surface had become one rosy glow.

" You love him," said Miss Thorpe with a penetrating whisper that was neither heard nor observed by the others. Col. Robert and Major Royce, the ordnance officer, were coming through the gate.

" You love him," said Miss Thorpe, in the same tone as before, fixing a glance upon Phœbe's rich color and her eager, tremulous eyes.

All rose to meet the officers. More chairs, looking like relics of a railroad accident, were brought out, and conversation became general.

While in Florida, Mr. Prescott had heard Robert relate his history after his sudden departure; but he thought it better that the ladies should hear it from his own lips. So, after a few general comments upon the scenery and the novelty of the surroundings at a military post, the colonel was asked to give an account of himself. *Conticuere omnes;* and he repeated, though more fully, the story we have already told.

" I know well how strange it seems to you to see me in uniform; but I hardly know how it would seem for me to assume the character of a clergyman again. I think I had never before found my place in the world."

It was true: he looked every inch a soldier.

The shyness and reserve of the student had disappeared, and his manner was as firm and assured as if he had been brought up in camp.

"Still it was no whim or fickleness that moved me to enter the service. It was a paramount duty, I thought."

Phœbe winced at the word. Duty was the one thing he thought of.

When he mentioned his escape on horseback, with a dozen of the enemy in pursuit, Phœbe became intensely interested, almost beyond self-control. Then, when he told of his floating down the Edisto River on a log, moving only by night, and lying hid in tree-tops by day, making his way among reptiles, and subsisting upon raw potatoes given him by some negro in hiding, she was still more agitated.

Miss Thorpe remembered the fever-dreams, in which Phœbe related with dramatic vividness the same thrilling scenes; and, firmly planted as she was upon the basis of reason and fact, she could not repress a sudden thrill at the coincidences. Had those lovely eyes followed a lover, and seen what was going on a thousand miles away?

But she thought it best to change the subject. "You have not told us, Mr. Prescott, about Col. Roderick."

"No," he replied. "I have not seen him since the morning of the battle, as he rode by at the head of his regiment. He still had a bandage on his arm, and there was a mark over his temple. He had grown thin and wiry, and quite heroic too, in his appearance," looking at Col. Robert.

"Yes," answered the colonel, — "a very distinguished-looking officer; a man of sterling character, and high reputation in the army. Poor fellow!"

"But you don't say what has become of him," said Phœbe, startled anew.

"Does she love him?" thought the colonel. "Let us see how she bears it."

So, fixing his eyes upon her, he continued, "After the last fatal charge made by his regiment, I saw the men coming back without their officers. There wasn't a mounted man left. I inquired for Col. Roderick." Here Mr. Prescott moaned, and the colonel stopped.

"Do you mean to say he is killed?" exclaimed the women in a breath.

"No, I trust not, but wounded, and a prisoner."

"You poor, dear, good man!" sobbed Phœbe upon Mr. Prescott's shoulder. "This will kill his mother." And again she heard in the recesses of memory, "Was it for you that I have lost my son?" Robert would have almost given his life if he could have read her secret soul; but her eyes were like wells, not to be fathomed by a gaze.

"Search was impossible," said Robert, "as the enemy held the field, and fired at those who went to look for the wounded, or to bury the dead. There were not surgeons enough, for such a disaster had not been anticipated; and that was why this great boat-load of agony had to be brought here. We all got back to Jacksonville as well as we could. A sorry time we had. The general, in consideration of the coming of my uncle and friend, and that I might visit two ladies whom I had known, put the steamer under my charge.

"You will wonder why, with all these reports, I still believe my namesake to be alive. The morning we left, a rebel flag of truce came in to camp to confer about prisoners. I made the inquiry. 'No, they had no such officer.' But I found a colored servant with the party, and watched my opportunity. Upon describing Roderick to the experienced darkey, he said, 'Oh, yes! cunnle of de colored troops! Dey,' pointing to his master, 'don't count *dem*. Our cunnle don't 'low *dem* to be off'cers. He hurt mighty bad; but he tough: yes, he tough. He git well if dey don't send him to An'sonville.' I was sure he had recognized Roderick. God help him! for his captors won't."

"Poor Eleanor!" ejaculated Mr. Prescott. "Her life is bound up in him. I hope he'll get home alive."

There was silence for a few moments. All were thinking of the absent mother.

"We shall renew our inquiry through the next flag of truce," said the colonel; "and I hope you will have good news to carry home."

" If the day could have been long enough! If no call to duty intervened! If all the company save one could be temporarily banished! If there were to be no to-morrow!" So thought the colonel, as he looked at the vision of exceeding beauty just out of reach. The steamer was to return at once. Only an hour of liberty was his. What were her feelings towards him now? The thought went surging around in his mind; and, though he had faced many dangers, he would rather encounter the whole over again than leave the idol of his heart with the momentous question unsettled. It was an anxiety too great to be borne. Perspiration came upon his broad forehead, and wet his temples. Perhaps he was externally calm, but within there was a fury of contending feelings. It could not continue. He stepped off the veranda as calmly as he could, walked about the garden, picking a blossom or a shining leaf here and there, wiping his forehead meanwhile. Then he walked towards the house, no more tranquil at heart, and handed the bunch of flowers to Phœbe. " Think of me!" he said in a soft and deep tone.

" Are you going?" she asked tremulously.

" Yes, in an hour. Won't you walk a few minutes in the garden? you may have some message —for Roderick." He was ashamed of the ebullition of jealousy before it was off his lips.

With a look at Miss Thorpe, Phœbe stepped off the veranda.

"This may be my only minute," he said passionately. "To-morrow, — do you realize it? — I shall be with my regiment — what is left of it. Where next, who knows? We are only pawns in this terrible game. Now, Phœbe, tell me, you were surprised, but were you *pleased*, with the change? Are you glad I entered the service?"

"I am glad you are brave, but sorry there is need for so many sacrifices. I think of the country as a mother mourning over her sons."

Phœbe was attentive, even alert; but her face was still flushed from weeping, and a mist of sorrow still dimmed her eyes.

"I did not go to the war to win you: the woman I love would not be won in that way. But don't think me heartless, or indifferent to the fate of others, — of Roderick, — if I say that I cannot bear the thought of going back without knowing your feelings towards me."

"Oh! in this moment, with these aching hearts near us, with what is before you, how *can* you? I pray you, Col. Prescott, until we meet again, to be satisfied with sympathy and good-will. I am sorely pressed: I hardly know on what ground I stand."

"Thank you for your kind words! I have been hardened in manner, perhaps, by my experiences; but you know my heart is yours. That is the only hope I have, to deserve your love: otherwise I should think death in battle the great prize."

"Oh! do not talk in this wild way. How can I

listen after that dreadful experience of last night?
— *here*, encircled with a ring of fire; with every
thing in the future uncertain; with Mr. Prescott
sitting yonder; with that mother away there in
New England — Poor Roderick!"

Robert was by no means deficient in sympathy,
and his sorrow for the hard lot of Roderick was
unaffected. But a train of thought, that reached
far back to that interview when his rival told him
he meant to win Phœbe, now took fire, and began
to blaze like a line of fuse leading to a magazine.
This unusual journey, undertaken in winter, amid
the scenes of actual war, with every possible dis-
couragement, and against all manner of obstacles,
undertaken not only by the step-father, but by a
delicate girl, — what did this all portend? The
party had not come to search for *him*, the lost
clergyman: no, it was to see Roderick. Doubtless Phœbe had instigated it: there must have
been a correspondence. Phœbe had betrayed herself; and now to his earnest plea she had only
responded, " Poor Roderick!"

The very earth seemed to sink beneath him.
How foolish he had been not to see the meaning of
the journey before! The light of his life was extin-
guished. Fighting henceforth. He heard the
heavy undertone of the steam from the wharf: it
resounded as if it were the foundation-note of
some colossal organ, infernal in quality, and appalling in its suggestions, — fit accompaniment for the
agonizing chorus of war.

He went again upon the veranda.

"You hear the signal! My time is up: I hope to come here again, if you remain long. Be sure of my best efforts to find Roderick. We shall all meet in happier times. God bless you!"

With a hearty farewell to each the colonel took leave. A few minutes later, from an upper window Phœbe saw through swimming eyes the great white steamer heading southward.

CHAPTER XXVIII.

IT was a high misdemeanor to have one's house open in summer, even with all the profusion of grass and shrubbery that were to be seen from the front windows; and Mrs. Prescott had intended to have been away with the world of fashion at the seaside. - But it was now June; and she had been detained in the city, waiting for the long-expected return of the two colonels. Her son Roderick was now at home, and Robert was with him. Roderick had been a prisoner in the stockade at Florence, and, being apparently at death's door, the Confederate officers had agreed to his exchange. Robert had been ill with a fever, and, besides, had been wounded, and was granted a furlough. The colonels had come on from Fortress Monroe together, only a few days before the date of this chapter.

The luxury of sleeping in real beds they had enjoyed to the uttermost, and could not be induced to rise for breakfast before eleven. Then Robert, who had two sound legs, helped Roderick, whose knee had been shattered, down the stairway to the breakfast-table that was spread for them near the conservatory. And then Roderick, who had two practicable arms and hands, prepared the viands at table for Robert, whose right elbow and wrist had been injured by a shell. Roderick's features had become as sharp as a pickerel's during his illness and imprisonment, and he ate ravenously, as if on a wager. Robert had grown grave, and had the bearing of a man of middle age; or, if he had not, he thought he had, which amounts to about the same thing. Since his great sorrow, he had schooled himself to an unusual sobriety of speech and manner. The quenching of an absorbing passion is not done without such an effort as leaves a visible impress of the struggle.

Probably he suspected that he had been in the wrong, and had proceeded without tact in his last interview with Phœbe at the island. He began to remember that he had accepted the theory of her preference for Roderick without the least proof. It might be, after all, that he had foolishly run away from his own happiness. In the interval he had been closely scanning that former lady-killer, to observe whether there was any change in his manner when the name of Phœbe was mentioned. They had met once, Miss Thorpe having called with Phœbe; and Robert saw no indication of an understanding, — none of the glances nor flushes, nor the eager speech, that betray the accepted or the interested lover. It was in a happy-go-lucky way that Roderick spoke of Phœbe and of every other person and topic. In short, the preacher-colonel began to believe that Roderick had really renounced his pretensions, and he accused himself of being a suspicious idiot.

While they were breakfasting upon lamb-chops and peas, with a pint of claret between them (ordered by the doctor to save Robert's scruples), the door-bell rang, and our young friend Amory rushed in. The greetings were hearty, as between men who had a common ground of respect and attachment; and, after the visitor had repressed the sigh that came at the sight of their injuries, he sat down by the table.

"And so you are really home again! When I heard they had you cooped up at Florence, I feared it was all up with you.—And you, Robert, you are rather peaked. We must have you padded and rouged. Are you both out of the service?"

"I am not," said Roderick. "When my leg is better, I am going back to see the end of it. I mean to be in at the death, if I don't get hit again."

"Oh, I see! you want a general's star.—But how is it with you, Robert?"

"I haven't made up my mind. I may go back to my regiment; or I may take a place on the staff; or I may resign. I shall consult my father and uncle."

"Then you'll resign, *I* know. Your father and mother are on pins and needles about you. Your mother wants you to resign, and preach."

Roderick laughed; then, seeing the looks of Amory and Robert, he said, "Oh! Robert is *good* enough. He is cleaner than any chaplain in the army. But a man who can handle a regiment as he can, *to preach!* I think not. He ought to be a corps commander."

"I don't know that ability is any disqualification in the Lord's service," said Robert gravely.

"Of course not. But it's one thing to rattle off Scripture, and quite another to move a body of men against a battery."

"What do *you* say?" said Amory.

"I think," replied Robert, "that, if my duty had not called me into the field, I should have been glad to serve my Master as father and mother wished."

"But now," said Roderick, "that you have found your place among active men, you will let the timid. scholastics do the preaching for you. Isn't that so?"

"I shall think about it," said Robert. "By the way, father and mother are coming to-day, I believe."

"Are they, indeed? And, as Mary is here, we shall have a family party. So jolly!"

Roderick looked amused at the animation of Amory, but said nothing.

"How is Gibbs?" inquired Robert, with a gleam of merriment.

"Fatter than ever," said Amory, rubbing his hands; "and his nose is more coppery. But that's all the copper he has. I got his stock, or rather Mr. Prescott and I together, at 1¼."

" And how is it now? "

178½.   Don't you read 'The Advertiser'? "

" No, I confess; not the stock-reports.   They don't interest me."

" You ought to; else you can't properly enjoy Gibbs's sufferings.   That sign of ours — how it burns him!   Gilt letters just across the way."

" How is his business? "

" Gone to pot.   The old clerks made a new concern, and got the pick of all the mills.   Gibbs kept only those that owed him, and he has to carry them.   Oh! he's been catching it.   I expect the Miantonomo is going to fail.   If it does, he's done for."

" My uncle, then, has no share in the mill business? "

" I didn't say that," replied Amory.   " The new team wanted his name, and they needed capital. It's Prescott & Co. still, by Jupiter!   It's sweet for Gibbs, you believe! "

" Yes," said Mr. Prescott, entering, " the old house has a new foundation and new prospects."

" Shall I? " said Amory mysteriously, after a pause.

" Yes, if you like," said Mr. Prescott.

" Well, then," said Amory, with a little conscious air, " if you two colonels have had your fill of war, you are invited to take places in the Corinthian, — one here, and one at the mine; or you can alternate.   What do you say? "

" What do *you* say? " inquired Roderick.   " You have legs."

"What do *you* say? You have arms," was the answer of Robert.

"We'll sleep over it," said Roderick.

"Yes, till noon, I've no doubt," said Mr. Prescott, with a twinkle.

"Plans for the future," mused the lover, with a cautious look at his comrade, "and no mention of Phœbe. Can he love her still?"

Here there was a new and pleasant interruption. Mary came floating in like a pink blossom on the wind, said hurriedly, "Papa's at the door," and then swiftly went into the hall, followed by her brother Robert.

Roderick remained sitting, though strangely affected; for he could not rise without help. Mr. Prescott stalked to the window as he heard the door open, and affected to look for signs of rain; while Amory pulled out his handkerchief, and buried his face in it. The mother and father were meeting their long-lost son. No one within hearing could listen unmoved to the sacred maternal joy and grief that flowed in mingled tides. The mother's strong nature was subdued, and gave way in passionate sobs upon the neck of the son of her heart. This was her boy, her beloved, and he had come back, — had come back in honor; and here was the brave fellow's lacerated arm. It was too much. God was too good. In His arms her boy had been safe. He watching over Israel slumbers not nor sleeps. He suffered not a foot to be moved. The pestilence that walketh in darkness, and the destruction that wasteth at noonday, had passed by him. Thousands had not prevailed against him, nor had ten thousands made him afraid. Yes: God had saved him from the slings and arrows of the mighty; and now he was to testify to His goodness, and rejoice in his loving-kindness. "Like as a father pitieth his children, so the Lord pitieth them that fear him."

So the divine instinct hurried the great-hearted mother on, until uncle Solomon took her gently by the arm, and again and again pleaded with her, "Come, come, Zeruiah! come now, do! Be calm, and let Robert go and sit down. You'll wear yourself out, and him too. Come, don't cry any more! He's here, and safe: 'tain't as though he was down in Andersonville, lookin' for a place to lay his bones."

By and by, completely exhausted, the mother was led to a seat in the drawing-room; and there she sat, still in her travelling-suit, with her eyes closed, rocking slowly, and murmuring her prayers and thanksgivings.

The father found his way to the window, and silently grasped his brother's hand; then, beckoning to his son, they two sat down in a corner. Even the humorous old man had been in tears by sympathy with his wife's strong emotion; but, while the drops still glistened on his leathern cheek, the old spirit rose, and he shook himself as he said, " Your mother allers has 'em ready,—

them texts. She shook 'em over ye as ef she had a pepper-box full."

Mary had stolen near Amory for sympathy during this scene; and they withdrew to the adjacent room, where they were soon busy catching butterflies.

Mr. Prescott meantime walked about, dropping a word here and there.

"I say, Amory," said he, "have you finished that poem? It's odd if lines about sparrows don't pair. Perhaps you and Mary will rhyme together, and become a poem, or at least a couplet, yourselves."

"We've a glorious poem, — in prospect," said the happy man.

Mrs. Prescott now appeared, and persuaded her sister-in-law to retire for a while in order to take off her bonnet and shawl, and compose herself. No one now remained but the two elderly men and the two colonels, and the conversation became more cheerful.

"Hugh," said uncle Solomon, "Robert tells me you've got a good thing in that 'ere copper-mine."

"Yes, brother Solomon, — better than raising poultry, or hauling cord-wood to the village."

"No slip-up in it, I s'pose?"

"I think not. Ask Amory about the size of the hill, — all copper."

"I'm ginerally skeery about stocks. Dan Drew, or one of them oppyrators, last summer got hold of our minister, and made him think he was goin' to make his fortin; and he told the deacons, and they told the squire; and so it went round, and they all bought sheers: and if that crafty feller didn't jest clean out our village!"

"It's a way they have. People don't steal any more: that's simple and vulgar. They only get up stock companies."

"Wal, I've got a little, not much, — a thousan' or two, — and I've been gittin' six or seven per cent for't. P'raps I'll draw it in, and git the vallue in sheers."

"If you like. And I'll make over an equal number to Mary. I have just offered Robert, here, and Roderick, chances to go in. There's room enough."

"Of course you'll *go* in; won't you, boys? I kin call you boys, now that you hain't got your eppylets on. How is it, Roderick?"

"Uncertain, uncle Solomon. I want to see the war out, and Davis and Lee here in Fort Warren. Time enough to make money after that. Besides, mother has been talking of my going to see my English relatives. I haven't decided."

Once more Robert thought, "A trip to England, and no mention of Phœbe."

CHAPTER XXIX.

Signor Belvedere was back again from Europe. He had aired and brightened his rooms, and had restored the flower-pots to the windows. The bird had been brought home, and the piano was in exquisite tune. The sheaf of rapiers, fencing-foils and canes, hung over the mantel. The chairs were in picturesque disorder, and the secret closets newly filled with house-keeping articles.

He had dressed himself with extreme care, and had combed his beard until it fell in soft, white waves over the purple necktie. For the first time in this country, he wore an unusual ornament,— a heavy medal of gold on his breast. His closely-fitting black frock-coat was trimly buttoned, and a small crimson ribbon was just visible in the buttonhole of the lapel. Then, with the ceremonial glossy silk hat (which he detested), his costume was complete. Selecting the slimmest of malacca sticks, he drew on his buff gloves, whistled to his bird, and descended to the street, making a figure as striking and as graceful as one often beholds. He walked leisurely to Mount Vernon Street, and reached Mr. Prescott's house a little after twelve, just as a carriage left Miss Thorpe and Phœbe at the door.

Phœbe had entirely recovered her health and spirits, although her experiences had given her an unusual maturity of expression in one so young. Since her return from the South, she had resumed her place as a music-teacher, but passed a day or two each week with Miss Thorpe. They had now come in compliance with a request from Signor Belvedere, who had in a characteristic note informed them of his return, and expressed a desire to meet them at Mr. Prescott's.

He was more stately than ever; and, though his manner was gracious, his self-command was perfect. No one not in his secret could have told whether he had come to give a lesson, to attend a funeral, or negotiate a treaty. Phœbe felt her heart beat loudly as she walked up the steps, and Miss Thorpe had completely lost her self-control in the protracted suspense. The pale and anxious lady wished she could have the Italian illuminated from within, like a city clock at night. She was vexed that he could smile like a fiend, while she was in such an agony. Clearly he had missed the chance of distinction as a diplomatist.

Phœbe and Miss Thorpe were shown into the reception-room, where they met Mrs. Prescott, resplendent in the newest of morning costumes. She noticed first the complementary colors of her visitors' white chip hats, — hyacinthine pink upon Phœbe's, and purplish lilac upon Miss Thorpe's, — and saw how each lent beauty to the other. She next surveyed the new brocade curtains, the fresh laces, the rich mossy carpets, the regilded picture frames, and dwelt a moment on the glimpse of gorgeous colors seen at a distance in the conservatory. Yes, all was as it should be, and she was sure her friends would find themselves harmonious figures in a charming *parterre.*

The three ladies advanced into the larger room: both parlors had been thrown open together, as well as the breakfast-room and the conservatory. Signor Belvedere attended them, holding on to his hat as if it were the cover of a jewel-case, or a gift he was to place before some shrine.

The two colonels were at the breakfast-table, which had been cleared of every thing but the crystal claret jug, and to that Roderick continued to pay his devotions. They were playing backgammon; and aunt Zeruiah, hearing the rattle of dice, lifted her eyes, and groaned. She had expostulated against the sin when the board was first brought, in vain. Her solemnity had returned, and it oppressed her like the band of artificial hair that rested on her broad brows. Amory and Mary Prescott were still in the small adjacent room, apparently engaged in some literary exercise that was excessively amusing. Sounds like "kiss" and "bliss," and "love" and "dove," were heard at intervals, with occasional bursts of laughter inexplicable to all but the rhymers themselves.

The two elder Prescotts were in the back-parlor, and, after the usual compliments, resumed their seats. It was evident to both that the meeting

of the guests was not accidental. Uncle Solomon
was full of admiration for Phœbe, but Signor
Belvedere was a puzzle to him. The eyes of the
honest countryman followed the lithe, courtier-
like movements of the Italian with undisguised
curiosity.

"Guess he's one of them foreign lords, ain't he?
Looks like one. I remember, in a picter where
Clumbus was tryin' to show how he was goin' to
discover Ameriky, there was a man like that, only
he had tight breeches on."

The reply was a mere nod; and uncle Solomon
continued his comments, especially wondering
how "a man with airs like them are could demean
himself to teach singin'."

The various groups were in some inexplicable
manner drawn together by the delicate art of the
Italian. A word to this and a smile to that person had the effect, after a time, of concentrating
the attention of all. He had neglected no one in
the apartments, and had even quite won the admiration of aunt Zeruiah by his skilful posing of
her son Robert in the attitude of a Christian hero.
All were in the front parlor, or within hearing.
The colonels laid aside their game, and came forward together, — one hobbling with a crutch, the
other with his arm in a sling. The sight was new
and touching; but the sufferers were cheerful,
almost merry, over their misfortunes, and carried
the matter in such a high and nonchalant way as
to take off the pathetic impression. Phœbe and

Miss Thorpe greeted the heroes with warm words and with looks of tenderest sympathy. Signor Belvedere meanwhile was stealthily watching the girl, believing that her countenance would betray her, and show to which of them she was attached. But, though Robert was his favorite, he could not observe that she was any warmer in her manner towards him than towards Roderick. She did not show her feelings.

Then the young men, in turn, related something of their adventures; and, while this was going on, Signor Belvedere had a new light upon his former perplexities. For he remembered vividly the scenes when Phœbe in her delirium had described what she saw. It was Robert, not Roderick, whose thrilling ride for life she had followed with the lenses of love's second sight. It was Robert, not Roderick, who had been hunted through the swamps, and had paddled, while blistered and hungry, down the river to the sea. It was the image of Robert, not Roderick, that had attracted her, and made her willing to brave the wintry sea in search of him. And, with all this undying passion in her breast, she had met her lover without an unmaidenly thought, and left him to learn her heart by trial at home.

He looked up at Mrs. Prescott, and smiled, as he saw with what intense interest she was regarding the drama in progress.

He looked again at Phœbe. Her tranquillity did not deceive him any longer.

"Noble girl!" he said to himself. "Pure and discreet, she will die before she will speak. It is the soul of the daughter of a great race. She could be a heroine, a Joan of Arc, if need be." How he admired her, adored her! He would have been proud to kneel to her as to a queen.

The Signor further questioned the colonels as to their purposes, and heard from them what we have learned already. Only Roderick, as he was always more affected by the latest notion, was a little less firm about seeing the end of the war, and appeared to be waiting to know more about the English relatives.

Here Mr. Prescott interposed, and mentioned his offer, which the Signor heard with surprise. He looked at the speaker and at the young men. It was like a dream to be told that the ridiculous copper stock had come to have a value, and was to make all the family rich.

The demeanor of the young men in presence of the charmer was perplexing to Mr. Prescott.

"The young dogs!" thought he. "I wonder which of them, after all, is to get my niece! I can't think Roderick really meant to give her up if he ever really cared for her. He is gay and off-hand, no sighing lover surely. And Robert, though he is nervous and hectic, is grave and silent. Has she jilted them both?"

Robert was more and more astonished at the manner of Roderick. Was it claret now, as it had been commissary [D] before? There was no tremor, no eagerness of expression, no tenderness, in his voice. He might have shown as much agitation at the sympathy of the housemaid. Then glancing at Phœbe, Robert saw, or thought he saw, beneath the apparent calm of her countenance. His soul rose to mid-heaven at the thought. Yes, he *had* been a blind idiot.

"Roderick is almost impertinent," thought his mother. "How can he be so indifferent when so much is at stake? I should like to pull his ears."

"They have conspired: I am sure of it. They have exchanged confidences while in camp together, and have agreed to slight me," thought Phœbe.

"The dandy has become *blasé* and hardened, and the preacher has grown worldly," thought Miss Thorpe. "I liked him as a poetical enthusiast better."

"I wonder if those coxcombs think such a girl as that is to be had every day for the asking," said Mr. Prescott to himself, as he looked at the pair who were lolling on the sofa. "In my time I would have leaped a barnyard gate, merely for one look of hers."

Aunt Zeruiah with a heightened color said in a clear voice, —

"Whatever others may decide, I hope *my* son will not be deceived by the riches and vanities of this world, but will turn his face toward God, and preach his everlasting gospel."

Uncle Solomon, as usual, quieted his spouse,

and she proceeded to cool her cheeks with a broad
and breeze-compelling fan. The city dame smiled
as the formidable implement was spread, and
wondered if its like could be found anywhere
except in a museum.

"You know, madam," said Belvedere, addressing
Mrs. Prescott with more than his usual formality,
"that I had some strongg rea-son to make a
winter trip across the At-a-lantic. I wish-ed to
know the truth about the parentage of our beloved
Phaybe. You have-a-thought, with some rea-son,
that she was your niece. I am compel-led to tell
you she is not." There was a general murmur.

"No, madam : your brother Roderick Manning
marri-ed the Countess della Torre, then a widow,
and with one very young child. That child was
nam-ed Phaybe, and she is La Contessa. It is this
girl,— our Phaybe. She is La Contessa. Her
mother did bear a child to Roderick, her second
husband ; but that child di-ed in infancy. Phaybe
is not a Manning, — not your-a niece. These
thinggs I have surely learn-ed, both in England and
in Italy. There is a small estate, an an-cient house,
—you may call it a castle, — and a vineyard, which
is the seat of the Della Torres, and which will belong to the Contessa here. A similar good-fortune
awaits Col-onel Roderick. His uncle Ralph Manning invites him over, as next heir, to make the
house his home, and bids me tell him he has pick-ed
out a beautiful and a rich youngg lady for him."

As he uttered these words, the Signor looked at

Roderick and Phœbe, and glanced from the one to the other.

"No bond between them that will kill by being severed," thought he.

Robert's breath was coming fast; and his face would have been deadly pale, except for the bright spots in his cheeks.

Poor Miss Thorpe! Now, that Phœbe was not the niece of Mrs. Prescott, was her turn coming?

"But, Phaybe," Signor Belvedere continued, "you have not ask-ed me about the Della Torres. Have you no curiosity about your father?"

Phœbe found herself strangely calm while all the company were so excited in her behalf. She thanked her generous friend, and answered that she would be most grateful to know about *both* her parents.

"Aha!" he replied. "One at a time. Of the father I will say he was Count Ferdinando della Torre, the son of my elder sister. No other male relative of the name survives. On the other side — the Cavalcantes; I am the head of the house. I am the Cavalcante. You are the daughter of my nephew, the next heir of my blood, the daughter and the best belov-ed of my heart."

He raised his arms, and in so doing showed the decoration on his breast. He looked towards Phœbe, and she rushed into his fatherly embrace.

The scene was a part of one of nature's own dramas; and, when Phœbe looked up, she saw only a circle of faces bedewed with tears.

What Robert felt in that moment it is impossible to describe. He had begun to repent his abrupt breaking-off the suit when they were .last together. He had seen that Roderick was not her lover; and, under that inscrutable loveliness of feature, he thought there might be, after all, concealed a deep and tender regard for him. But he had vowed to himself never to renew the question; and now that she was a countess, and with an assured future in the land of her birth, how *could* he ask her again to be his wife? He had cut himself off from all that he desired on earth.

"And now," continued Signor Belvedere, "as to the unfortunate mother, the countess, whose hard-a fate it was to die in a tenement-house, after seeing the death of her husband and of the off-spring of their love; to die afar from kindred, and without the offices of the church, and to leave her remaining child in the care of that poor but great-hearted Irish angel, — as to that mother, I have-a been able to learn nothing. I visited the place where her first marriage took place. I saw the records of the church, and the book of the notary. The entry of the marriage-contract is there; but some one has cut out the name of the bride. Why, I cannot say; but so it is. I found the baptism of Phaybe, and the names correspond with those found in the mother's prayer-book."

"Oh, if you were only my poor sister's daughter!" said Miss Thorpe in an outburst of motherly feeling.

"No one knows that she is not," answered Belvedere meaningly. "I have often remark-ed that in her are blended the best-a traits of both English and Italian races. It was then I thought she had an English father and a mother from my own country. But now my own blood is accounted for; and it may be that the strain of English beauty and of English high bearing comes from an American mother, and perhaps even from the lovely prima donna whose loss you have so long lamented."

"To think we shall never know!" said Miss Thorpe pensively.

"You are more than aunt, and more than mother even!" said Phœbe impetuously. "I shall always claim my share in that portrait; and I have a place *here*," fervently embracing the childless woman.

"And so it's a great lady ye are!" broke in Mrs. Maloney, who had been waiting in the hall, and could restrain herself no longer. "The Lord bless ye, and the blessed Virgin kape ye!"

"Dear Mrs. Maloney," said Phœbe, turning, and seizing her hands, "I am glad you are here to wish me joy. We will never part again,—not if you will live with me."

Mrs. Maloney retired, courtesying, and quite astonished at her temerity in speaking out unasked.

Signor Belvedere (as we shall still call him) was standing by Phœbe, chatting gayly, and cooing like an elderly pigeon, with an air of immense satisfaction. He fixed a look upon Robert which appeared to signify unmistakably, "Come!"

That bashful and despondent youth saw and wondered. He had remained by Roderick, because he was naturally bound to aid him in locomotion. Perhaps Roderick also saw the same invitation in the Italian's eyes, and meant to take himself out of the way; for he said, " Here, Robert, help me to mother, if you can do it with your left flipper. Your legs are all right. I have something to say to the old folks. Land me, and leave me."

As Roderick was going out of hearing, Amory observed in a burlesque philosophic tone, " This family's fortunes show that the best-laid plans gang aft aglee. Miss Phœbe wished to be a public singer. Look at her: she is La Contessa. Robert was sure he was going to preach. Look at him : he is every inch a colonel. Mr. Prescott hoped he would beat Gibbs, and had no faith in copper. Now, he didn't beat Gibbs until the Corinthian had become the pillar of his fortunes. Mrs. Prescott was going to have a niece and perhaps a daughter-in-law; but that is turning out otherwise. Good-fortune comes, but not as we expect. For instance, my being named for a poet was to no purpose; yet I hobble on to prosperity in prose. Man steers the ship; but the tides and winds he can't control. — You observe, I am acting as Greek chorus."

" Make a sonnet on it," said Robert.

"No, I thank you. The proverb is enough, —
'MAN PROPOSES.' Poetry whistles itself. I
sha'n't try to whistle it any more."

After a rather painful progress, Roderick sat
down between his parents in the privacy of the
smaller room. He looked rather flushed and
excited. Claret, surely, was to blame.

"Mother," said the dutiful son, "it's best to
have a fair deal. That affair has blown over.
I've seen how Robert is bound up in her; not
that he talks, but he mourns. I know he is getting out of the notion of black, — a moulting
theological crow — but he's all right. He saved
my life more than once. I won't contend with
him, — not for bravado, as I once set out to do.
I have a speck of honor. No: I'll either go back
to my regiment, or I'll go over and see my uncle
Ralph. Perhaps the girl he has picked out for
me isn't as pretty as Phœbe; but we won't
enlarge on that point. Now, not a word! I was
afraid you might do, or say, or look something.
Let the play go on. Count me out. Will you
help me back into the parlor?"

"Yes," said Mr. Prescott. "But, Roderick,
you've had too much claret."

"Perhaps I have, and that's the reason I tell
the truth. *In vino veritas.* I'm not strong on
my pins yet, in any sense."

Mrs. Prescott had been extremely agitated; but
the new turn of affairs brought some consolations.
If she had lost Phœbe, she would be yet repaid

by seeing her son a landed proprietor in England, perhaps a baronet, or even a peer, by and by. And she wondered if he could wear his colonel's or general's uniform when he came to be knighted.

Mr. Prescott was astonished that Roderick should voluntarily renounce such a darling as Phœbe, countess or no countess; but he thought it might be just as well, for he felt pretty sure as to her preference. But the young men were heroes for the day, both of them; and he was half in a melting mood as he walked about.

Aunt Zeruiah, in a whisper to her husband, asked, " Is that gal Phœbe a Papist? And, even ef she *is* a countess, won't she have to jine the pope's church before she can git her property over there? Ef she's a darter of the Scarlet Woman of the Revelation, I don't want her to be a-marryin' my son."

Uncle Solomon laughed, and told his wife not to talk in that way, for fear her sister-in-law would think she was denouncing the oratory. While Belvedere and Robert were talking apart, Phœbe felt that two deep and earnest eyes were fixed upon her, although she did not at once raise her own to meet them. Soon, however, she looked frankly at the honest face of her lover.

Did Signor Belvedere find it necessary to converse with Miss Thorpe? At all events, he had moved his position nearer to her, and discreetly turned away from his Phaybe: in fact, a general movement was in progress, and the company were forming new groups.

Phœbe and Robert found themselves near the conservatory. The flowers were bright, but they did not see them. Scarcely a word was said. As spirits have no vocal organs, their thoughts may be exchanged as by the efflux and influx of light, and their feelings may be mere emanations. Robert swam in delight as he saw in Phœbe's face the look that answered his own. It was an effort, for his breath seemed to fail him; but he managed to say, —

"Are you going to Italy?"

"Yes, if you go with me."

THE END.